DEAD
IN THE
WATER

SIMON BOWER

John
Enjoy the read!

Simon Bower

MIDDLE
FARM
PRESS

First published in the UK in 2018 by Middle Farm Press

British Library Cataloguing-in-Publication Data

A catalogue record for this book is
available from the British Library

ISBN 978-0-9928896-9-2

Typeset in Palentino Linotype © Heidelberger Druckmaschinen AG

Published by Middle Farm Press

Author: Simon Bower

Managing Editor: Kate Taylor

Printed by Think Digital Books Ltd.

For Laure

PART 1

You can only connect the dots in your life
by looking back - not forward…
Connect the dots and find what you love.

Steve Jobs

1

Unidentified woman

Sunday, 24 July. Golfe-Juan, France.

By the time she hits the frothy Mediterranean water, she is already technically dead. Her heart ceases to circulate the blood inside her body, and she is aware of how comforting the water is as a strong sea breeze blows across the nape of her neck, left bare as she lays face down in the water.

She can hear music, muffled and distorted, coming from a late-night harbour bar. Despite her waning consciousness, visions of the past week – the boat, her friends, cocktails, laughter, fighting, sex – flash before her.

Why is she in the water? Is her mind playing tricks on her? Where is everyone? Surely they would pull her out soon?

As the acrid water fills her mouth and nose, she is powerless to prevent it, but a wave tosses her over and as the water laps over her face, she sees someone. A face. Yes. They have come at last.

Moments later, as the face blurs, she sinks deeper and deeper, where there is no longer sight nor sound, and her memories of the past week will be lost forever.

2

Me

Sunday, 7 February. London, England.

Five months earlier

I had been with my girlfriend for five years, living under the same roof for three. It was her idea to break it off, but I didn't put up a fight. Our relationship had become one of bitter contempt and insincere apologies and the default position of artificial remorse had really started to grate. I had never been one for sincere regrets, not to her or anyone else in my life. An aspect of my character that inevitably and consistently jolted already unstable foundations.

So last February, when she unexpectedly announced that she would be moving to Manchester due to a promotion in her expanding marketing firm, she followed it up with the not so unexpected suggestion that we call it a day. On the following dull Sunday morning, she had loaded any possessions that meant anything to her into our (now her) motor. As I sat on the electrical meter box watching the ceremony (my offer of help had been rejected), I felt empty. We had never travelled – save a day trip booze cruise to Dunkerque –

and I had ideas of us one day taking off. A five-star resort in Mexico, or diving in the Seychelles. Unlimited cocktails, clubbing late into the night, an air conditioned bungalow with a Jacuzzi bath, marble floors, and a king size double bed. So when I watched the final items – a shoe rack, some plates and the espresso machine (that pissed me off) – get loaded into the back seat, and she turned and said "See you Charlie. Have a nice life. Don't be such a tosser with the next one" I actually felt rather relieved. A new chapter was beginning, and I liked new chapters! They were clean and fresh and uncomplicated, if only for a while.

A few days later, while peering outside into the cold, damp winter's day in Hackney, I decided what I needed was to get the fuck out of there and find some fun in the sun.

My faithful dog-eared wall map looked down at me, full of opportunities and reminders of where friends now lived. When we left Nottingham University, there seemed to be a mass exodus from Blighty. One had buggered off to Canada. Another had taken a year out in New Zealand and never showed his face again. And after a couple of years in New Delhi, Jerry de Menzies had ended up in the Philippines. Jez was American, for whom university had just been a distraction and a step towards a glamorous expatriate lifestyle in Manila, the country's capital. He was always destined to lead a charmed life. I knew from gazing enviously at his Facebook posts that he enjoyed the convenience of a personal driver and a detached bungalow with central air conditioning and a kidney-shaped pool.

I was from a simple upbringing – my dad had lost his business and fortune when I was eleven years old and I recalled little of the domestic comforts we enjoyed up until then. After the company went down, I had left my swanky private school and joined the local state one, and this was the level of affluence I had enjoyed since. Looking at Jez's recent post about a new maid had made me look around my newly-designated bachelor pad (which, as it turned out, I would only have for a few more weeks), noticeably void of full-time servants, and I decided that it was time to get a new lifestyle, fast.

My online bank had informed me that I had the princely sum of £391 to spend before invoking my well-oiled overdraft so I proceeded to search for the best air fares to Manila, and after a quick WhatsApp with Jez, I had secured a return ticket.

What I didn't know when I clicked 'Buy Now' was that my little Far Eastern sojourn was the unleashing of a runaway train that would change my life in unimaginable ways.

Friday, 12 February. Manila, Philippines.

I resented not having paid greater attention to the flight schedule. The eight-hour layover in Beijing Capital Airport gave me the unexpected opportunity to absorb Chinese airport culture. One-third of a day should have been ample time to transfer to my connecting flight. I set about time wasting, I bought a disposable dust mask to blend in. I tried the chair designed to provide massages. I pissed about failing to get an hour's free Wi-Fi. When the airport gate for my red-eye Delta Air Lines codeshare flight to Manila finally appeared I set about navigating the impossible signage. At first, the security line seemed to be moving, but a guy with a beard and a woman with a baby ground the whole show to a lengthy stop. With growing frustration, it struck me that I would not make my next flight. Taking no prisoners, I elbowed my way over elastic fences towards the checkpoint, to the sound of much huffing and pleaded with the security staff to fast track me through. As the gate was closing, I slammed my passport and boarding card on the red counter and shortly after felt a sense of total elation as the plane door was closed behind me. I stuck the 'do not disturb' sticker to my seat back and swiftly drifted into a deep sleep before we had even left the hot tarmac. My much needed slumber was, however, short-lived as the courteous cabin crew broadcast a numbing, dream-invading announcement that breakfast and Duty Free were to be served. So, I sleepily nodded to the offer of breakfast, unable to enunciate my preference for

5

croissant over a porridge congee served with the sides of pickled vegetables and fermented tofu. Bugger.

Pissed off with the wake-up call and uninspired by breakfast, I let out my frustration at the first air stewardess that passed. Her name tag read 'Chrissie'. She apologised in a slippery American accent and snuck me over a croissant – lifesaver.

Arriving at Manila's Ninoy Aquino International Airport, Jez's driver was waiting for me. He efficiently transferred me from the airport, navigating the heavy traffic back to the gated community that Jez called home. Filipino drivers seemed to take a combative approach to getting around the city's traffic. My driver explained in broken English that the first rule of the road was that 'bigger wins', as he swung the wheel hard, sending a three-up scooter careering into the littered verge.

Jet-lagged and feeling the effects of the complementary in-flight drinks, I was snoozing in the back of the car when I was roused from my travel-induced doze by a large stick cracking against the window. Shitting myself, I found the source of the noise to be a bedraggled young street kid, hard at work, begging at the traffic lights. I told the driver to get moving.

Narrowly avoiding a smash-up with an overloaded 'jeepney' bus, we parked up at the white-painted steel security gate of the expat neighbourhood where Jez lived. The guard undertook a half-arsed inspection around the vehicle after which we were gracefully permitted to proceed. The driver brought the white Toyota to a standstill on a small concrete driveway outside a modest house framed by trees that looked like they were recently planted. Jez and I embraced in a man-hug. "Jez de Mez!" I offered with a good-to-see-you voice.

Jez looked hardly a year older despite the seven years that had passed since we last saw each other. As I looked around, I perhaps saw why: a gym in the den, a pool outside. I kept wondering where I had screwed up so badly. By then, I rented an unremarkable room in a shared house in North London. In my hall there was a bike, a decrepit stand-up vacuum cleaner and a wooden stool with a pile of junk mail on it. Outside, there was a tiny concrete yard, where the bins and recyclable bottles took pride of place. It was a notable contrast from what I saw before me.

The bungalow was designed with a large central lounge, kept cool by climate-controlled air, and had been done out with cold unforgiving brilliant white tiles on the floor. Everything was spotlessly clean and smelled of recently-applied bleach. Jez showed me to the guest room where I decided to crash out on the freshly-pressed Egyptian cotton sheets. Just for a minute.

Four and a half hours later, at 5:30pm according to the unfamiliar clock beside me, I woke wondering where the fuck I was. My body had involuntarily shut down and I knew that once I recovered movement in my limbs, I would feel totally energized from it. Gathering together my consciousness, I looked in the mirror. I was not entirely sure I liked what I saw; unlike Jez, my body was starting to show signs of age, wrinkles taking root and a hairline sneaking away from my brow. My clothes were well-used, as were the bags under my eyes… and what did I have to show for it? I needed to get a life.

Having awoken from my extended siesta, I entered the lounge wearing the not-so-funny-now T-shirt with a crude laddish comedy slogan on it. I wore loose shorts, instinctively scratching myself and rubbing my hair after my afternoon catnap, when I was faced with a spectacularly attractive woman wrapped like a burrito in a fluffy purple towel. My mouth opened to say something profound, but, "Oh!" is all that came out. Jez hadn't mentioned a woman.

Jez appeared from the kitchen and clarified the situation. His younger sister had grown bored working in a coffee shop in the off-season in California's Laguna Beach. She had taken a couple of months of unpaid leave to consider what to do with her life and was temporarily a habitant chez Jez. She immediately struck up conversation, "Hey, you must be the famous Charlie!"

"I hope famous and not infamous," I attempted, instantly castigating myself for spouting such a well-worn cliché. She made one of those non-smiles, like she had tasted something unexpected. Not in a good way.

"Jerry's told me all about you" she continued. Naked night-time swims in the Nottingham Canal?" A drunken flashback jumped into my mind, where I had shed my clothes in honour of the smelly water. I donned a sheepish grin.

"Breaking in to a hairdressers' at midnight?" she continued.

"Ah, well, no... someone else had already broken in, we were just looking around," I explained, "Until the police showed up."

"Climbing up scaffolding at the town hall to steal a flag?" his sister added with a cheeky smile. I am not sure Jez had done me any favours here. I did my best to suggest Jez may have exaggerated.

"We gave it back the next day," I offered, giving Jez a look.

"Only because you worked at the town hall on Saturdays and they recognized you on CCTV," chimed in Jez, laughing.

"Not after that I didn't." I said with a smirk towards his sister. Anastasia 'call me Ana' looked at me inquisitively. With that reputation preceding me, I realised that I could act up the part and be every bit the happy-go-lucky buffoon that she was now expecting, although in truth those days were long gone. My act certainly seemed to be working. Ana offered me a large glass of Tempranillo and over dinner Jez and I filled her in on old times, which I am glad to report she enjoyed as much as we did. Jez cried off to bed, citing an early client meeting the next day and left Ana and me, duly fuelled and feeling the heat.

We chatted by the pool, which was soothingly illuminated with phased underwater coloured lighting. The day had barely cooled off, the temperature still a tropical 23°C, no clouds disturbing the night sky. I was absorbed by Ana – when she smoked a cigarette, she did so with such elegance; when she attempted to swat a mosquito, her vain efforts amused me; and when she recounted tales, I was captivated. It was after 10pm when the conversation turned to swimming.

"So, you like swimming unencumbered?" she joked.

"Skinny-dipping? That was a long time ago, I was seriously inebriated!"

"Are you 'seriously inebriated' now?" Ana was taking the piss out of my accent – I had never noticed that I sounded so distinctly English until being the odd one out.

"The maid is still here." I offered, sheepishly.

"She's gone," Ana corrected me, fixing a determined gaze.

"Jez might..." and I trailed away at the stupidity of that excuse. Having sounded sufficiently reluctant, I thought, it was time to go for the kill – the most obvious line in the world, "You first…"

"That would be too easy, Charlie, let's play a little game instead. I'll get the cards, you know the rules!"

As Ana dealt five playing cards each, I found the tension and excitement overwhelming. Was she just teasing me, a hustler at poker, and just planning to humiliate me? Perhaps the maid had not departed after all? Would the video clip be on YouTube before the sun went down in London? Did I give a shit?

Ana kept herself in shape and was sporting an impeccable bikini tan. Over the coming hour, I studied her breasts, finding them to be pert; small but perfectly tantalizing. The game passed quickly, with me winning more than losing and within a few rounds there was nothing more for either of us to take off. As I reached down to get my San Miguel beer from the marble style terrace, I could not help myself instead sliding my fingers delicately from Ana's heat *heel* to her calf. Smooth and slightly moist, I progressed to caressing her leg with my full right hand when I stole a moment to study her face. Her eyebrows were making a quizzical impression, her mouth hanging slightly open. I bent down further to kiss her ankle when she grabbed my head by both sides and brought me up to kiss her flat stomach, something I found perilously erotic. Ana was breathing deeply through her mouth by then, moving my head in circles around her middle. Not able to hear or see anything, I busied my hands, trickling my fingers along each side of her back. Still cupping my ears firmly and with each deep exhalation a movement, she edged my face down towards her perfectly waxed Brazilian, where I needed no further invitation.

The sex was exceptional. I would go as far as to say the best I'd ever had. And unless I'm a terrible judge of these things, I'm pretty sure it was the same for her.

Later that night as I drifted off in my bed, I had one last thought.

Jez must not find out about this.

3

Chrissie

Sunday, 14 February. Forest Hills, New York, USA.

Forest Hills had been Chrissie Morris' home since she moved to New York three years ago. Arriving with an 18-month-old toddler, she wanted somewhere sensibly priced for New York City that was safe and still fostered a community spirit. Forest Hills seemed to check all of the boxes. She lived in a newish red brick seven-storey condo on Booth Street. The building looked identical to the one next door and the block next to that, but it was clean and the neighbours were respectable professional people.

As a single mom, she was always struggling to make ends meet. After income tax, social security and Medicare she took home a little over $3500 per month, and her rent and maintenance charges immediately gobbled up over half of that. Chrissie's two-bedroom apartment was kept immaculately clean; she rented it out through Internet B&B sites when she was out of town. It was an inconvenience locking her personal things into Anabelle's room, but the extra $100 per night meant she had money to pay the childminder when her shifts fell at awkward times.

Chrissie loved her job. Being a flight attendant with Delta Air Lines allowed her to see the world, although it was becoming increasingly difficult to be there for Anabelle. She had started to look at short haul cabin crew jobs and occasionally other things altogether – she would love to own a florist shop – but financial priorities limited her options.

She was just back from a JFK to Beijing, round trip, via Manila, which was a long trip for her, and too long away from Anabelle. Several of the customers had been real idiots, like the guy complaining about Chinese breakfast being served on a flight from Beijing, but Chrissie found she had a temperament to calm grumpy clients. By the time she got back to Forest Hills, her virtual paying guests had already 'checked out' and she managed to catch a few hours rest. She collected an ecstatic Anabelle from the childminder's apartment at lunchtime.

"Mommy!"

"Hi my favourite girl in the world! Have you grown overnight or have I got smaller?" Chrissie teased.

"I think I've grown, because I ate my broccoli," Anabelle suggested. The conversation continued in a mother-daughter fashion, Chrissie asking enthusiastic rhetorical questions and Anabelle lapping up the attention.

In her early twenties, Chrissie had never imagined herself being a mother, but when Anabelle came into the world she found that it was the most rewarding, exhilarating experience of her life. She had not tried to track down the smooth guy from the one-night romance in Hong Kong. She didn't want him involved – Anabelle was her daughter and hers alone, and she was extremely protective of the girl.

Friends also played a very important role in Chrissie's life, compensating for the lack of family. She had an openness to cultivating friendships with anyone she met – old, young, banker or cleaner, because she took no relationship for granted.

They were in the elevator, leaving the childminder's building, when Chrissie thought she'd treat Anabelle to something fun:

"Why don't we…" she started, and Anabelle helped her finish…

"Go to the Hall of Science! Can we Mommy, please can we?"

Normally, they only visited NYSCI on Friday afternoon to benefit from the free entry, but Chrissie was keen to make it special that day.

"Come on, let's get there before everyone else does!" Chrissie said, running from the building.

Almost skipping with happiness, Anabelle proudly held her mom's hand, and they took the Q23 bus up 108th Street. Anabelle rushed around the exhibits and hands-on learning materials, but her main aim was to get to the playground within the grounds – one of the finest play areas in the whole of NYC. Slides, seesaws and sandpits amused Anabelle for the first hour, then she remembered the fog machines and ran off towards those.

Chrissie loved to see her daughter like this, full of life. It was a different story at 6pm when they got home; she was like a zombie, worn out from the day's activities and ready for bed. Once tucked up, Chrissie sat down with a well-deserved glass of Napa Valley Chardonnay.

4

Ana

Sunday, 14 February. Manila, Philippines.

Anastasia de Menzies was born to an Irish-American dancer, Siobhan O'Keele, and a Mexican labourer, Pablo de Menzies Ruiz, 32 years ago. At the time of her birth, her parents were already struggling to keep up with the overactive Jerry in a cheap suburb of San Diego, California. Pablo lasted only three months. According to what her mother told her later, he had walked out of the duplex one morning when Ana was sleeping, supposedly to go to work, and never returned. Much later, after her mother had some fleeting poorly judged relationships, she told Ana that she had tried to track down Pablo, with no luck. So Ana grew up learning to fend for herself, and she always had her brother Jez, who she knew would do anything he could for her. And here she was, aged 32, relying on him to put her up in his home in Manila.

Ana had enjoyed a day sightseeing around the Philippine capital. Her brother's driver had taken her around several sights, including a special souvenir shop, especially for tourists. It was all so cheap! The driver had left her at Maria's Gift Emporium while he went to pick up a friend of Jez's at the airport.

That friend turned out to be Charlie Dunster. When she first saw him, scratching himself and looking distinctly hung-over, she thought 'what a total loser'. However, his understated British charm grew on her during the course of the evening. He was quirky, reasonably intelligent and his intense blue eyes sent her crazy.

It occurred to Ana that she hadn't had sex for over three months and the thought of a no-strings-attached holiday romance was appealing. She wondered if Charlie would take the bait. She would have to be careful not to come on too strong; a buddy's wasted sister could be a man's worst nightmare.

The drunken university exploits that they had blathered on about through dinner hadn't done him any favours and she had realised that if there was going to be any action at all, she would have to take the lead. Strip poker would do the trick.

The sex was perfunctory at best – more like the mechanical sex of a long-married couple rather than a racy first fuck. Of course, she did not reach orgasm, but she thoughtfully faked it for him, not once, but twice. It should bring her good karma. And it had been Valentine's Day after all, not that he seemed to be aware of it, so a good day for sex.

Although 'no-strings' was appealing, she saw a spark of potential in this guy. Sure, she had to lead him along, he was so prudishly British. But she could not help wondering if this was the perfect partner she had been seeking all these years. The Clyde to her Bonnie, she chuckled to herself as she fell asleep in the next room to Charlie.

5

Fournier

Tuesday, 16 February. Golfe-Juan, France.

Agent Fournier prided himself on his bread and butter police work. His supervisor described his best attributes as tenacity and diligence. His peers said he was like a shark that instinctively sensed blood. He himself savoured the other officers' tongue-in-cheek praise, their sarcasm passing him by. Agent Fournier did not remember all the cases that had gone cold during his career, his selective memory only recalled the high-profile wins.

In fairness, most of the cases that came his way were thoroughly trivial. Last week, he was told to close the case of Mme Garcia's car tyres being deflated twice in a week. He felt he would have found the culprit, but results take resources and both were scarce in the *Préfecture de Police* in the French commune of Vallauris Golfe-Juan. Like many detectives, Agent Fournier was jaded by the seemingly never-ending cuts and reorganizations sent down from the top by the *Ministère de l'Intérieur*. Every five years a new government was formed, and correspondingly, every five years someone had a better idea. The cost of the reform itself never seemed to feature in the ministry's calculations.

Agent Fournier pondered why, given all the thought that had gone into the structuring of the nation's police force, no one had spotted the blatant duplication of running two federal police forces with almost identical mandates: the *Police Nationale* and the *Gendarmerie Nationale*. He was aware that both forces dated back to the Middle Ages, but despite numerous battles, and a not insignificant revolution, somehow, the two bodies continued to co-exist side by side in the modern day. Who ever heard such nonsense? But in all 28 years as an Officer of the Law, he had never met another French man or women who shared his view.

"Mais, ils sont différents," they would argue, "One is the government, and the other is the army". This struck Agent Fournier as *ad antiquitatem*: a common fallacy whereby something is deemed correct on the basis that 'this is right because we've always done it this way'.

His international views made him few French friends, but did enchant the non-French. His ex-wife, from whom he had been divorced for nine years, hailed from Texas. They had communicated with each other in English, principally owing to her apparent mental block to learning French. It had resulted in Fournier speaking passable English, with the occasional American inflection mixed in.

Agent Fournier often found himself daydreaming, an upshot of a job that entailed many troughs and precious few peaks. The irony of Inspector Ayad pulling him off half-finished cases, like Mme Garcia's tyres, because it was not worth the time was offset by the fact that once off the case, he sat effectively idle, filing papers, watching the clock and waiting for the phone to ring.

For now, his phone stubbornly refused to spark into action, however much he stared at it. Luckily for Fournier, that would soon change.

6

Me

Friday, 19 February. Boracay, Philippines.

I was lying on a deserted beach, seven thousand miles from home. Next to me lay the bewitching Ana, darkly tanned and wearing a fluorescent orange bikini. It had been three days of sensual bliss on this romantic Philippine island. I felt like the luckiest bastard on Earth.

Jez had been pretty pissed off when he found out about our activities the previous Sunday. Neither of us actually told him. The day after we met, Ana and I had sent the maid home and prepared an evening meal for the three of us, while Jez was at work. Looking back, I guess that had been the first clue; conspiracy to prepare a meal.

Our body language had obviously changed since the previous day, we were comfortable occupying each other's personal space, and our conversation was utterly complementary. We were already supping gin martinis when he arrived and Ana asked if he wanted one.

"You two are looking very companionable..." he started. Ana and I exchanged what must have been guilty looks, since he followed it up with "Oh, for fuck's sake!"

When Jez returned from his room fifteen minutes later, he had mellowed, or, perhaps, realized he was not gatekeeper to his sister's body and mind. Chastity belts were not in vogue. "Right, well I'd better have that martini then," Jez accepted, "unless three's a crowd?" he added sarcastically. His face resembled that of a disappointed dog, like one or other (or both) of us had betrayed him, but he soon cheered up, recounting some of the benefits of his expatriate lifestyle.

Later in the evening, Ana informed him that we'd decided to go away for a few days. Jez asked in my direction, "Where to?"

I had no answer for him as up until that moment I had no idea I was planning to go anywhere. In fact, I was already 'away' and quite happy in the luxurious flat, not out spending money I didn't have. Saying that, in a moment of rare forethought prior to leaving England, I had raised the limit on my MasterCard, providing me with access to around £2000 of extra credit for emergencies. Certain that a romantic weekend with Ana constituted an emergency, but unsure how much of this boondoggle would be my financial responsibility, I thought I'd try to minimize the outgoings.

"Where's a good place near here?" I ventured. I had been thinking about a jungle hut a couple of hours away in a (hopefully free) car, but Jez had his own idea, revenge perhaps, that left little room for negotiation.

"You've gotta make it Boracay. It's absolutely perfect. I was there a couple of months back – sandy beaches, cosy beach bars with excellent cocktails, plenty of top accommodation..." stretching to reach his iPad, he added, "Leaving tomorrow you say? Leave it with me." So that was that.

Boracay turned out to be an idyllic island an hour's flight from Manila, operated by AirAsia's regional service. I was worried about the 12,400 Filipino Pesos for both tickets being put on my card, but it went through okay. Then I discovered that it converted to less than £200, which, to be honest, was a relief.

We landed in the morning at Kalibo International Airport and wandered through the terminal. I was impressed that Ana packed light and we proceeded *Past* passed the luggage carousel. As we negotiated a faulty sliding door that signalled the line between air conditioning and tropical heat, we were set upon by six or seven drivers.

"Where you going? I take you there, good price."

"Where you from? Americano? I know Houston..."

"Come with me, my car over here."

Thankfully, the hotel that Jez booked offered a free pick-up service, and we batted away the taxi touts and headed towards a slightly less feverish throng of drivers holding name boards. Never shy of a prank, Jez had ensured that our board read Mr. and Mrs. Dunster. This seemed a bit presumptuous, but Ana pointed and giggled so I went along with it. The hotel was called

DEAD IN THE WATER

Sandy Beach Resort, which, as a name, appeared to satisfy perfectly what we were seeking.

The driver led us to his minibus, and as the only passengers, we had our choice of seats. We sat beside each other, holding hands, pointing and marvelling at the simple abodes that lined the equally primitive unpaved road. Our 'cottage' was located near the sea with paradisiacal vistas into the Tablas Strait. As the staff showed us the bungalow, Ana dived onto the bed with excitement. Yes, this would do just fine.

There is not that much that can be said about our three days and nights on the island. Each day seemed to settle into a cycle of sun-sex-sea-sex-sun, only side-stepping that enviable routine to drink delicious cocktails and eat locally-made food – rice with fish, rice with mussels, rice with chicken, rice with soup, rice with rice. Desserts made up for any monotony in the starch department – the quality, taste and variety of fruits was astounding – custard apple, guava, guayabano, kalamansi – I hadn't heard of half of them before.

The love making on day three had been especially stimulating. Without saying as much, we took turns to morph into increasingly adventurous positions, trusting the other with their desire. Sliding into her from behind as she looked out towards the bay had made her writhe with pleasure. Reverse cowgirl was her idea, and one of her best!

After we were both well satisfied, we laid spooning on the bed. I felt totally at ease with her. Keen to show her, I uttered the words that I do not volunteer easily, "I think I might be in love with you, Ana de Menzies."

She didn't seem to acknowledge the gravity of my declaration, instead muttering "Why thank you, Mr. Dunster." Then she took the pillow talk in a curious direction, whispering, "Charlie, have you ever thought about ending someone's life?"

"Ha! um, well apart from the odd despot or dictator, not really, no." I offered.

"Seriously, for love, or for money, or for revenge," she continued, "if you thought you could get away with it?"

"Um, no I can't say I have. Have you?" I asked, half dreading the response.

"Yes, sometimes."

At the time I shrugged off the comment as silly, but looking back, I should have taken it very seriously.

7

Ana

Friday, 19 February. Boracay, Philippines.

Ana found herself really enjoying Charlie's company, so, on a whim, she told her brother that she and Charlie were going away for a few days. There was no great premeditation to her announcement, but once Jez had rumbled her previous night's intimacy with Charlie, a) she did not really want to carry on under Jez's nose, and b) she reckoned she could get Charlie to pay for it. "Let's see how serious he is," she had muttered to Jez.

She put Charlie's mediocre performance during their first sexual encounter down to first-night nerves and/or stage fright. She had been pleased to discover that he could learn with a little careful guidance. Using few words, over the next three days, she taught him how it was the journey, not the destination that was important, and how orgasm was not the only 'key performance indicator' as Jez would put it.

Whereas at the start, Charlie could not wait for the penetrative chapter of love making, by day three he'd gone too far the other way and she had to hasten his resolve. Ana taught him about joys of her tropical bird's feather tickler, which she kept in a glasses case and never travelled without, typically reserving it for her own personal use. However, sharing the feather with Charlie brought intimate sensations all over her body that could easily outclass his intuitive approach. As he teased the feather from her fingertips along her inner arm, down her flanks (as Charlie liked to refer to them) crossing to her inner thigh and through the calf to her toes, she had to congratulate herself – the tutor had guided the protégé. Likewise, Ana calmed him down, by applying pressure behind the ear, she was able to slow down his excitement, intensifying the whole experience.

On their final day on the island and her penultimate day in the Philippines, the inevitable happened. She had known it would. He said those embarrassing words, "I think I might be in love with you, Ana de Menzies." She hit back with the killer line, that should slow him down!

Frankly, she was not even sure they would see each other again after this little mini break was over. Long-distance relationships never worked. Yes, she was enjoying the moment, but that may well be all it was. A moment. A fling. Casual sex.

8

Fournier

Tuesday, 15 March. Golfe-Juan, France.

Agent Fournier had been twiddling his thumbs for almost a month when he received a call from the harbourmaster at Golfe-Juan. He reported suspicious activity on a catamaran moored in the outer harbour, a part of the marina which he referred to as 'the cheap seats'. Actually, moorings were still appallingly expensive, but compared to the jetty-side moorings, they were inexpensive. The 'suspicious activity', he was told, amounted to four well-built men, whom the harbourmaster did not recognize, boarding the sailing yacht when the owner had clearly advised him that no one would be using the boat until May.

Relieved to have some real police work to do, Agent Fournier clutched the keys to his fifteen-year-old Police issue unmarked Renault 19 and moved, almost with a spring in his step, to his reserved parking spot on the street side, next to the *Mairie*.

Out of season, Golfe-Juan was a skeleton of its summer self. There were many parking spots to choose from at the harbour, however Agent Fournier exercised his prerogative and bunked the old Renault up near the fire hydrant. Purposefully, he strode towards the harbourmaster's office.

Although the Maritime Gendarmerie existed for open water maritime policing, when the incident lay within the harbour area, the land-based police were often first on scene. They kept a meagrely powered old patrol boat for such eventualities, although it was rarely taken past the harbour walls. Should any fugitive take off into the Med Sea proper, Agent Fournier's boat would not offer any opportunity to chase anything faster than a sailboat – and anyway, once outside of the harbour, it would fall solely under the Maritime Gendarmerie's jurisdiction.

The harbourmaster pointed to the 40-foot sailing boat and observed, *"Ils sont encore là,"* – they are still there. He explained that they had arrived around 25 minutes earlier and appeared to be preparing the boat for departure. Using binoculars, he had witnessed the men using bolt cutters to gain entry to the cabin. Boat theft had been increasing in recent years, particularly with sail boats, which were harder to secure. If the thieves could get access to the sails and could rupture the anchor chain, they were away.

Agent Fournier seldom enjoyed the benefit of a fellow police officer accompanying him – all thanks to the cuts from the top. Everyone knew it was safer and better – and far less boring – to operate with a partner, but outside of the big cities, it was more and more common to be rostered solo.

The harbourmaster told Fournier that the men had arrived by way of an inflatable rental speedboat, a so-called RIB, equipped with a powerful outboard motor. Using the harbourmaster's binoculars Fournier could see them attempting to hoist the main sail. Typically, a skipper would motor out of harbour, so hoisting the sail within the harbour walls was, at a minimum, unusual. Fournier tried to imagine what they might be up to.

The detective knew better than to presume too much when first arriving at an incident. The scope for making incorrect assumptions was just so vast. He also knew that he had to be ready for anything; when things turned sour, they invariably did so quickly. He pulled back the cover on the pitiful outboard motor and primed it.

His vessel was conspicuous – large white letters denoted *GENDARMERIE* on the side. Its maximum speed was around 15 knots, with no head current – one of the reasons it had been taken out of regular service. This fine velocity tailed off dramatically if it was going against the flow. As Agent Fournier neared the compromised boat – about 50 yards out and a good minute away, he became aware of a commotion on board – an argument between men. One muscle head was accosting another, while his two co-conspirators looked on. The shorter of the two onlookers noticed Agent Fournier first, judging by his reactions. Within an instant, all four had piled into their high-powered RIB and gunned the engine.

Agent Fournier was helpless to do any more, he was not authorized to give chase in open water, and anyway their boat would outpace him from the start. He called it in to his prefecture and also informed the Maritime Gendarmerie.

He found his sea-faring colleagues annoyingly blasé about it. *"La prochaine fois, Agent."* – next time, officer – was the response he received, which hardly inspired visions of a pursuit in an ultra-powered speedboat. Instead, it conjured up a picture of a familiar cosy café in Juan-les-Pins, two cigarettes and two coffees with two sugar cubes.

Dejected, Agent Fournier nevertheless secured his patrol boat adjacent to the catamaran. The cat was a beautiful vessel, but not in the league of billionaire's row, near the harbourmaster's office. The yachts that people moored here blew his mind. It cost over €1000 to stay for the night, which, he figured, is peanuts when your vessel is worth over €100 million. But the running costs must get noticed even by the richest owners – for the grandest yachts up to half a million euros to fill up the tanks alone! Incredible.

On board, he photographed some discarded tools and the minor damage caused, and returned to land to explain what he'd found to the harbourmaster. He made a note of the boat's name – Shooting Star.

9

Me

Saturday, 23 April. Lauterbrunen, Switzerland.

After Ana took her flight home from Manila, it wasn't the same. I had hung around for a few more days before deciding that trip was no longer satisfying me. I was looking for some greater excitement and purpose.

A couple of months later, the season was right to resume my interest in aerial thrills. The Lauterbrunen valley had vertical cliffs almost 1km high, with glistening rampant waterfalls scattered along its length.

Despite his 56 years, my Uncle Len cut an athletic figure of a man 15 years younger. While he enjoyed Dom Perignon and Châteauneuf-du-Pape, he exercised daily and watched carefully what he ordered during his business lunches.

As agreed, I met Len at the bottom of the cable car that ascended the mountain. I had arrived first, by virtue of staying in a small *gasthaus* in the village that was two hour's drive from Basel airport. Len reached the car park in his Tesla electric sports car (the bastard) an hour later at 7:30am.

It had been my idea to take our air exploits to the next level, and although an experienced skydiver, I was new to BASE jumping. I knew that it was not illegal in most cantons of Switzerland, although we went along with the local custom and bought 'landing cards' which a mate had said helped the local farmers to relax about the deluge of jumpers landing in their fields whenever the sun came out.

A wingsuit looks a bit like a wetsuit, but comes with wings. The idea is to jump from planes or high mountains and experience the most dangerous buzz available to man. They have been around for ages in various forms: long after Icarus's desire to fly, an Austrian geezer named Franz Reichelt used his experience as a tailor in Paris to patch together a primitive wingsuit for the benefit of a 1911 silent movie. A dummy was meant to be used for the test flight from the Eiffel tower, but crazy Franz decided to don the tailored feathers himself. He lingered on the edge of the Eiffel Tower for a moment on a barstool, wearing only his flouncy invention. Then he stepped over the barrier and plummeted to his death below, creating a hole in the frosty ground almost a foot deep.

Evidently, there was some fine-tuning to do.

Nearly 100 years of industrial evolution had done the trick and my wingsuit, thankfully, was a massive improvement on Franz's frock. The Lauterbrunen valley in Switzerland was recommended as a hot spot for trying such activities.

"Are you sure about this, Charlie?"

"Getting cold feet, Len?" I teased.

"Not at all, not at all. Just don't want to show you up…"

Our banter was still good-natured and I had arranged for a local kid to come with us to bring the unwanted kit back down. He was about 18 and knew some of the most popular BASE jumping spots. We took the express cable car and then the train, and by 9:30am we were standing at the edge of the ravine.

Len and I paced around looking at the breath-taking panorama that surrounded us. His bald shiny dome was reflecting the morning sun as he peeled off his detachable hiking trousers and North Face fleece. It should be noted Len is the sort of guy you love and hate. I spent the first part of my life admiring him, and now I'm starting to sway the other way. Today, though, it's going well.

The nearest peak was Jungfrau: the mythical young virgin's mountain. We could see the highest European railway station at Jungfraujoch with its 9km tunnel, a remarkable achievement of engineering completed around the time of Franz's deadly stunt. A little further away, we could catch sight of Mont Blanc, towering in its majestic white way, looking like a sugar pile. The rocks around us were dry and the early morning mist had lifted to reveal the sort of vista that you see in coffee-table books. Those high tumbling cascades lined the inland cliff walls, bringing perspective and a dewy animation to the scene. For ten minutes we strode from one side of the precipice to the other. Finally Len broke the silence, singing a Macklemore line, "This is fuck-in' awesome…"

We had rented the same type of suit – a latest model Tony Suits X-bird. It had a protruding tail wing which allowed it a glide ratio of over 4:1, meaning we should get 4km of range from a 1km vertical decent.

Kitted up with helmets, goggles and a parachute, we stepped towards the edge. I thought it was the ultimate display of man in concert with nature. My heart was beating fucking overtime. Len just seemed to want to get on with it. He jeered, "What's the matter McFly? Chicken?"

I looked up to the sky, formed fists with both my hands and yelled, "On three – one, two, three," followed by a sound that was not a word, more a primeval chant. We were side-by-side, airborne, and I was descending fast – nothing like the advertised ratio. I looked down and wondered whether this was it – game over. I knew the dangers of the sport, we both had friends who had hit the deck, dead on scene. Watching the rock face passing my line of vision at an alarming pace, I let my unconscious guide me.

I had been flying like a wounded bird for just over a minute – it seemed much longer, but my watch and altimeter confirmed the case. I flicked my wrists back and extended my arms up and out, stretching the webbed canopy taught. This important action repaired my ratio, I finally started to enjoy the sensation, ripping through the air, feeling like Superman. A split second of peripheral awareness informed me that Len was tracking slightly ahead of me in terms of the horizontal trajectory, but still higher up. Endorphins were pumping hard through my veins.

The noise was absolutely deafening, like trying to hear someone on your mobile phone when a gale's whipping up. My vision was also struggling to process the terrifying speed we were maintaining, my eyes running as my watch informed me we hit 100 miles per hour. It is a truly exhilarating feeling. I was still around 400m from valley floor when I suddenly felt a terrifying blow to my body. Startling.

I struggled to work out if I had hit something – a bird? The canopy of a parachute? Was I close enough to hit a tree branch? Or had something hit me? Another person? Wildlife? I was confused, barely able to see, while the wind rush and blinding sun was disorienting me. I was scared shitless that final impact was imminent.

As I brought myself together, it became clear that it was Len, the imbecile, that had collided with me from above.

In what can only be described as pantomime fashion, minus the donkey, I found myself with Len in my arms like a groom carrying a bride across the threshold. Now that I knew my problem, my next thought was to eject this unwanted parasite from my tired arms, or both of us would die within seconds.

With adrenalin taking over, I grappled with his limp body searching for his main or emergency chute cord. I could not imagine bringing the two of us safely to the ground as one unit. My window of opportunity to do anything at all was closing every millisecond, as we plummeted at a glide ration of 1:1 towards the valley floor.

In a moment of self-preservation, I came to the conclusion that I could not save the both of us. The best utility I could get out of this was my own life, although by that moment even that option was evaporating. Suddenly, an image of Ana laying post-sex flashed before me: "Have you ever thought about ending someone's life?" Impulse took over, Len was unconscious. I should at least give him a chance.

With my last burst of energy, I pulled my chute, and somehow, as Len fell away, I caught his emergency chute cord. The violent movement, or perhaps the lower altitude and decreasing speed brought him back, and as I saw him slow, his eyes were like golf balls

We both took clumsy landings, alarming a cattle herd, but we were alive. Len crumbed into a weeping heap as the shock of what just occurred caught up with him. His good fortune coupled with my intervention had saved him, and he knew it.

That evening, as we said our farewells to return to our respective homes, Len uttered in a kindly voice that he would 'take care of me.' I began to wonder what that meant.

10

Tuesday, 26 April. Golfe-Juan, France.

Agent Fournier drove the five minutes back to Vallauris-Golfe-Juan Police Station. Inspector Ayad had been in the office all week, and that arrangement was not suiting Fournier one jot. He had become accustomed to working on his own and did not appreciate Ayad hanging around, poking his nose where it wasn't needed. He wished Ayad would tap his irritating pen and chew his never-ending gum in another station in the Antibes district. He could no longer endure it.

Nothing had come of the boat break-in back in February. He had written it all up, together with recommendations of how it could be investigated further. Ayad had instructed him to file it. No return on investment, he had said. Fournier could not understand the logic of it – the cases he selected, the cases he let go.

He had just returned from investigating a spate of tagging near the railway station. Youths either living locally, or perhaps coming in by train from Nice or Cannes, had taken to spray painting their signatures on the railway walls and freight cars. Some of the graffiti was admittedly much more than tags – it was street art. Nevertheless, Fournier had no time for any of it. He had reviewed the CCTV recordings, but it was not possible to identify the culprits under the hoodies they wore. The perpetrators predictably fled when uniformed officers showed up.

Fournier slumped down into his old, ripped swivel chair, behind a desk that looked like it was from a different century. Well, it was. A hot flush came over his face. He had planned to log into the case database and update what he had discovered, but he was interrupted as he felt the left side of his face beginning to twitch uncontrollably. It had become an unwelcome but increasingly familiar sensation over the past six months, and he knew what was to follow.

His heart started thumping like a brass band's drum, boom-bom, boom-bom, boom-bom, probably a pulse of 120 – quite a beat to dance to. A feeling of anxiety ran through his veins. Then he blacked out.

When he came to he felt like he was waking from an all-night French wedding. He knew he must cut down on the booze, but that was far easier said than done.

And he should get some proper exercise.

And eat more healthily.

Depressed with how that life sounded, he went outside for a cigarette.

11

Scott

Friday, 6 May. London, England.

It was just another day. Scott was the first to rise at 6am with the previous night's wine and whisky still pulsing through his bloodstream. He took the dog for a long walk, out of the neighbourhood, past the store and along a track that made him feel like he lived in the countryside, not the 1980s housing project he called home. The only other humans up and about at that hour seemed to be joggers – a pastime he could not fathom. Runners seemed to think they shared some sort of affinity with him, Scott with the dog, them with the sweaty well-toned bodies, but reality could not be further from the truth.

He had discovered that doing the honourable thing and exercising the Labrador also relieved him of the tiresome duty of waking and dressing the girls. When he returned, breakfast was in full swing, so he stuffed a capsule in the machine, pressed the button and downed the contents freshly presented to him.

Scott Dunster picked up his phone and checked Facebook. He was supremely envious of the posts his brother, Charlie, had been publicly taunting him with. Why did he even look? The latest read "Thanks for the great idea, Scott." and showed him in the Philippines, with a stunning woman at his side. Arsehole.

He looked down at his bulging midriff. It distressed him, but he couldn't think of a way out of it. He hated running. He hated exercise. And he had convinced himself that his daily jaunts to the Nag's Head were essential in his mental well-being, that they made his life a little more interesting. He considered a diet plan that restricted breakfast to coffee and a cigarette and that he would maybe add a portion of salad to his considerable daily lunch.

Scott had grown up with great aspirations. His father's estate agent business had provided a charmed early upbringing for him. When it had imploded after Black Wednesday in the early 1990s, he and his brother Charlie had to get accustomed to a more humble existence.

Some years later, Scott left Southampton University with a First in Geography. He found a contract job with a mobile phone provider, planning the optimal positioning of mobile phone masts.

His work that day could be described as ordinary, unspectacular, mundane. There was no pressure, but no pleasure either. He told himself he would leave his career and follow his dreams – but he knew that it was never going to happen. In ten years, the girls would both be away at university, he would be in his fifties, and would ride out another 15 years to his retirement. Knowing his luck, he would then succumb to a terminal disease before he turned 70. Reenergized to live for the moment – or perhaps in the past – he texted his brother to see if he could conveniently be called upon for some reason or another – DIY, form-filling, fixing the bike, he wasn't fussy.

By 6pm on that pivotal Friday, Scott had made his excuses with his wife and taken the bus to Oxford train station. The train was one of the new lighter trains, little more than a bus on tracks – two carriages clickerty-clacking through the plush home counties of southern England. Scott had worked on the project to get mobile coverage on these trains, so he felt duty-bound to surf the net on his smartphone, which had the results of draining the battery at an alarming pace. He was pleased with the 62-minute duration of the ride, but mystified that it cost the same as flying to most European capitals – still he figured he would not be in a fit state to drive home later. He reached Charlie's newly-acquired, shared, home on Bermondsey Terrace in London at around 7:30pm, dumped his bag and the brothers set off to a nearby pub, wittily named *The Office*.

Charlie was legendary in his brother's eyes for always having the latest technology – particularly when it involved cameras or social media. Scott had not even noticed the badge-like object on his lapel, about the size of a 50 pence piece. Charlie informed him that this was the Narrative Clip, all the rage, he said. It housed a five megapixel camera that takes a picture every 30 seconds.

"What for?" was Scott's first question.

"It records your day, who you meet, what you see."

"And then what?" Scott continued.

"You can share the more interesting ones on Snapchat, Twitter or Facebook."

By the self-satisfied look on his face, Charlie seemed to think this reason was evidence enough. Scott wanted to keep asking 'what for', but at that point an acquaintance of Charlie's slapped him hard on the shoulder, sloshing a good quantity of beer onto Scott's trousers.

"Hey, buddy, how's it going?" The friend appeared to be American.

"Bob, let me introduce you to my brother, Scott."

"Good evening, Sir," he said, which might have been mocking or could have been over polite in an American sort of way.

Bob turned out to be quite the entertainer. Beer spilling antics aside, he was never lost for words, ideas or where to go next. He had been living in London for six years, but had lost none of the bouncy twang. And he was Canadian. How was a man to know? Luckily, Bob had an answer to that too.

"Canadians say 'eh' at the end of a sentence, making the semblance of a question. Like, 'we should be going, eh?'" Bob explained. Scott wished he hadn't asked.

By the time midnight came, the three of them had patronized five different pubs ('You're a great pub, no, really…' a poor joke that Scott never ceased to over-use) and had made their way to the Roxy Bar. Scott realized he would miss the last train back, and made no discernible effort to catch it – a night on the sofa it would be. The goddess behind the bar poured them three more mópets – or tequila slammers for the uninitiated – with the obligatory lime and salt. Bob seemed to think this was a splendid idea. Scott was too wasted to argue. The bar had taken a decidedly blurry turn and when he returned from the men's room, there were two girls talking to Charlie and Bob. Unsure where they came from, he opted to ogle at them, or perhaps through them, but the conversation was moving too fast for him, and his contributions earned only scoffs and tuts from the girls. Had he drunk that much more than the others?

On the next visit to the toilets shortly afterwards, on a whim, he decided it was time to depart. His body was on auto-shutdown after quite a few pints, the awful choice of a vodka-based cocktail, a slightly more enlightened pick of a margarita, and the nail in the coffin of two shots of tequila. Recounting this sorry tally as he stumbled towards the tube, he realised that, other than a few nibbles, he had consumed only a liquid dinner. He promised himself to make a sandwich once he reached Charlie's kitchen.

His lucky break came when he caught the last underground train, saving a good £40 on taxi fare, since he could not fathom the night buses even if sober. The Underground guard stared at Scott in his unsteady state, and for a moment he thought he would be denied entry, then the man just returned to swiping his phone.

Reaching Charlie's door, each step was a small step for most people, but a huge leap for this man. Putting his hand in his pocket, he felt the colour drain out of his face. In his eagerness to vacate Roxy's and its cheap tequila, he had neglected to ask Charlie for a key. He grabbed his phone and made the call. Annoyingly, his earlier train surfing came back to bite him as the phone shut down, out of battery just as Charlie answered.

Never one to be outsmarted by bad luck, he approached Charlie's front door. It was locked, as expected. Stepping down to the basement door, via a set of concrete steps with a wrought iron barrier, things were looking decidedly more positive. The double door was ancient with paint peeling away from the frame. As he shook it, he could see that it was not going to put up a great deal of resistance and appeared to be poorly secured. Pushing it back and forth, it was almost open, and with one drunken shove, Scott was satisfied that it gave way, splintering the frame, and securing his passage towards a much needed kip.

It was at that point that he heard the most tremendous ear-piercing scream, and suddenly everything went black.

When Scott came back to consciousness, the Metropolitan policeman was saying, "Nice and easy, mate, nice and easy." Then he added, "Now give me your left hand, thumb first." Clearly fingerprints were order of the day. Scott became aware that he was crying, which was a foreign sensation for him. He wondered what on earth had happened since he had last been lucid. Had he passed out? Had he fallen asleep? Is there a difference? As he scratched his head to ponder this important thought, an instinctive, "Fuck!" slipped from his lips.

The policeman, who had been so mellow just a moment ago, gave a firm warning: "Any more of that and you will add breach of peace to your problems." Scott, thrown by this unsolicited advice, managed, "Sorry, Officer." although he was sure he had read in the paper that it was now his basic human right to swear at will to a police officer.

Within an hour, he had made his statement of his memory of what happened, with Police Constable Duncan Welks helping him with the blanks. He had been trying to enter his brother's house, no, he was not resident there, and no, he did not have a key. Given the late hour, he decided to gain entry, yes, it could be considered breaking and entering, via the basement doors. No, he was not aware that his brother's housemate was in that room, *her* bedroom, sleeping at the time. Indeed, it was easy to understand her shock and horror that she would no doubt have experienced, and he did not blame her for striking him with a solid wood African carving, which had caused him the painful concussion (not a passing out, then).

Although he had come around physically at the house, he held no recollection until he reached the police station. Indeed he admitted the offence. Scott did not see much point in having a solicitor get involved, if, as the police constable offered, he could receive just a caution and be out once he sobered up.

The sooner the whole issue was over, the better.

12

Ana

Saturday, 7 May. London, England.

After their whirlwind romance in the Philippines, Ana wasn't sure if she would make the effort to see Charlie again. Since she found little difficulty in attracting good looking men, why bother with this man on the other side of the Atlantic? But there was something intriguing about him, his sarcasm, his desire to improve his lot in life. What's more, he was infatuated with her, which meant she could get him to do pretty much anything she wished. Ana left sunny California the previous evening, landing at London Heathrow around 9:20am. The contrast could not have been more marked. Horizontal rain, low cloud and a stagnant air welcomed her to the English capital.

Charlie was waiting for her at Terminal 2. She thought he looked far more ordinary in his native setting. Gone were the bright shorts and 1970s sunglasses, replaced by jeans, sneakers and a T-shirt; he looked like most of the other guys! Nevertheless, she was pleased to see him as they made out, in the kissing sense, on the concourse and she wondered what journeys lay ahead for them. Charlie seemed to be good at finding adventures.

The subway seemed to take forever, the Piccadilly line then the Jubilee line, Charlie told her. Eventually they reached his rented accommodation – a room he rented in a shared house. She was impressed with how modern and well-tended the place was. On entering, after passing both of Charlie's bikes and a tote bag in the entrance hall, she was struck by the pureness of the common areas – tastefully presented artwork was hung using fine wire from the high picture rails. Slightly worn thin grade hardwood floors provided warmth and vibrant matching red sofas were set to completely envelop the unwitting sitter.

By that time it was almost midday, and it was at that moment that Charlie insisted he needed a shower to freshen up after a long night, so, wondering how it could have been longer than hers, Ana snuggled down into one of the sofas and flicked though something called The Big Issue. A short time later, Charlie's housemate passed en route to the kitchen, saying, "Hi!" and looking like she had something to say.

The housemate turned out to be the vivacious Stella Cooper, and within minutes, Ana felt she was reuniting with an old school friend. Perhaps it was the shared homeland that they talked about – the mighty USA – that made them so comfortable in each other's presence. Stella told her that she had grown up on Chicago's South Side where her dad worked at the Port of Chicago. Like

DEAD IN THE WATER

most of the residents on South Side, Stella was African American, and she recounted how her uncompromising father instilled in her a deep sense of responsibility and work ethic that she said explained her studious nature. Ana found it contrasted with her own almost Bohemian upbringing, where she was given free rein to follow her whims although now her mother frequently told her that she had failed to reach her potential, especially when compared to her brother, Jez.

Stella, suddenly seeming to remember where she had been going before she met Ana, jumped up and grabbed a bottle of Shiraz and two glasses, filling them both and handing one over, exclaiming, "Cheers – to beating men unconscious." Flustered as to why she was celebrating such a violent toast, or perhaps because it was still 4am for her and she was not at her most alert, Ana spilt her wine, staining her blouse.

"Shit!" Ana muttered, mostly to herself.

"Oops, here," Stella said, offering a paper towel.

"I can be so clumsy. Look at me! Sorry Stella, what are we toasting again?"

"Last night, this creep broke into my room at one o'clock in the morning, Mr. Gooma smacked him on the head," explained Stella.

"Who's Mr. Gooma?"

"Oh, yes, good point. He's an 'it' under my spell: a tribal head carving from my aunt's village in the Senegal."

At that point, Charlie walked out from an exceptionally long shower, blue towel around his waist, speaking animatedly into the phone, "No fucking way. You're not serious! Well, when you buggered off, Bob and I went to a club, then I figured a greasy spoon on the way to the airport to meet Ana would fix me up. Figured you were going home, since you did not ask for my keys." There was a pause, in the audio as far as Ana was concerned, then, "Well frankly, I did not study the time of the last train to Oxford – next time I'll be sure to check!" he continued, goading his brother. Charlie was listening and laughing to his brother's tale when he seemed to notice Stella and Ana were gawking at him. "I'll call you back."

"Charlie?" Stella broke the empty airwaves and disrupted the four staring eyes.

"Yep?" Charlie replied, knowingly.

"Did I hear you say -"

"Were you eavesdropping?"

"I hardly had a glass to the wall, Charlie, you were broadcasting right next to me…"

"Still, you didn't have to listen." Charlie was just playing with her, because he knew he was holding the solution to her personal game of Cluedo. "If you want to make a guess, you have to return to the centre of the board."

"Okay, well I know it took place in the bedroom, in *my* bedroom."

"Right so far!"

"And I know it was the African carving, and not the lead piping."

"Right again!" Charlie was enjoying this.

"Just not sure of the perpetrator – who was that on the phone?" continued Stella, seeing a little humour in their one-two that Charlie seemed to be milking for Ana's benefit.

"Well if you are not going to make -"

"Charlie!" Stella shouted, her amusement fading fast.

"Okay, okay. It was my brother, Scott," Charlie revealed.

"Mr. Middle-aged-phone-man that you told me about?"

"The very one."

13

Len

Saturday, 7 May. Geneva, Switzerland.

Len Hubbard was at the office on a Saturday, catching up on his official and unofficial work. He looked through his many emails. One caught his attention, it carried the subject 'Your daughter'. He remembered that he had received two letters from a woman in New York, claiming that he was her father. Len rather liked the idea of suddenly winning a daughter, after a lifetime of believing he was childless. Despite this, he had thrown away the letters that she had sent. But this time there was a photo. And his potential daughter-to-be was beautiful.

Back in the 1980s, Len was married to his first wife. He could not remember a time when he was faithful to her and nor could he remember specifically a romantic liaison with a Joyce in New Orleans. Hubbard did have some moral standards, albeit comparing to a low bar. He decided to suggest a DNA paternity test. If she *was* his daughter, he would like to know.

Len despised Geneva as a city. The attraction was discreet private banks that were more than willing to turn a blind eye for a cut of the cake. This little fiscal arrangement suited him perfectly. His businesses were built on financing ethically-challenged start-ups, and making big returns when it worked. More recently, his Board position for an expanding oil trading company had been lucrative, buying oil products at knock-down prices from the desperate Russians, and selling to anyone that wanted them. Stoilco Trading Cie boasted a significant number of employees on precarious contracts and prided itself on its cut-throat business approach, and although his role was non-executive, Len knew every major deal that was signed.

The oil trading executives in Geneva were a motley bunch of money hungry maniacs who considered shady business ethics par for the course during economically difficult times. Len Hubbard was no exception and the plummeting cost of a barrel of oil cost Stoilco dearly when they backed the wrong scenario. His personal fortune had correspondingly suffered, both because of declining share value at Stoilco, and thanks to some new senseless bilateral agreements that the Swiss authorities had signed promising to hand over the names of tax minimizers to some European nations.

Companies like Stoilco chose Geneva as a business headquarters, owing to its race-to-the-bottom corporate tax schemes. This more than made up for higher staff salaries required to sustain lifestyles in the Geneva area. However, Len's estate differed from his peers as he bowed to the pressure of his wife Mia, agreeing to set up home in the frontier region of neighbouring France.

It took Len Hubbard half an hour to drive back to the house that locals had named 'le château' and stood, looking out over the garden of his nineteenth-century renovated farmhouse, located in the idyllic French village of Echenevex. At the end of the garden, a group of four were teeing off on the popular eighteen-hole golf course that bordered the source of the Allondon River further over. As his wife, Mia, entered the conservatory, he lit a Cuban cigar and bemoaned her choice of living location. "Sweet Pea, my accountant has been on the phone again, we really must consider moving across the border to Switzerland." Hubbard had been a rough-cut diamond when they had met, who had refined his London East End accent over the years, now sounding more 'mockney', a hybrid dialect more frequently used by well-bred boys wanting to sound a bit rough.

"You can consider it all you like, I will not be leaving our home! I love it here, Len," she pointed, "up there we have the ski resorts of the Jura Mountains and over there Mont Blanc."

"Precious, listen to me, the Canton of Vaud has nice views too. Michael Schumacher is rehabilitating there, the founder of IKEA had his home there, they've had Phil Collins, Charlie Chaplin, Ernest Hemmingway – it can't be too bad. Let's take a look at the weekend?"

"Over my dead body!" retorted Mia.

14

Chrissie

Saturday, 7 May. Forest Hills, New York, USA.

Chrissie and Anabelle were up before 7am even though it was a Saturday. Chrissie had the weekend off and the two were planning a trip to see Anabelle's grandma in Philadelphia. Since Chrissie did not own a car, they would take the train.

They boarded the Acela Express at Pennsylvania Station in New York. Anabelle loved any adventure and taking two trains in one morning ranked as highly as the moon landing. Chrissie, her dark hair trailing behind her, felt a sense of immense pride holding the hand of her cute, smart four-year-old daughter. All the strangers' adoring looks made her feel like a celebrity. Anabelle could even make gangbangers break into a smile. Today she was sitting opposite an old lady who was full of questions, "Where are you going, sweetheart?"

"To my grandma's."

"Is that mummy's mummy or daddy's mummy?"

"I don't have a daddy." That shut the teacher up for a while, but it always gave Chrissie a pang of guilt when her daughter told anyone that.

Sitting on the train, Chrissie thought through her own attempts to find her father. She first tried a few years ago, using a name her mum had given her. The name was Len Hubbard and she thought he worked in the oil and gas industry at the time. Chrissie had Googled and searched the name on Linkedin. There were 54 men going by that name on Linkedin alone, however one profile stood out as broadly the right age and industry: Len Hubbard, Independent Board Member, Stoilco, based in Geneva. Chrissie had hand-written a letter and posted it to the company address, but she never heard anything back. She tried again around two years ago. The second time she opted for an element of certitude. That letter started:

Dear Dad,

32 years ago you had a brief relationship with a woman named Joyce Morris while on business in New Orleans. My mother has told me all about it. Nine months later, I was born. I am a flight attendant, I live in New York City with my two-year-old daughter.

As the weeks and months passed, she had felt immense disappointment that her father had not even acknowledged her letters. After thirty-two years, surely anyone would want to make contact with their offspring, however they were conceived?

Chrissie had started cyber-stalking the Geneva Len Hubbard, finding out anything she could about him. His picture was on the company website along with various press articles, mostly concerning hob-nobbing with politicians, businessmen and so on. One of the press articles included his email address, which seemed preferable to sending a Linkedin message.

Two weeks earlier, Chrissie had tried to make contact again, this time by email. She attached a photo showing herself, her mum, Joyce, and her daughter, Anabelle. It looked like a decorator's paint colour palette, Joyce on the left, her plump black face making it difficult to see the definition of her features. Chrissie, a delicious chocolaty mixed race colour, she thought, black hair and bright shiny teeth. Anabelle on the right was lighter again, her biological father a Scandinavian co-pilot. Her message included a clear invite for her father to get in contact by whatever means suited him.

Her thought process was interrupted by the old lady resuming her interrogation. "She has your eyes, don't you think?" Unwilling to egg the woman on, Chrissie made a wide artificial smile, half nodding, which seemed to do the job and conclude their discussion. She took the chance to pull Anabelle's reader from her small rucksack which was complete with soft floppy ears and a dangling trunk. She set about enjoying her daughter's learning.

In what seemed like no time, the streamlined Amtrak train pulled in to 30th Street Station in downtown Philadelphia a little after 9:30am. It was a gorgeous clear spring morning and they exited the airy high-ceiling station by the Market Street exit and strolled across the bridge over the river. They took the water's edge path downstream to Schuylkill River Park, and then it was just one more block to Lombard Street.

Joyce lived in a white-walled 480-square-foot condo in the Fitler Square neighbourhood. Her one-bedroomed home in a six-unit block suited her perfectly, the sofa-bed providing extra space when Chrissie and Anabelle came to stay.

"Hello darling! What a beautiful day! Come in, come in."

They had some soda and ate some cookies that Joyce had baked, at which point Chrissie surreptitiously checked the messages on her phone. Her mum's phone was of the antique variety, so she was not aware of what Chrissie could be doing. There were two messages, one junk, the other sent by HUBBARD, Len. It read more like an acrimonious memo to a colleague, rather than an emotional letter to a long-lost daughter.

Dear Chrissie,

Sorry for not writing before, my secretary did not pass your earlier letters to me. Of course I remember Joyce Morris in New Orleans, a fun and adventurous girl – I hope she is well. While I do not doubt your best intentions, of course, it would be unwise for me to take your claim at face value.

I suggest as a first step, you get a DNA paternity self-test kit. Please send swabs from you and your

mother to me at the address below, and I will do the same and process them here. I will send you a copy of the results.

All the best,

Len.

Chrissie's heart raced like she was on a first date. She ran to tell her mum, who took the news in a more matter-of-fact way.

"Okay dear, I know how important this is for you," she looked at the LinkedIn profile image on Chrissie's phone, "and that is definitely him."

"Can we get a test kit now?" pressed Chrissie.

"What is it, a urine test, or what?" asked Joyce.

"Just a swab of the mouth – takes five minutes."

"Let's go then – there's a Walgreens just along South Street, let's see if they have one of these D and A tests," Joyce agreed.

"DNA," Chrissie corrected. She loved her mum's ability to switch to whatever her needs were at any moment, but she often mixed up the details.

At the chemist, Chrissie bought a DNA Paternity Test Kit for about $30. It all seemed so easy. She read that the results would not be legally binding, but she did not think that would matter. Chrissie was bursting with excitement, and hoping that there had not been a mix-up. The world suddenly seemed enormous, as she began to think that her search for her father was one in a billion.

15

Mia

Saturday, 7 May. Geneva, Switzerland.

Mia Hubbard was the antithesis of her husband. It was truly remarkable that they ever married 15 years ago when she was a timid 24-year-old. She had her own career and refused to be trapped under the wings of her businessman husband. She also liked to keep her finances separate to her husband's. She said it was her insurance if he ever left her, but, there was little chance of that, she thought.

After she had graduated with a Juris Doctor law degree from Georgetown University, she joined the United Nations High Commissioner for Refugees as a Human Rights Officer. Although Mia had never borne children, she had certainly tried with Len. When it did not work, she had undergone fertility tests and had been was assured that she was in 'full working order', the phrase the gynaecologist had used after the results came back. Her husband had consistently refused to take a sperm count test, declaring that he had no doubt about himself. "I can assure you there is nothing wrong with me," he told her. The inference was clear – but as far as

Mia was concerned, he should harbour at least some of the responsibility.

That day, Mia's auburn hair had its trademark windswept look. She dressed in her beige pantaloons and what Len called her power jacket. She agreed that the scarlet short-style garment cut her a dominant figure. She had picked it up on sale at Balexert shopping centre in the summer, and brought it out whenever she made a presentation to a large gathering, or had to negotiate.

Her presentation was at a conference at the United Nations *Palais des Nations* on migrants' rights in Europe. She left her Mini, as usual, in the parkade below the Nations square. She exited the parking via the steps and, prompted by a memorial rock, paused to remember the victims of Srebrenica.

Mia passed the familiar jumping fountain jets that danced in the square. It was a hot spring day and playful children were rushing in-between the water getting thoroughly soaked in the process. She stood for a moment and looked at the sandwich boards of that day's protest. Mia knew that each day, the United Nations and the Canton of Geneva permitted one protest to take place. All very Swiss; all very organized. Today more than 4,000 protesters were assembled in front of the United Nations office demanding international investigations into Tamil genocide – various media organizations were reporting the story.

As she gathered her thoughts for her speech to the assembled dignitaries and government officials, she looked upwards to see the severed chair leg, a memorial for those who have been maimed or killed by landmines, or 'anti-personnel devices' as the manufacturers prefer to call them. The injustice in the world of big business collaborating with governments made her blood boil. She coped with her husband's business activities by blinkering herself from it, because, despite all his foibles, she loved him.

She was first aware that she was being followed as she paused again to look up at the full assembly of flags adorning the UN entrance. She had been mesmerized when a flag was raised for Palestine. Her stalker had dark features and a broad aquiline nose. He was shorter than her, but far more solid, no doubt as a result of regular bodybuilding. In a move intended to disguise his real intent, he swiftly took out his phone and proceeded to take a 'selfie'. How quickly that word has entered into everyday vernacular. She momentarily wished that he would step backwards into the road and join the 49 unwitting casualties that had been accidentally killed taking selfies in the previous year.

She upped her tempo and entered the *Palais* through the staff entrance, which was far more direct than using the visitors' Pregny gate and came with the added bonus that her would-be assailant was not able to pass security. As she walked past the flags, she could see him raising his phone to take photos, or perhaps a video.

Mia did not report it, since there was really nothing to say, and she was pressed for time to reach the conference. After waiting in the side seating for what seemed like an hour, she delivered her planned speech to the assembled guests flawlessly.

She made many friends and many enemies with her discourse, pointing the finger at certain countries for doing too little for refugees from Syria. She insinuated that the European Union's response to cut a deal with Turkey to trap the refugees there was a breach of human rights. Some applauded, others scowled. She left with her head held high.

16

Saturday, 7 May. Oxford, England.

Scott had returned by train from London on the 7:48am Great Western. He had decided against calling Charlie, and anyway, his phone was still flat. The facilities in the Holborn Police Station drunk tank clearly did not run to electrical sockets. Something for the suggestions box, he thought.

After the duty officer had returned Scott's wallet, credit and debit cards, out of date condom and his belt, he had sat on the steps outside the station and closed his eyes for several minutes. What on earth had become of him? Drunk as a skunk and a night in the cells? He should never have accepted that caution – but maintaining no criminal record seemed like a good exchange at the time. Looking at it now, any wet-behind-the-ears solicitor would have made child's play of dismissing the charges. Anyway, it was done, and it would not get back to his employer.

At Paddington train station, he nipped into the chemists. He needed something fast for the sorry state he found himself in. Scott reached for the Nurofen display, and was swept away with the point of sale marketing, as his hand got attracted, almost magnetically, to a product he had not seen before, packaged as Nurofen Express. That sounded like just the job, he hoped it lived up to its name. He completed his rudimentary shopping with a bottle of home-branded water (no need for imported French stuff) and a king size Twix.

"Bad night?" queried the plump cashier without looking up from her smartphone, beeping the products past the scanner.

"Bad night" repeated Scott.

He was fairly happy with his less-than-terrific plan to avoid Charlie and the inevitable ribbing, and more importantly to avoid that crazy housemate woman with the African tribal carving, or whatever it was that knocked him out. As the train was leaving Paddington Station, Scott realized that his overnight bag – with his precious mobile phone charger – was still at Charlie's. It was another of those, 'Oh, bugger' moments, like when you arrive home from the grocery store, only to find that you have neglected to purchase the one item you initially needed. Like the ill-fated supermarket run, he conceded defeat, after all, his few possessions were not truly lost, and Charlie would surely return them soon. He would call him later that day.

Walking home from Oxford Train Station to get some fresh air took an hour at his gentle, fragile pace. Scott stopped at his usual newsagents to pick up a copy of the Daily Express and some daffodils that had seen better days. He figured he had better show willing with Alison to make some effort to revive their moribund marriage. Although only ten minutes later, he would wish that he had not taken the trouble. The realisation that his house (and car) keys were in his overnight bag was his nadir. The temporary key loss was compounded by the unexplained disappearance of the spare set of Ford keys some months earlier. So the result of all this was that he had to ring the doorbell of his own home at 9:54am on that dismal Saturday morning.

"Look what the cat dragged in" – Alison had this irritating habit of speaking in idioms.

"I bought you these," Scott tried with a half-smile, handing her the yellow flowers.

"These! For me! Oh, you shouldn't have." The sarcasm dripped off every word. "I must get the phone looked at since clearly it's not working."

"My phone was dead."

"Says the man who never travels without his charger. Where's your bag – and where the fuck were you last night?" Alison's mind seemed to be functioning significantly faster than Scott's that morning. Scott just could not keep up. Damn the slammers.

"At Charlie's." Scott ventured.

"And you just forgot your bag as you left his house this morning? One thing to pick up. Oh! I've forgotten it!"

"I left it on the train. I'll call them," Scott lied. The words of his dad were rattling around his head – 'When you're in a hole, son...'

Scott was struggling to compute whether it was better to admit the reality of receiving a caution for breaking and entering, *and* for being kept in the drunk tank, or to leave an obviously leaky story, which would undoubtedly lead Alison to conclude that he had spent the night with a sleazy tart called 'Fay'.

Imaginary tarty Fay won the day.

17

Ana

Thursday, 12 May. London, England.

The invite came by snail mail, falling on the bristled entrance mat from the letterbox on another rainy May morning, together with a photo of a 40-foot long white catamaran that was anchored in an idyllic Mediterranean cove. Its cream main sail and bright red spinnaker could be seen folded in place. The photo was taken from an elevated position, most likely the photographer had climbed the steep rock face which could be seen surrounding the natural harbour.

The invitation read:

Dear Charlie.

Come join us on the Côte D'Azur for a week you will never forget!

Meet at the marina in La Spezia, Italy for seven nights on the sea, ending in Antibes in France. Bring a girl and sunscreen! July 16-24.

Adios, Len.

Ana saw it first, Charlie was at work. Ana had never sailed before, but the thought of a week on that boat sounded awesome. When Charlie returned home from work, she bounded up to him like an over-eager puppy being thrown a tennis ball, "Charlie, guess where we are going in July?"

"Mad?"

"The Italian Riviera! And, the French Riviera! The Riviera!"

"You don't look like you're kidding…" Charlie muttered, his eyes scanning left to right looking for an explanation.

"That's because I'm not!" she beamed and flung the invite through the air. Charlie fumbled the catch and it dropped on the floor. Having to reach to pick it up spoilt some of the enjoyment from the moment, but as he studied the text, he could not deny the accuracy of Ana's story.

"A week sailing on the Med! Excellent! Can you come back to Europe for it?"

"I wouldn't miss it for anything!"

These simple yes-no moments can (and did) change her life.

18

Scott

Friday, 13 May. Oxford, England.

Scott arrived home first; the girls had ballet lessons or prance and dance or whatever after school. He scanned carelessly through the post. A book arrived that he had been waiting for, entitled *Seven Steps to Enjoying your Mid-Life Crisis*. Hopefully it had the answers he was seeking. He had become vehemently in touch with his own mortality recently, scared witless at the thought of impending death, and the many ailments that might take him down. Cancers of all flavours troubled him intensely, liver malfunctions, nervous system errors, digestive meltdowns. The list of diseases bringing an unscheduled expiration to the people he knew seemed to be ever growing. Who would be left?

The book had been delivered by Deutsche Post DHL and a utility bill reminder was headed *Électricité de France,* or EDF, as the company prefers to market itself in the UK and he was prompted to start thinking about Europe when he happened upon a postcard, concealed behind a flyer for reasonably priced car loans:

Dear Scott and Alison.

Bring yourselves to the Mediterranean for a week of bad behaviour!

Meet at the harbour in La Spezia for seven days learning to sail. Don't forget the suncream! It's July 16-24.

Ciao, Len.

He was pondering what to do with this amazing invitation when he heard a key in the front door lock. Scott looked up guiltily to see Alison and the girls. "Hi Dad!" chanted Maisy and Charlotte in unison.

"You look like a fox with lamb wool caught in his mouth, what have you done?" began his wife.

"Just looking at this reminder, looks like we forgot to pay the electric bill," Scott bluffed. Well, that much was true.

"Looks like *you* forgot to pay it, that's your department together with duvets and windows," chided Alison. How was it that everything took a turn for the worse so quickly? "Now move out of the way, we are trying to get into the house," she scowled.

Scott folded the postcard and slipped it into his back pocket in one deft movement. Getting an invite to a sailing yacht on the Med just made his woeful day a whole lot better. But there was no way he was wasting it on his wife.

"Peter needs to stretch his legs, who wants to take him out?" It was a rhetorical question from Scott about the family's dog, but he was setting himself up. Silence rung around the house in response. "Okay, I'll take him." Smoothly done.

Outside with the leash in his hand and his Bluetooth earpiece in place, he used speed-dial to make the call. "Hey Charlie, I got a postcard from Uncle Len today."

"You got one too! Excellent. Ana and I are stoked to be going." Scott wondered at which point Charlie had started using Australian lingo. Probably a result of living in London. "The boat looks beaut!" This has to end.

"Stop with the bloody Crocodile Dundee stuff would you?" ordered Scott, in mock anger.

"Sorry, mate," exaggeratedly Australian.

"Listen, it came addressed to me and Alison, but frankly things are a bit shaky between us at the moment. The thought of a week in a confined space with her – well it's just not going to happen. I'm going to tell her I have a conference that week," Scott rattled off.

"Okay bro, whatever," Charlie didn't seem to care one way or another.

"Can you think of anyone else who might want to go in her place?" There was a silence. "And I wasn't thinking of your drinking buddy Bob."

"Oh." Then, "I'll have a think about it. I'll let you know."

"And mum's the word this end." Scott ended the call.

19

Len

Wednesday, 8 June. Geneva, Switzerland.

Len Hubbard's businesses were built on a bedrock of corruption and unscrupulous dealing. Whilst outwardly on the board of the oil trading company, Hubbard also ran offshoots and side entities that he maintained for a variety of reasons, not least of all to boost profits during a period of ailing oil prices.

Guillaume Poyet, a slight man with a light complexion, had been causing him problems for some time. Hubbard had invested his own capital in Poyet's venture to provide dubious clean-tech solutions to a group of investors. Meanwhile, Poyet had put his neck on the line, promising returns of at least five per cent, irrespective of the waves that might hit the market. His main plan was centred on the premise that governments and businesses were falling over themselves to be a part of the green revolution. However, Poyet overestimated companies' interest in such corporate social responsibility projects.

In short, the returns were not there and Hubbard wanted his one-third stake of the one million Swiss franc start-up fund, per their verbal agreement. Unfortunately, Mr. Poyet did not see it that way. Poyet was an entrepreneur, he was used to presenting his business plans in the most favourable light, but what he wasn't used to was Hubbard's unconventional and harsh means to get what he sought.

Geneva is a surprisingly small city, for a conurbation with such a household name. It counts less than 250,000 residents in the city, and even including all the neighbouring satellite towns in Switzerland and France, it peaks only to one million wealthy inhabitants. Workers in the region are involved with one of a few principal sectors: finance, luxury goods, oil trading, pharmaceuticals or the United Nations.

The city centre is serviced by only one main shopping street just across from the Mont Blanc Bridge, where the luxury marques of Swiss watches congregate. The shadiest area – which by any other city's standards is positively salubrious, is Paquis, located between Gare Cornavin and Lake Geneva. Hubbard deliberately chose this area to meet his business associate, Poyet.

On that day, Hubbard arranged to meet the man at a café on Rue du Levant and bought him a glass of beer. He put it to Poyet that he was withdrawing his funding. It was not a request.

"Sorry, Mr. Hubbard, it will take time to devolve your investment."

"That's not what we agreed."

The conversation went largely round in circles, which Len had no patience for. "Guillaume, this is my last offer to settle this amicably."

"Like I said, your disinvestment will take time, Mr. Hubbard. I will see what I can do."

"Right," said Hubbard casually, like he had just understood directions to the airport. "Come, I want to show you something," and he led Poyet towards the lake, along Rue de la Navigation shaded by its tall buildings. After a block, and apparently without warning, they were jumped by a heavy-set assailant sporting a beanie hat. He left Len alone, but dragged Poyet down an alley. The attacker did not talk while he laid into Poyet, pummelling him in the abdomen with punches strong enough to bruise but not severe enough to cause any permanent damage. After all, this was only the first warning. Beanie hat ignored the victim's cries and questions as he fell to the ground, damaged. When Poyet stopped yelling, the man kicked him in the gut, and took his wallet.

Len gave Beanie hat the smallest nod, indicating the reprimand was adequate. Indeed, Len knew the man very well.

Back at the office, Len started through the stack of mail balanced in his in-tray. His administrative assistant normally opened his letters, but she had left the specific item he was looking at untouched, owing to its red and white 'confidential' sticker. The other corner indicated the name of the DNA clinic.

The formal page inside showed the assigned case number and the name – his name as well as the alleged mother and offspring. Then the later stated:

Summary of Findings.

Based on the genetic testing results below, the combined paternity index (genetic odds in favour of paternity) is 49,600,000. The probability of paternity is 99.99% as compared to an unrelated, untested random man of the same race.

Len thought, 'Holy crap! I'm a dad! It's a girl!' For perhaps the first time in his life, Len felt a surge of responsibility for someone other than himself. He immediately made an appointment with his lawyer and decided not to tell Mia about it.

20

Me

Tuesday, 15 June. Laguna Beach, California, USA.

I had been bored shitless on planes for almost 12 hours when we touched down at Los Angeles LAX. I suffered the fundamental economic problem of having seemingly unlimited wants in my world of increasingly limited resources. Thus it was that, to save money, my flight route included two stops.

Flying west, I experienced a state of perpetual daylight that came about with my follow-the-sun flight path. The first plane departed London Heathrow just before noon and I landed in Los Angeles late afternoon, but it sure seemed longer than that.

At LAX airport, wandering through the stereotypically American arrivals hall, I noticed Dunkin' Donuts, Western Union and Wendy's. These are international marques, I know, but put them together in one row and you have USA-in-a-box. It's not a classy ensemble. When at London Heathrow, I noticed Harrods, Burberry and a caviar bar, spot the difference.

What was less usual, but still supporting the three American Bs – big, best and bargain, was the array of 58 flat-screen televisions creating a 90-foot long filmstrip. The films seemed to be focused on travel. One of them was particularly surreal. It followed a household plant being checked in at the baggage counter it chronicled the airport from the plant's point of view, navigating tricky luggage belts and what have you. Anyway, fascinated as I was, I really just wanted to make my way to Ana and climb into bed with her.

It had been four weeks since I last saw her in London, and I have to admit that I missed her a lot. We texted, sexted and kept in touch with a whole raft of social media, but a friend in the flesh is worth ten in the ether. Our first embrace, witnessed by the Mexican family next to us, was a physical and sensual cuddle, Ana's shorter body naturally giving me a mouthful of her bouncy hair.

In her car on the way to Orange County, she came across far more American than I had recalled. The accent seemed harsher, the self-assurance even more pronounced, and the unabated cheeriness was just so absolutely refreshing after the dreariness of Londoners. Everything is just such a depressing drag in the UK compared to the US, where the day is just 'so fucking awesome'.

In Ana's rattling old open-top Mustang, we took Interstate 405 south then Laguna Canyon Road to the Pacific Ocean. First stop was at what Ana called her crash pad. It was on a backstreet, quite a few blocks from the sun-soaked beach. Ana could hardly wait to get inside the door, and we left my small cabin bag in the miniscule 'trunk' in order to get to a state of undress even quicker.

There must have been something about the warm air and pent-up anticipation, because it was not my best performance by a long shot. Even Ana, usually so complementary, wrinkled into an overacted frown and whispered like one might to a hungry dog who had spilt the contents of his food bowl, "Oh, Charlie – you were too excited."

Friday, 18 June. Laguna Beach, California, USA.

The week I spent in Laguna Beach can only be described as other-worldly. We knew that Ana had to work every day except Monday, an agreement that she had struck up with her boss in order to take yet another week's vacation the following month.

A typical day during my getaway would see us wake, make love, have breakfast, more sex, then down to the beach where a constant stream of friends and acquaintances – including, so I learnt, some ex-lovers – seemed omnipresent. Ana told me how she hadn't limited herself to lovers of one gender – "Why would I do that? Don't be such a prude!" – and introduced me to two female more-than-friends. At 3pm, Ana's shift started at the coffee shop, where she worked until closing time. It was a cool, hippy-esque joint and happily the owner did not object to me hanging about sipping ice tea for several hours a day.

On Ana's day off, she suggested we could go to Universal Studios, Disneyland or one of the many nature parks in the area. But in the end we just cruised down the coast towards Mexico. We had lunch listening to crashing waves at Solano Beach and dinner with the view of a vanishing sun on San Diego Bay. We spent a lot of time talking about the future, what we value in life, and how we could get what we wanted. Driving back with the top down on the coast road, I felt like a movie star, next to me, chewing gum was the co-star of my life.

Those dreams were cut short two days later when I landed back at Heathrow, my souring mood only kept afloat by our next planned reconnaissance only three weeks later, which couldn't come soon enough.

21

Me

Friday, 15 July. Europe.

The time passed quickly back in the office and I was glad when the all-important date came. It was Ana's idea to take the train – she had arrived the day before on a direct flight from Los Angeles and I think the idea of travelling by rail across Europe was more romantic than an orange-themed budget flight. It was certainly much more expensive and took all day, rather than an hour and a half and the price of a pizza.

In London, Ana, Stella, Scott and I boarded the Jubilee Line at Swiss Cottage and alighted at Baker Street, then used the Circle Line to Kings Cross St Pancras. Scott had driven down from Oxford the night before, telling his wife of the smartphone world congress in Madrid. He hoped that she would not check if such an event actually existed.

Inviting Stella had been Ana's idea, since they had struck up a friendship in the short time they had known each other. Scott was not consulted, but neither did he complain, especially after the unfortunate breaking and entering incident.

Our Eurostar train wasn't until 8am but Ana was in a panic. She seemed to think that St. Pancras would be like an airport. However, after exiting passport control, there was really very little to do for the remaining hour before our scheduled departure time. I bought a small sample of the most expensive coffee in the world, and Ana decided now was the time to buy half a litre of bottled water sourced from Evian.

We had hardly sat down when an elderly lady at the opposite table sparked up conversation, asking me to place her baggage above her head (on the luggage rack). But once she started, she wouldn't stop. I felt like I'd been put next to Aunt Ethel on the table plan at a mate's wedding. Yes, she had been to the Cinque Terre in Italy for her honeymoon. That was back in the sixties, much more popular now. When she went it was completely unknown. I wondered why old people always tell you how good it used to be, but that you have basically missed the boat. I liked Coldplay's early music, but not since they made it big, and so on. As I drifted into a morning daze, I left her banging on to Ana about Girl Guides in the 1970s, and how these days, girls could attend Boy Scouts. What was the world coming to?

I woke from my shut-eye and we were racing through northern France at over 300km/h. Scott and Stella were debating loudly about whether or not Scott's break-in to Stella's basement room was in any way justifiable, or simply plain imbecilic. There was no malice in Stella's voice, incredulity, perhaps, but not nastiness. I had heard her recount the tale to every visiting guest over the past two months, so it had entered the mystical realm of house legends. I got the distinct feeling that the undoubted shock of waking to a drunken, but peaceful, intruder was well worth the story mileage.

We passed across Paris, using the Metro, then took a fast train out of *Paris Est* station. Against my better judgment, our route took us through the cities of Strasbourg, Basel, Zurich and Milan. Finally, we arrived into La Spezia in northern Italy at 9:30pm and collapsed into the budget hotel that we had booked near the station. Scott and Stella had booked separate rooms. I have to tell you, Ana and I made the most of ours.

We were all eager to get started.

22

Scott

Saturday, 16 July. La Spezia, Italy.

Scott enjoyed his breakfast of Italian breads and some wickedly strong and pathetically small coffee. The four tourists hailed a cab for the short hop to the marina.

Charlie was clutching his invite card close to his chest, like he thought it valuable, but in fact it served well to steer them in the direction of the correct catamaran. Scott could still not believe this was happening. Beautiful sunshine – damn, forgot the sun cream – great company, and the prospect of a week to enjoy himself on the Med.

He enjoyed Stella's company, but he would be surprised if she thought he was anything but a middle-aged fool. Still, it was a pleasure to be away from Headington, his wife and the mobile phone firm.

They spotted Len at the furthest mooring in the entire marina and lugged their wheeled bags along the concrete docks and then the wooden slatted jetty. Len was undertaking preparatory boating tasks, there was a hosepipe connected to a faucet in the marina and he was wielding a tough bristled broom. On the boat's stern the words, 'Shooting Star.'

"Here's the crew!" shouted Len enthusiastically. Then, "Welcome aboard – careful on the steps, they're slippery."

"Hi everyone!" It was Mia. Scott had always found her to be such a caring, thoughtful person, which despite his welcoming show, is not something many people would readily volunteer about her husband, Len.

"We're looking for work as deck hands, do you know anyone interested?" Charlie, playing it up.

Ana walked the gangplank first, "You must be Ana, shoes off on deck!" a friendly reminder from Len. Next up Stella, followed by Charlie then Scott.

Len showed the group to their berths, one cabin each for Scott and Stella, and shared cabins for the others. As Stella and Ana were talking with Mia, Len reeled off facts about the vessel.

"It's a 2005 Leopard 40, designed by Morrelli and Melvin. Its twin hulls are 40 feet in length and it was built in Cape Town, South Africa. These boats are light and fast," Len paused to see if his guests were listening. "Hence her name… because of nimbleness she can ride easily over waves and her sharp bows and clean underwater profile cut cleanly as well, to minimize drag."

Charlie asked, "How long have you had it?"

"I've had her for two years, I replaced everything when I got her, since it had been a charter boat before that. Mostly, we just sail in the Med – down the Croatian Coast, island hopping in Greece. That sort of thing - it's a lot of fun."

"She is beautiful, Len. How far will we go?" asked Scott.

"The route we're taking is about 200 nautical miles – we'll be in Golfe-Juan near Antibes next Saturday night." Len stated.

The week was set to be a corker. What could possibly go wrong?

23

Len

Sunday, 24 July. Golfe-Juan, France.

The week had been consumed audaciously on the catamaran and much water had passed under the metaphorical bridge. It was a little after 6:45am on that fateful July Sunday when Len Hubbard slipped out Ana's double berth and tiptoed down the yacht's tight corridor towards the master suite that he should have been sharing with his wife. He took due care and attention not to unnecessarily wake any of his on-board guests and thus be forced to engage in an inconvenient conversation about his whereabouts during the night. His significantly younger wife, Mia, had long been aware of his constant extra marital indiscretions, but nevertheless, he preferred to keep under the radar.

The fact that Ana had taken an interest in him the previous evening had been a surprise. He had thought that he had caught her flirtatious eye when preparing cocktails and had tried overtly to return it, but then, perhaps he had imagined it? During dinner, he had believed that his inner calf was suggestively caressed by Ana's upper foot, but again, could it have been unintentional? Ana had clearly had an argument with her boyfriend, Charlie, and he had eventually announced that he would be sleeping in galley that night. So, Len had taken the risk to rap on Ana's cabin door a little after 1am. She had silently answered the door in her slinky burgundy negligée and a saucy smirk; Len knew he was heading for another notch on his virtual bedstead.

It had been a great night with Ana, but it was over and time to return to his wife, with whom he had endured an awful 24 hours. Len was not totally sure if anyone was watching him as he arrived back at the master suite, but he peered in, saw an empty bed, and turned back around. He began the process of searching the boat for Mia, eventually heading back to the berth from which he had only recently crept out.

"Hi again! Sorry. I'm actually looking for Mia – have you seen her?" asked Len.

"No need for excuses Lenny… if you're still not satisfied… " purred Ana, lunging forward to kiss his neck.

"No, seriously, Ana. She's not in the master suite. I can't find her anywhere."

"Has anyone seen Mia?" Len yelled loudly to the rest of the boat.

Charlie opened the door of the bathroom, Stella and Scott poked their heads out of her cabin.

"No" they all replied in symphony, or close enough to it.

"Can't find Mia," spat Hubbard curtly, to no one in particular.

"Is she in the other bathroom?" offered Ana but Len's decidedly furrowed brow informed her that he had checked that.

"Have you looked on deck?" tried Scott rather redundantly, as Len was climbing the stairs.

That morning, Hubbard completed his fruitless search on deck. He was rubbing three days of stubble between thumb and forefinger, gazing to the jettied harbour of Golfe-Juan on the Côte D'Azur, when he spotted the patrol boat approaching, with *GENDARMERIE* marked boldly on the side.

His heart skipped a beat. He knew his wife was dead.

"*Bonjour, nous sommes de la Gendarmerie Maritime. Nous avons quelques questions pour vous.*"

The five remaining passengers – Len, Charlie, Ana, Scott and Stella – all froze, startled, and Scott muttered, "What the…"

Hubbard broke in, "Oh, God! What's happened?"

The police sergeant attached to the Juan-les-Pins station of the *Gendarmerie Maritime* boarded the Hubbard catamaran without further invitation. The male policeman held up his warrant card.

"*Agent De Brun et Girot, Gendarmerie Maritime.*" His partner remained in place on the ramp of the official boat and accepted the introduction with a rudimentary nod.

She was young, perhaps mid-twenties and was clearly trying to look in control of the situation. Agent De Brun was older, mid-thirties with a well-toned body and a seaman's tan. Their uniforms looked similar to that of their land-based counterparts, although there had been some cunning modifications along the way – most notably, shorts.

"Parlez-vous Français?" A question to all.

Hubbard spoke close to no French, despite living in France for ten years. He had found that living where he did and with a wife and accountant that dealt with all administrative matters, he could get along just fine with a few words. Charlie spoke passable high school French, but apparently he decided that his interpretation vocation could wait. The others spoke a smattering of restaurant-level French between them, but not enough to explain themselves to a policeman. Thus, the group answer was a resounding, *"Non."*

"Do you have a full guest list of *passagers* aboard?"

Hubbard was first, "No, err – we have been looking for my wife – has something happened to her?"

"And who is your wife?"

"Mia Hubbard," responded Len, factually.

"I may have some unfortunate news for you. We were alerted to a body floating in the sea this morning near the harbour of Golfe-Juan." The long vowel sounds seemed to Len to be pronounced short and the short vowels all long.

Hubbard froze while Ana uttered, "Jesus."

Scott looked thoughtful and summarised, "Holy shit."

As Stella sat down and started to cry, Charlie asked, "Are you sure it's her?"

"We believe it is Madame Hubbard. Monsieur Hubbard, could I ask you to come with me to help identify the body?" It was not in actuality a question.

As Hubbard grabbed his shoes, wallet and somewhat unnecessarily, sunglasses, Agent De Brun spoke to the remaining four guests.

"At this time the death is being treated as possibly suspicious, so I must ask you to come with us to the shore."

Agent Girot started the twin 200 horsepower motors with Hubbard and his guests safely seated on board. While Girot was at the controls and De Brun was untying the boat, Len caught his guests' attention. He knew he would not have long. "Look, guys, we need to keep this simple."

Scott, Charlie and Ana nodded like they knew what he meant, and Stella, looking somewhat more hesitant, acknowledged with a half nod, looking up and to the sky as she did. At that point, Agent Girot gunned the engines, leaving the sailing yacht rocking in its wake.

Len wondered who the police would focus their investigation on as he scanned the faces of the other passengers.

PART 2

Mistakes you can learn from;
sins stay with you forever.

Corey Taylor

24

Me

Tuesday, 2 August, location unknown.

When I regain consciousness, I instinctively, but ineffectually, try to gasp for much-needed air. But I can sense a thick, effective sticky tape pulling on the stubble surrounding my mouth. I crave to stretch my jaw, just for a moment. I try to throw a rejuvenating yawn, but it's just not happening. They say when you yawn, your brain cools off and your motor functions restart. I'd like them to restart now. I desperately want to quench my thirst; water would be fine. When I suck in air through my nose and gulp to swallow, a grating pain sears down my throat, like waking from a heavy night out. 'What the fuck has happened?'

Prising open my eyelids is somewhat successful, which is a small solace, one mildly tarnished by the palpable lack of view. So this is what it feels like to be sightless. Years ago, a friend of mine was diagnosed with a degenerative eye disease. She told me that it wasn't all darkness, being blind. She said that she sometimes experienced glaring shades of red and yellow, breaking up the monotony of eternal darkness. And to be honest, that is pretty much what it feels like right now. I am fairly sure I have been blindfolded with a rough fabric, perhaps a scarf.

Evidently, I am in transit, the groan and some fumes of an overworked diesel engine filling the space around me. Whoever is driving this shit piece is doing so with reckless abandon, swaying between lanes, eliciting the occasional horn of frustration. Judging by the fairly constant speed, we appear to be on a motorway, or at very least a dual carriageway. The ribbed rumble strip, designed to keep drivers — and hostages — from dozing off, is working a treat.

As I continue my self-assessment, I realize that my right arm is numb to the core. The blood in my left arm has ample circulation, although my left biceps muscle is in intermittent spasm, no doubt from being trapped behind my back. My wrists are tied together. I manage to dislodge the blindfold by scratching the back of my head against a protruding notch on the side of the vehicle, whilst simultaneously making an incongruous surprised expression with my forehead to shift the material upward. It does not shift very far, something on my head is impeding it, but at last I have some visionary sense restored.

From what I can tell, I am in the back of a van. I am wearing my Lycra cycling shorts, the type that has a sewn-in padded seat. Since I am not inclined to don them for any other activity, I conclude that my last conscious actions involved my bicycle, which now comes into focus on the other side of the cargo space.

My mind is becoming rapidly cogent; whatever induced my sleep, thank fuck, appears to be wearing off sharply. I *remember spending the week on the catamaran and Mia's death. Straining my thought process further, I recall an old lady looking pitifully at me, and a mother with a pushchair turning the child away from the scene. Then a voice, "It's okay, it's okay." A strong French accent, "I take him to l'hôpital". Am I in France? No, he wouldn't be speaking English. I'm in England then. Am I on my way to hospital? Is that why we are travelling at speed? No, I've been gagged, blindfolded and restrained. Have I been kidnapped?*

I can feel something preventing my sore head from resting comfortably on the floor of the cargo hold. I realise that my prized, wind-tunnel-designed helmet is still strapped reassuringly to my head. It is one of those state-of-the-art models, with a live streaming helmet-cam incorporated into the polystyrene moulding. So someone other than my captor could be aware that I am here…

25

Fournier

Sunday, 24 July, 8:20am. Golfe-Juan, France.

One week earlier

Agent Fournier was wondering what drunken tourist case would land on his desk next when he got a call from the Maritime Gendarmerie in the nearby coastal resort town of Juan-les-Pins. A corpse had been found floating in Golfe-Juan harbour that morning, which was the most interesting thing to happen during the year. Fournier knew that if the case was elevated to 'suspicious death,' then the case would be reassigned to the *Police Judiciaire*.

The *PJ* were well known for swooping in and treating the local cops like chambermaids. Fournier despised handing cases over to the *PJ* if he could help it, precious little interesting happened as it was. In France, the District Attorney, or the *Procureur* as the position was known, played a key role in the case from the start of the investigation, unlike in some countries. The DA had agreed to let the local police establish the basic facts, and then she would decide if the case merited the costly arrival of the *Police Judiciaire*.

As Fournier placed the archaic handset back on the body of the device, he felt that irritating rush of heat to his face. The sensation was followed by the familiar twitching, then a hollow sinking feeling in his stomach and a thundering thumping of his heart. "*Putain!*" he muttered, "Not now!"

Fournier had only blacked out for a few seconds. He was fairly sure about that. If he was honest with himself, he knew he should take some medical tests, but he was feverishly worried about what they might reveal. Having lost too many friends and colleagues, he harboured no illusions of immortality. Rather, he was acutely aware of his transient state in this world and as far as he was concerned, ignorance was bliss.

After taking a few deep breaths, he jumped up energetically and drove down to the harbour. His task was only to establish the basic facts, but who would complain if he laid a little groundwork? From what he had been told, the DA was already leaning towards calling it accidental death, which would leave the case with him anyway. As he turned the well-worn key, the dilapidated blue Renault's engine sparked into life, which surprised him as much as it startled the passing elderly shopper pulling her tartan wheeled shopping cart.

Down at the quayside, Fournier's maritime colleagues Girot and De Brun had shepparded the five remaining friends towards a restaurant's outside seating area, which was not yet open for business. They could

were

only sit on the tables, since the chairs was chained in a stack. Agent Girot was earnestly engaged in conversation, acting the counsellor, it seemed, more than the investigator. This suited Fournier, since he would need to tow a fine line to keep this his case. A fleeting mention of arrest would immediately signal to the DA the escalation of the case, and that was something he did not wish to encourage.

One by one the friends were presented to him. Len Hubbard, the English husband of the deceased. Bald, but clearly fit and tanned, he was probably in his early fifties. Something about him made Fournier uneasy. Although he had recent growth stubble, he was no doubt normally clean-shaven, probably some business fat cat. White shorts and Fred Perry T-shirt, he looked like he enjoyed life.

Scott and Charlie Dunster were brothers and nephews of Hubbard. Charlie was impeccably in shape, a toned abdomen like his uncle, and was in his early thirties. He was wearing flip-flops, Bermuda shorts and an open shirt, displaying a bronzed waxed chest. Scott, by contrast, had the whole hairy beer barrel in place of the six-pack. He looked like his brother, artificially inflated by 50 per cent. The chin was sagging, the cheeks were full and a general puffiness was leant to his demeanour, illustrating a man who had let the aging process and probably too much drink take its certain course. Fournier had learnt the term 'moobs' last year, and, if he understood correctly, this man had a serious case of them.

Anastasia de Menzies was introduced as the girlfriend of Charlie. For some reason this elicited conspiratorial eye contact from Hubbard. Her Hispanic looks resembled a younger, slimmer Penélope Cruz – toned bottom with B-cup breasts that her fluorescent yellow bikini barely concealed. A brunette, her dark complexion did not completely hide that she had clearly enjoyed the sun that week.

Finally, Ms Stella Cooper, who was attractive in a different way. African-American, she seemed to be in shock about the news, perhaps even withdrawn. Fournier would probably place both the girls in their early thirties. He planned to understand a lot more about these suspects back at the station, but for now, he needed to inspect the body of Mia Catherine Hubbard.

Agent Fournier's role was simply to determine if there was evidence of foul play. If there was, it became a murder case. If it became a murder case, he would play no further role, as it would be handed to the *Police Judiciaire* homicide team. The body had been hauled out of the water, and Agent De Brun was standing by it. Someone had carefully placed a towel, which sported a brightly-woven sexy image, seemingly incongruous considering the grim reality that lay below it. The saucy beach towel was, however, preferable to every passer-by getting a glimpse of the stiff. His male and female colleagues known colloquially as '*les femmes de ménage*' would arrive shortly and zip the corpse into a body bag and tidy up. At least one Crime Scene Investigator was on her way although that was a procedural formality in such circumstances.

For the meantime, Agent Fournier pulled back the towel to reveal what he assumed to be Mia Hubbard's body. The corpse was horribly bloated and thoroughly lifeless. The victim must have increased in size by half. The body would be bagged and sent off to the morgue, where the local pathologist would make his conclusion and report back to Fournier and the *Procureur*. For now, Fournier had the opportunity to pick up his own clues.

An aqua coloured bikini was on the corpse, with a pair of 'shorties' in addition. Between the swimsuit top and the bottom, puffy abdominal scratches revealed, perhaps, a recent fight. The top had underwiring, providing the wearer with a little extra lift, although that would not help her now. Her face was grey as concrete, even the lips were a dark purply grey. On the left side of her head, there was a visible wound, blood having clotted in the hair – at least, it was no longer dripping. On the right side, Fournier could see another lesion just above the ear. Accidental deaths nearly always had some visible abrasions, so, thus far, nothing to point either for or against death by misadventure.

The victim was wearing an expensive-looking necklace – not that Fournier knew a high-street nine-carat chain from a diamond-encrusted pendant. Nevertheless, in his humble opinion, this one looked like it had set its purchaser back some serious wedge. Nobody had removed it, implying that a bungled mugging was unlikely to be responsible for this grisly mess.

This theory was further bolstered by the Cartier watch adorning her right wrist. Probably a *gaucher*, then, like him. Only around ten per cent of the population was left-handed, but within that percent were a disproportionate number of geniuses, or so he liked to believe. Leonado Da Vinci, Albert Einstein, Aristotle and Pele. He preferred not to dwell on studies suggesting that left-handers were also over-represented at the other end of the intellectual scale. Left-handers were obviously extremists!

He looked again at her dreadfully swollen abdomen, not the fault of a careless junk diet. The legs were also as chunky as tree stumps, not likely to be her preferred ante-mortem look. Other than that, her body had no asphyxiation signs visible, no stab wounds, no gun shot injuries and no lacerations on her throat or wrists.

While it was not his place to demonstrate the cause of death, as far as he could see, it was a standard drowning. The toxicology report would reveal more – it could be a deliberate or accidental overdose of legal or illegal drugs. Suicide could not be ruled out, he must remember to check for a note, but no one had mentioned a letter of any kind. Besides, if she was looking to finish herself off, there would be more reliable ways to achieve it than floundering then foundering in the harbour.

An accident still seemed quite possible. He had a case years ago, where a young man had drowned trying to swim underneath the length of a boat. His shorts had snagged on the monohull's keel, trapping him under the sea and ensuring his watery end. He wondered what this woman's story was.

Until the pathologist gave him anything useful, he would try to get to 'know her' – which would have been markedly easier twelve hours earlier.

26

Me

Thursday, 21 July. Monte Carlo, Monaco.

Three days earlier

At 6pm I could honestly describe the day as one – perhaps *the* – best of my life. I uploaded the images from our day's sailing on the Med captured by my Narrative Clip to Facebook, and before the day ended, I had 31 *likes*. Practically viral. But things were about to go pear-shaped.

Len had been less of a dictatorial arsehole that day, which set the morning well in motion. We woke in the outer harbour of Savona, Italy, and were destined to cross international waters into France. I thought that since Christopher Columbus grew up here, it would be the perfect spot for a naval adventure. As usual, Len was the first up, bounding around the boat. Ana and I slept in the port aft cabin, which, while barely big enough for the small double bed, was as cosy and airy as it was minimalistic. Above us, half the ceiling was taken up with a massive clear skylight, which provided the only luminance, and ensured that natural light woke us each morning, given the absence of a blind.

Ana and I were engaged in what could also be described as a navel adventure (the pleasure seemed to be more hers than mine) when I thought I saw a shadow shift. Looking up, I witnessed Len giving me the thumbs up and donning a broad imbecilic grin. Because I was still obscenely drunk from the previous night's prosecco indulgence, I altered the course of Ana's impending orgasm, and gave a weak thumbs up in return. Ana was none the wiser.

Breakfast was a smorgasbord affair – Stella had been ashore and shopped at the Piazza Goffredo Mameli, where she picked up passion fruit, papaya, mango and other tropical fruit that brought back memories of that island in the Philippines. She also got some fresh locally-made yogurt and organic granola. In paper bags were Italian *maritozzi* breads, which seemed to be buns filled with chestnut cream, and *cornettos*, the Italian croissant. Everything was washed down with long espressos and freshly-squeezed orange juice, all on board a beautiful catamaran moored for that morning in the harbour of Savona.

Len steered us out of the harbour using the twin motors, and we set sail within a few minutes. Mia was pulling up the main sail, and I was on the jib sail. We were given a 12km/h south-easterly breeze, gusting up to 18km/h, so our travel in a south-westerly direction was relatively easy going.

We tracked a course along the Italian Riviera a few miles out from land and moored at a harbour in the town of Albenga for lunch. After admiring the hundreds of spires, we set off again, passing the sprawling Imperia and the terracotta buildings of Ventimiglia, all glistening majestically from our vantage point on the water.

Every half hour or so we switched direction, with Len yelling "gybe!" and shortly thereafter the heavy boom at the bottom of the main sail swung violently to the opposite side as we tacked back. Len reckoned that getting cracked by that heavy metal bar on the head would send you clean overboard, at best.

Once at sea, there was little to actually do of navigational importance. Consequently we lounged around the boat, barefoot, and read, drank beer and chatted in the summer sun.

At 6pm we reached our rest spot for the night – in many ways the pinnacle of the whole trip – the Principality of Monaco. I was immediately struck by the outlandish opulence of this ridiculous city-state. It is a location that boasts most Formula 1 drivers, numerous tennis stars and many business owners amongst its residents. Unlike our other overnight stops, it was not possible to anchor further out, so Len had booked some weeks ago to secure a mooring at the Port de Fontvieille. He told us that while it was still stupidly expensive, it was fantastically cheaper than the main Port Hercule, with its multi-million dollar super yachts and direct casino access.

27

Fournier

Sunday, 24 July, 8:58am. Golfe-Juan, France.

The female corpse had been spotted by a morning jogger at 7:34am, who was running along stone bricks that constituted the harbour's edge. The runner had been quite shaken by his discovery. He went by the name of Olivier Montfleury, a local man who worked in a boat shop. Fournier had his coordinates, should they be required.

Montfleury had called it in, dialling number 17. It rattled Fournier that the country used different emergency numbers; 18 for Fire, 15 for Medical and 17 for Police. It seemed that no one could remember which to call. He heartily approved of the pan-European multi-lingual 112 emergency number. Fournier had seen a transcript of the recording, written in French. Translated, it began:

> **"Good day. This is Olivier Montfleury. There is a body..."** [pause, caller struggles to retain composure], **"There is a body floating in the marina."**

The Maritime Gendarmerie was already at sea near Juan-les-Pins, so on receiving the alert, they about-turned their patrol boat and were first on the scene. They mobilized the harbourmaster to stay with the body; he turned out to be the owner of the corny beach towel. The harbourmaster was most helpful in making the initial identification of the body. He had seen the woman with the group going to shore the previous day aboard a small landing dinghy.

Agent Fournier needed to extract Hubbard from the group in order for him to identify the body. While this should ideally be done with a pathologist present, if there was any chance it wasn't Mrs. Hubbard, he needed to know right away. Fournier strode towards the group, imagining what Hubbard was thinking, wondering if he had played a part in his wife's death, quietly observing the man as he approached him.

"Monsieur Hubbard, could I ask you to come with me to identify the body?"

The man was either a fantastic actor, or he was genuinely distraught. He uttered only, "Sure," but his face was a picture of torment. They returned to the body at a far more solemn, respectful pace. Hubbard braced himself. Fournier felt like he was a morbid magician, about to reveal the fate of this man's future, with or without his wife. He leant forward and took both corners of the towel. Initially Hubbard made no change to his facial expression, but a look of immense grief slowly overcame him. "It's her," he confirmed.

Fournier's poor reputation for solving cases could not be attributed to a lack of effort. If he was deficient in investigatory skills, he countered that with pure determination to find the truth. For the victim's sake, he would use all his experience, nerve and verve to uncover the fatal events.

With the assistance of Agent De Brun, Fournier had relocated the group to the station. The *Gendarmerie* was much larger than it needed to be, a throwback to grander times. There were a number of interview rooms, that were almost never used, but that day they would see action. He believed it would take the pathologist some time to confirm malicious intent, if he did at all, so he began by looking at everyone on board. The husband seemed somewhat of a ruthless soul, a businessman from Geneva. Call it detective intuition. Perhaps his initial assessment of Hubbard was unfair and simply jealous bigotry on his part. He appeared to carry an air that he was untouchable, and somehow above this current investigation. But he was right in the middle of it, as far as Fournier could see.

Agent Fournier would also look back into that incident earlier in the year, where four suspicious thugs had been arguing on a boat; and quite possibly the same boat, it struck him. Without the suspicious death ruling, Fournier could only realistically ask the tourists to stay in the area for 48 hours – and even that might be difficult. He did not hold much hope of Inspector Ayad authorizing their detainment for what appeared to be a routine boating mishap. The victim was reported to have drunk a fair amount of alcohol – the toxicology report would confirm that later that same day.

Based on experience, Fournier had chosen to interview each of his suspects separately to see if there were any discrepancies. If any one of them was a murderer, they would need to invent a story. Agent Fournier felt he was good at spotting liars.

And so it was that Len Hubbard found himself sitting across the table from Fournier in Interview Room 1. Technically, he was voluntarily giving evidence and he had not objected to their 'conversation' being videotaped. Like most of his colleagues, Fournier tried to delay the arrival of the lawyers for as long as possible, so he needed to interview Hubbard carefully so he felt at ease and didn't rumble the tactic. If he lawyered up, Fournier simply did not have the resources to crack him. So he planned to keep it nice and amicable.

After stating the date, he spoke clearly for the tape, "This interview is being conducted by Agent Georges Fournier ID 36229. Mr. Leonard Francis Hubbard is in the room of his own free will to give a video statement of what happened the night his wife, Mrs. Mia Catherine Hubbard (nee Van de Merwe) died, on 23rd or 24th July."

Agent Fournier paused to catch his breath.

"Mr. Hubbard, first of all sorry to hear of the unfortunate news concerning your wife. I have a few questions. As you know, Mrs. Hubbard's body was found in the harbour this morning. I understand she had been staying on a sailing boat this past week. Whose boat was she staying on?"

"It's my boat. A 40-foot catamaran."

"How long have you had it?"

"I bought her two years ago this July."

"And you had been on board since last weekend?"

"Last Saturday, yes. July 16th."

Fournier pressed on, "How was your relationship with your wife prior to her death?"

"No big problems, we've-" he corrected himself, "we'd been married fifteen years. Of course, we had disagreements like any couple, but nothing you would call major."

"Any physical violence? Psychological abuse?"

"No, she wasn't too bad." Hubbard smirked. Fournier was not amused.

"From you, Mr. Hubbard."

"Good God, no, of course not. No, none at all."

A happily married couple, Fournier thought for a split second before his cynical side overrode that idyllic myth. 'No such thing!' he thought. He would believe Hubbard more if he said she was an unreasonable witch and a nightmare to live with!

So far, Agent Fournier had only got some background. He had not established the timelines – the time of death, the suspects' exact whereabouts and what on earth was happening on that yacht. But it was going to be hard to get that information without putting the wind up them.

"So, Monsieur Hubbard, tell me about your evening and night yesterday." Hubbard recounted a full 24 hours, from morning through to that moment, which was tearfully boring. Fournier found himself drifting into daydreams at times. He was having trouble separating the fluff from the facts. He decided to let him carry on, until he said something interesting – which took about 25 minutes…

"So I went to bed, and frankly after all that wine, I was asleep by the time my head hit the pillow."

"So, when did you last see Madame Hubbard alive and where were the others?" he questioned.

"I brushed my teeth at the sink in the galley, as I normally do. The bathroom is quite tight, and I prefer to brush them there, and spit out over the side of the boat. Mia was engaged in conversation with Charlie. Scott and Stella had retreated to their respective cabins. Ana was there, but was either staring into space, or nodding off, I am not sure which. I don't blame her, Charlie can be an utter bore when he's had a few, and was droning on about how to get rich."

"So that was it, I suppose, last saw her alive while I was brushing my teeth. What a banal last moment together… I just can't believe she's gone." With that realisation came emotion, either forced or genuine. The tears rolled down his face, and Fournier stuffed a man-sized box of Kleenex under the suspect's face. He never knew what to do with a grown man crying. He was not going to put an arm around him, although that looked to be just what he needed.

"That would have been at around midnight?"

"About then, yes," Hubbard sniffed.

"And after washing your teeth, describe what happened next," Fournier pressed.

Hubbard looked at him like he told him he believed in UFOs. "I went to bed, Detective."

"You saw no one else after you went to bed, at about midnight?"

"Correct, Detective, now if that's all I could use some fresh air."

Fournier could not put his finger on it, but something was off-centre. It was certainly convenient that he was not aware of her disappearance – but on the other hand, on the boat, the other guests had said he was the one raising the alarm in the morning. He started to think about motives, and there seemed to be a number of reasons that Hubbard might want his wife out of the way. He was of a habit to think of motives as deadly sins:

Wrath – he might have had a fight and struck his wife in an act of rage, perhaps not realizing his own strength.

Greed – did he selfishly desire material wealth all for himself? His house? Or perhaps his life? Fournier had heard of people committing murder for a lot less.

Lust– was there another woman he was after? Was divorce not feasible for some reason?

He had to admit to himself, he felt baffled. He needed to keep in mind that Hubbard was with him willingly and he sought to keep it that way. Fournier decided to leave it there and try his luck with his next 'contender'. On the way out, he made a show of picking up the rubbish, the empty plastic coffee cups and a few used Kleenex tissues – they would come in useful. He could formally request a legal DNA sample once he was sure there was a match.

28

Chrissie

Sunday, 24 July, 9:32am. Madrid, Spain.

Chrissie received the news from Anabelle's childminder on her phone as soon as she landed in the Spanish capital of Madrid. Before she even reached passport control, she called her back.

"Hi, it's Chrissie, I just got your message, sorry to call you so late."

"It's okay, I am still at the hospital. The doctors say Anabelle's condition is stable."

Chrissie felt an unbearable inadequacy. Her daughter, Anabelle, at four years old was the most adaptable, adorable, clever girl she could imagine. And for once Anabelle needed her and she was not there. 'Worst mother in the world', she thought but, as she always did, tried to convince herself this wasn't the case.

Jasmine explained how at first it had simply seemed like a touch of flu. Anabelle was running a fever and had hot sweats and a mucusy cough. She had taken Anabelle, along with her own two children, to the local doctor in Queens, New York. The wait at the walk-in clinic was over two hours, but Jasmine had taken books and games to keep the three kids amused.

The doctor did not like what she saw: Anabelle was flaring her nostrils and wheezing with each breath. The doctor had sent them straight to the ER. Jasmine had dropped her kids with her mother and at the hospital she had tried again to reach Chrissie – but working on a long-haul flight, she was unable to take the call.

At the hospital, they had undertaken various tests, blood exams, chest X-rays and something called a pulse oximetry to measure the level of oxygen in Anabelle's blood. Then they took a mucus sample, which Jasmine said was a 'nuclear rusty green' colour.

Jasmine explained that the tests confirmed what the first doctor had feared – pneumonia. They had prescribed Anabelle amoxicillin antibiotics, in case the infection had been caused by bacteria, and other than that, all they could do was keep her in the ER for observation.

Chrissie was so grateful to have such a good friend looking after her daughter. She did not bother passing through Spanish immigration, instead and went directly back to the airside crew lounge. She asked to be on the first flight back to New York – it was the return leg of the flight she just arrived on, leaving two hours later.

On the way back to New York, Chrissie was not working, having taken special sick leave to avoid her own scheduled shift the next day. However, she could not sleep. She was worried about Anabelle. Half way through the eight hour flight, she did something she had never done before, she used the on-board credit card enabled phone to call her mom who had, it turned out, taken over bedside care at the hospital. Joyce let her know that nothing had changed, which did nothing to ease Chrissie's mind.

More angst was to follow.

When she landed at JFK, Chrissie took a cab straight to the hospital that was now known as New York-Presbyterian/Queens. As far as Chrissie was concerned they had the best paediatric care in the whole of New York.

Anabelle was sleeping when Chrissie arrived, and Joyce was eager to update her with all the details. She was told that Anabelle would be released later that day, all being well. It was critical that Jasmine had brought her in when she did – the doctors said that any later and Anabelle's condition would have been much worse.

Chrissie breathed a sigh of relief and was once again overwhelmed with gratitude towards the network of friends that she and Anabelle had.

Finding her biological father was no longer at the forefront of her mind.

29

Fournier

Sunday, 24 July, 9:52am. Golfe-Juan, France.

Agent Georges Fournier sat on the chair opposite Stella Cooper, but he turned the chair around first and sat on it backwards, something he thought might gave him an air of raffishness. Stella looked unimpressed.

Her posture was one of closed indifference. Her legs were outstretched, displaying their elegant length. Fournier had already noticed that she outsized him by a good inch or two. She had crossed her arms, perhaps deliberately, maybe not, expressing that she was not open to small talk with the detective.

Agent Fournier managed to elicit that she was born in South Africa, but moved to Chicago as a young girl. As a result, she held dual nationality. Stella had been the last guest invited on board, evidently when Scott either could not, or would not, bring his wife. The discussion moved on to the previous night, which was what Agent Fournier was truly interested in. Everything else was conversational foreplay, helpful to kick-start the process, but he was not expecting any lasting purpose to it.

"How long had you known Madame Hubbard," asked the detective. Stella looked thoughtful, making a show of furrowing her brow and scratching her neatly braided hair.

"Five days."

"How many times had you met Madame Hubbard prior this week?" pried Fournier.

"Zero," replied Stella.

"Okay. Let's talk about last night. Describe to me the last time you saw the victim?"

"The victim? Is that really what you're going to call her?"

"Madame Hubbard," confirmed Agent Fournier, trying to keep calm.

"She was talking in the boat kitchen with the others. I felt tired, so I went to bed."

"On your own?" queried the detective.

"Yes, on my own," replied Stella tersely.

"Was everyone else still in the galley when you went to your cabin?"

"As far as I recall."

"Did you see or hear anything or anybody before morning?"

"No."

The conversation continued in that vein, Hubbard probing with fairly open questions and Stella closing him down with short responses.

Fournier had hoped to get more peripheral information from the woman, but she was hardly cooperative. He asked if she would mind providing a DNA swab sample to potentially identify her if necessary, and she almost spat, "No chance." He decided he must work on his persuasive charm or this case would be closed as accidental death before the day was out. He considered the information he had gleaned from this interview, then concluded it was largely a waste of his time. His phone rang and he left the interview room and indicated to his assistant to send in some cake and coffee, to keep Stella occupied.

His mobile vibrated. It was the pathologist at Cannes morgue. He informed Agent Fournier that he had recently commenced the preliminary examination and had immediately observed remnants of skin under the fingernails. He also noted two abrasions on her head, one on the left and one in the centre at the back, quite different in characteristics. The pathologist also had a rough estimate of the time of death – between 11pm and 3am the previous night. He told Fournier he would keep him appraised with any new findings.

This death was no accident, thought Agent Georges Fournier as he turned his head back towards Interview Room 1.

30

Mia

Thursday, 21 July. Monte Carlo, Monaco.

Three days earlier

Mia was relieved to step ashore at the Port de Fontvieille in Monaco and to set foot on *terra firma*. It was also to be an opportunity to wear her Marc Jacobs *robe à fleurs* that she had carted all the way there. At such a venue it would surely be appreciated.

It was a fine summer's evening and with that the group's stroll along the dockside was blissful. Just after 7pm, all six of them stopped at a fashionable harbourside bar and ordered cocktails – Mia selected a Negroni – a blend of Campari and sweet vermouth served on ice. The night was balmy, and she did not need to wear her silk foulard for warmth, but it finished off her outfit, along with her Manolo Blahnik heels.

Len had been quite an embarrassment – captain of his freaking ship – and all the ego that went with it. It was so off-putting. When they had met, he was just an entrepreneur, trying to make a financial start-up company work, but somewhere along the way, he seemed to have developed some so-called business acumen. Frankly, Mia had little interest in his commercial success and, other than designer dresses and shoes, cared little about material wealth.

The evening meal at Le Petit Resto was a desperate disappointment. On the plus side, the Maître D' had seated Mia opposite Charlie, which suited her. He had a suave charm that had somehow bypassed her previously. Scott, on her right, seemed enamoured with Stella and she wondered if something was perhaps going on between them.

And there was Len, sitting across from, and flirting with, the beautiful Ana. Mia knew he had been unfaithful, and more than once. He was a dismal liar and she had even seen him on several occasions out for dinner with women, unaware that she had passed by and seen him. But she had decided years ago to turn a blind eye to his infidelity. She had discovered that she genuinely didn't care, her life suited her and she didn't want to be alone, and she was sure that at some point this knowledge would come in useful. She wondered if he had actually tried it on with Ana, or if something had happened already? They seemed overly at ease with each other. The moment that Ana ordered a tequila sunrise and Len said, "You know what, it's years since I've enjoyed a tequila sunrise, I'll have the same." she knew something had either happened or was on the horizon. He despised tequila.

The food was ordinary; set courses that came out one after the other, everyone having the same. It was meant to reflect that practice of small French *auberges* in the countryside, but here in Monaco, it was simply taking the foolish rich tourist for a ride. The *moules marinières, magret de canard avec sauce cerise* and *crème brûlée* were no better than she served up at a dinner party, but cost a small fortune. The wine, however, was outstanding. She had to give it to Len, he had chosen well. A quality champagne to start, copious vintage Châteauneuf-du-Pape with the main, and a late harvest Gewürztraminer with dessert. Len, of course, picked up the bill, no doubt imagining the gesture would somehow bring him one step closer to Ana's inevitable G-string.

Feeling more than slightly tipsy, Mia and the group chatted loudly, and listened hardly at all, as they headed towards the beckoning casino.

31

Fournier

Sunday, 24 July, 9:57am. Golfe-Juan, France.

As he entered Interview Room 3, Agent Georges Fournier realised that his plan of separating the suspects in order to prevent them from talking was essentially futile. He had not formally arrested them and thus they still retained their smartphones. Charlie was caressing his when Fournier entered.

"Texting someone?" he started, in as casual a nonplussed tone as he could muster, and not quite on board with the latest technological lexicon.

"Just posting on Facebook that I am being held against my will in a French police station," Charlie responded angrily. Then he broke into sneer, and added, "Only kidding, Detective, am I up next?"

"Charlie Dunster," he started, in the sort of tone one might address a brother or an old friend, "your friends have authorized a DNA swab, just so I can clear all the paperwork and get this case closed as an accident as soon as possible. Any objections from you?"

"Not at all, Detective," answered Charlie, "it would be my pleasure." The agent took an instrument resembling a cotton bud and took the sample before he changed his mind.

The detective then established that Mia Hubbard was Charlie's aunt, through her marriage to his Uncle Len, his deceased mother's brother. Charlie had thus known Mrs. Hubbard for quite a few years – probably about ten or so. Prior to that, Len and Mia had lived in South Africa, and Charlie had not seen them during those years.

Fournier found that Charlie carried a self-assurance with him, a coolness that things would fall into place. His blond flowing locks hung loosely, giving him the air of a less pointy Matthew McConaughey. In his flip-flops and board shorts, his aura was that of an aging surfer, and he often had a smart comment in response to the agent's questions. They had gone through Charlie's background and the week's events. Charlie had told him how they had begun their sailing trip in La Spezia in Italy the previous Saturday. They had spent a few nights stopping at different points along the route. Most days were spent improving their sailing at Hubbard's direction.

Charlie described how everyone was basically on Len's crew. Len was captain and they were his subordinates. This clearly did not sit well with Charlie, but he nevertheless described a leisurely week throwing trawler lines off the back and casting flies from the deck.

It all sounded quite enviable Fournier thought, up until the moment that one of the guests was murdered, that is. Fournier was contemplating his next fishing trip when he snapped out of his daydream and asked, "What do *you* think happened to Madame Hubbard, Charlie?"

For a split second, Charlie looked somewhat abashed, before affecting a thoughtful expression.

"You know, Detective, I think it was a terrible accident." There was no conviction in his words and Fournier wondered if that was what he really thought.

He tried to keep the interrogation moving along swiftly – perhaps he would slip up. "I see. And can you tell me about the last time you saw the victim?"

"Yesterday evening, around midnight. We all played some poker, then I think she went and joined Len in the master bedroom. At any rate, when I went to bed, she wasn't around."

"She could have been dead already then?" queried Fournier.

"Well, when she said goodnight, and headed towards the bathroom, she seemed quite alive. I don't recall seeing her after that, so who knows?"

"And then what did you do?" continued Fournier.

"Ana seemed sleepy, so I took her to bed." Charlie gave the detective a wink, as if they were in this together; men folk out in the world on a mission to sleep with any available women(folk).

"You returned to Ana's cabin, had sex, and remained in the room all night?" the detective persisted.

"That's sounds about right." replied Charlie, appearing to lose interest.

"Charlie, one more thing, then I'll leave you alone. The pathologist has called and it seems the victim has traces of someone else's skin under her fingernails. Any idea why?"

To Fournier's pleasure, Charlie's calm demeanour dissipated rapidly.

Agent Fournier left Interview Room 3 ever more convinced that something fishy was going down, but he didn't have anything of substance to take to the district attorney. He was going to have to lay it on heavy with Scott Dunster. Everyone appeared to be collaborating, but was that because they were all telling the truth? Or were they all simply given the same song sheet from which to sing?

None of the suspects possessed the profile of classical criminal. With the possible exception of Hubbard, they all seemed like people who could easily spend their entire lives never once crossing paths with the police. Perhaps this was just an unfortunate accident as the DA was inclined to believe, and all of this interrogating was just putting these people through deeper mire. But as a detective it was his job to be sure, to speculate, to enquire... and only when convinced there was no wrongdoing, let things go. Fournier needed to connect with Scott Dunster. He could spin a yarn about kids and marriage and see if Scott Dunster took the bait.

He entered Interview Room 4 ready for battle, only to find it empty. He asked his intern assistant, but she had been delivering cookies and tea to another suspect and had not noticed his absence. Trying not to show his infuriation, he walked the corridor and one by one asked Stella Cooper, Anastasia de Menzies, Charlie Dunster and Len Hubbard if they knew of Scott Dunster's whereabouts. Charlie muttered, "You're the detective, Detective!"

"*Merde!*" he said as he hurried towards the door. His progress was suddenly hindered by a familiar foe, as his eyes began to twitch. He sat down quickly and focused on his breathing, trying to stay calm. But he felt the customary stinging in his nose, a hollow feeling in his stomach, an accelerated pumping heartbeat. Then, darkness.

When he came around, he reasoned that it was probably one of his longer blackouts, judging by the spread-eagled position he had adopted on the plastic chair and the presence of the preppy intern with a disposable cone of mineral water from the cooler.

He batted the drink away as though everything was fine. Immediately his thoughts went to Scott Dunster. Might he have gone back to the boat to try and pervert the course of justice? Was Scott fuelled by Lust? Dazzled by Mia's sharp looks and smart persona, had he fallen head over heels for her? She rejected him? They fought?

Or was it Envy? Seeing how the other half live and striking out in a fit of jealousy?

He needed to get on board the catamaran, and decided that he wanted a tour guide. He put his head around the door of Interview Room 1, and signalled, "You mind showing me your boat?"

Len looked up, a glint returning to his eyes, and responded with a monotone, "Absolutely."

As the morning had progressed in Golfe-Juan harbour, more police and Maritime Gendarmerie had shown up, eager to play a part in the week's biggest story. Fournier had clocked Agent Girot at the boat and made a beeline for her – better that he had another officer to corroborate his actions.

Girot fired up the patrol boat to take Fournier and Hubbard the short hop to the catamaran. As they crossed the harbour, Fournier could see Agent De Brun on the harbour's edge showing the victim to the DA. Why had she seen the need to pay the incident site a visit? When they had spoken earlier that morning, she had explicitly stated she would not be spending her Sunday at any harbour.

On board the catamaran, Fournier became convinced this was the same boat that he investigated back in February. Shooting Star. He challenged Len, "Did you have a break-in earlier this year?" Len looked at him intently, making direct eye contact. It was Fournier that felt uncomfortable and looked at his radio as a distraction.

"I did." Len confirmed. "You think that might be relevant?"

"I keep an open mind, Monsieur Hubbard."

Once inside the living quarters, Fournier found it was more spacious than he had expected. Too busy herding all his suspects around, Fournier had not yet set foot on the yacht. Hubbard now seemed keen to provide him a tour. Since Fournier was not a boating man, port, starboard and bows or aft had always baffled him so he asked for things to be kept 'simple'.

There were four cabins on board. Len showed him Stella's berth first. There was a small bed with a glass of water beside it. A small round porthole permitted natural light to beam in, seemingly to bring a pair of men's boxer shorts under the spotlight. Next up, the other side of the bathroom, was the master suite, where Len and his wife had been sleeping that week. It housed a queen-size bed, the one in which Len claimed to have had such a deep sleep he had not noticed whether his wife had come to bed or not.

In all the times that Fournier had shared a bed with a woman, he could not remember one when he had not woken if she had pottered off to the toilet in the night – could someone really sleep that deeply? He asked, "Monsieur Hubbard, how is it possible that you would not wake when Madame Hubbard came to bed?"

"Detective, I sometimes take sleeping pills on board, as I did last night, but anyway, the fact that I did not wake surely points more to the suggestion that she never came to bed!"

"Interesting, Monsieur Hubbard."

Hubbard proceeded to Charlie and Ana's cabin and announced, almost triumphantly, "Ana and Charlie's bed!" Fournier took in the scene – a mess of biblical proportions. Among the clothes, bottles and tissues, he noticed two used condoms in the bin. "Seems Charlie's been busy!" he joked, but Len did not appear to share the pleasure of his levity.

The final cabin was Scott's, Len said. Small, like the first, this one was conspicuously different to the others. It could be that Scott was a fiercely tidy man, after years of fatherhood, but he didn't believe anyone could make a bed as faultlessly as a maid and with a hangover in the early morning. He set a mental reminder to ask Scott about it when he caught up with him.

The galley, as Len called it, was quite a mess too. Mostly it was bottles, glasses and clothes that littered the small countertops and seats. Fournier thought it looked like someone had broken in again. "Not had the chance to clean, yet," added Len, sheepishly.

"Please leave it for now, this is still the scene of an incident." Fournier emphasized 'incident' and studied Hubbard's face to see if an expression would betray him.

Len merely responded, "Okay, sure."

Fournier knew he should be watchful not to overstay his warrant-free welcome and he could not think of any useful follow-up questions that Hubbard could be expected to answer.

"Well, Scott doesn't appear to be here…" started Fournier, ostensibly to Hubbard.

"No one has been here," stated Agent Girot, apparently surprised that they expected to find anyone. Having a nose around the boat had been equally important to Fournier.

He announced it was time to leave and ushered Hubbard safely back on board the police boat. Then, with a flustered look, Fournier explained, "I forgot, I wanted to see the bathroom, but don't worry, I know where it is." Alone back on board the cat, he worked quickly. He photographed the pair of men's boxer shorts in Stella's room. Fournier inspected the master bed – Len and Mia's bed – and photographed and bagged some ginger pubic hairs that he found there. He then pictured and bagged the two condoms from Charlie and Ana's room, and photographed Scott's immaculately presented bed.

His little scavenger hunt, he was aware, would constitute flaky evidence. It would never be admissible in court, but time was not on his side and shortcuts were the order of the day. He would figure out a way to prove his suspicions procedurally later. At the current rate, the guests would be back on board by tea time, so he had little to lose. With his ill-gotten forensic booty, he flushed the toilet and headed back to the others.

"Sorry, got caught short." Fournier explained in a low voice.

Sunday, 24 July, 11:15am. Golfe-Juan, France.

It was 11:15am when Agent Fournier shuffled back into the station and dropped the samples for rapid DNA testing. He had grabbed a *jambon-fromage* half baguette at the *boulangerie* at the corner, which would have to suffice for lunch. Fournier was no wiser as to Scott's whereabouts and his unexplained departure was looking increasingly suspicious. Furthermore, Scott's bed had not been touched last night, and Stella had said that she was not with him. So, since Charlie and Ana were in a relationship, was Scott trying it on with his aunt? Of course that sounded more incestuous than it would have been; she was an aunt by marriage and was actually two years his junior.

Scott could have been with Mia, but what about the boxer shorts in Stella's room? Maybe some women use these as nightwear, he pondered, then had to admit that he was at the mercy of the DNA results, which take roughly six hours to come in after being submitted. Since the first swabs from Charlie and Len were deposited at 10:15am, and the skin, condoms and hairs at around 11:15am, all of the results should be back by 3:15pm But without Scott's DNA on file it may only allow him to eliminate Charlie and Len as chief suspects.

Fournier had missed his opportunity to speak to the DA, and her office appeared to have a phobia of returning his calls. Granted, it was a Sunday. In any case, she would not consider opening up a murder enquiry based on misplaced shorts and errant condoms.

He parked his sandwich next to the HP printer and headed back to the interview rooms. His intern had managed to keep everyone calm enough, although Len was now refusing to go back into an interview room. Fournier left him in the hallway and walked towards Interview Room 5. He was going to quiz the foxy temptress Anastasia de Menzies.

De Menzies engaged in a one-sided flirtatious display with Fournier, which put him on edge. He started by asking if she would be willing to provide a DNA sample. Ana was more than willing, replying in a husky tone, "Where exactly would you like to sample my DNA, Detective?"

He began his subtle interrogation in the same tack as the others – personal background and what happened last night.

"I last saw Mia when she went to bed. Must have been around midnight or 1am I think she joined Len in bed and that's all I know."

"And you? What did you do after you saw her go to bed with Hubbard?"

"Well, Detective, I was with Charlie in our room," she said, with a dry smile.

"Ms de Menzies, forgive me, but I'm just trying to understand. He showed her the photo from his Samsung Galaxy S5. This is a photo of your cabin, taken this morning."

"Looks like Baghdad, doesn't it?"

"Here's a photo of the bin," Fournier said, zooming in, "look, is that a condom I can see settled on top?"

"I believe it is detective, what is your point?"

Then Fournier panned across the zoomed-in image. "Was this Charlie's too?" he asked, gesturing at a second sheath.

"Ms de Menzies?"

"Well, errm, yes, must be," she mumbled, reddening sharply.

Fournier suddenly felt like he'd turned a corner.

32

Me

Thursday, 21 July. Monte Carlo, Monaco.

Three days earlier

The Beaux-Arts architecture designed mostly by Charles Garnier created a bloody classy and imposing welcome to the Casino de Monte Carlo. It seemed so much more stylish than other casinos I had visited. The casinos of Las Vegas, even the newer ones like Bellagio and The Venetian, were undoubtedly impressive, but somehow entirely fake and tacky. Vegas's Monte Carlo Casino is surely the greatest embarrassment of them all! The lunacy of Paris Las Vegas, even with its half-scale Eiffel Tower, was bemusing to me. Casinos in Sun City, Johannesburg and Atlantic City all followed a similar mould – the casino should be full of replica streets to awe the potential gambler, which inexplicably led them to part more freely with their holiday stash. But not the Casino de Monte Carlo. That was the real deal. James Bond's casino. Owned and operated by the royal family of Monaco. It was sophistication encapsulated.

DEAD IN THE WATER

By 9:30pm everyone had their game. Ana and Stella preferred the slot machines. I couldn't see the attraction of pulling down the one-armed bandit's limb. They told me arms were long gone, now hitting the button did the trick. Mia and I took a fancy to blackjack, whereas Len and Scott preferred poker. We all agreed that roulette was a good place to relax in-between more active games.

It was Friday evening and the casino was filled with a throng of wishful punters hoping the luck of the lady was on their side tonight. In an outer room, Mia and I saddled up to a €10 blackjack table, the game I knew as 21. Len, Ana, Scott and Stella dissipated quickly and we settled onto our padded stools for a game.

I had reserved little budget for gambling and was sufficiently worldly wise to expect to lose it. After the success of upping the limit on my credit card for Manila, the credit card company had thoughtfully doubled it again shortly afterwards. I was €200 down in the first half an hour, which I reflected was the cost of entry. I stood up, annoyed but solvent and walked away. I knew how to avoid getting trapped and was all too aware of the temptation to have a flutter as the drinks took their toll.

Mia was doing much better, and was over €400 to the black, by my count, although she had not followed what the book would do, and had been lucky to get blackjacks twice. I was no card counter at the best of times.

I met up with Scott and Len and they convinced me to play on. It was an easy sale. With casino chips in my hand, I knew that roulette had some of the best odds in the house.

Roulette served me well and won over two grand. It really seemed to be my night after all. Then I lost about half of the credit in one game – I had a really good spread when the double zero disastrously took the little white ball. There were actually tears from some at the table and the moustachioed croupier apologized as he raked in all of the bets, red and black included. A few games in a row, good fortune went against me. I walked away from the table at net zero. Scott suggested trying the private tables inside, so we both showed our IDs, and together with Len and Mia progressed into the coveted inner circle. The only real difference I noticed from the outer circle was generous complementary drinks and a €100 minimum bet.

Look, things went from bad to worse. I don't want to dwell on it, but in the next couple of hours, I lost three grand. My losses had just crept up on me and I kept thinking the odds would even out – but the casino could outlast the most determined gambler. When my credit card refused to grant any further advance, I asked both Scott and Len for a loan. Thankfully, on reflection, they both refused, besides, Scott was suffering similarly. Len and Mia were both up – where is the justice? The rich get richer, I thought. In the end, I had lost a staggering €4800. Scott himself was down some too. I really do not know how it compounded itself so rapidly, I wanted to scream, "Fuck you all!"

I felt absolutely crushed. I complained to anyone that would listen. I took my frustration out on Mia. Why should her fortunes flourish, when she had no need?

"Charlie, it's only money," Mia was only trying to comfort me. I just scowled at her in an angry, drunken way and walked away before I did something I would regret. I lingered by a high rollers' table, where a rotund Asian man was playing what looked like hundreds of euros each round. He had an entourage. I just watched on.

In a moment of inebriated reflection I muttered to myself that I was a 'fucking idiot', only it must have come out at a significantly louder than I had anticipated. The short balding Asian bastard stared at me as though he caught me with his wife. He said nothing, but his wide eyes moved from me, to two shit brickhouse bodyguards and back to me again. Within seconds, I found myself forcefully plunging down the entrance steps, desperately protecting my head. I came to a rest about two-thirds of the way down the steps. Then an unfeasibly large gloop of henchman's phlegm landed on me.

Shit.

33

Len

Sunday, 24 July, 1:15pm. Golfe-Juan, France.

Len Hubbard was outside the station, pacing up and down, when Agent Fournier exited through the double doors. Hubbard was fizzing with anger.

"Okay, look, we've been very cooperative. But that's it. Over. My wife has been killed in a terrible accident and we are stuck here in your unpleasant police station."

"Monsieur Hubbard, I am so sorry about these formalities. It is normal, you know, when someone dies. We have an obligation."

Fournier had resigned that his best hope was to get an incriminating statement from one of them and go from there. However, he did not have nearly enough to go on, so decided that the best course of action was to bluff it. He had established that Scott was up to something untoward and that he had failed to sleep in his bed the previous night. In addition, he had the evidence of ginger pubic hair from the Hubbards' bed, which did not fit their own hair colour at all. Too soon to reveal all that. He went for the early kill, aiming mostly

145

for the Lust/Envy motive: Scott Dunster the cold-blooded murderer.

"Mr. Hubbard, were you aware that your wife was having relations with other men?" demanded Agent Fournier, trying hard with pronouncing his Hs and presenting the question as a statement.

"Are you insane?" retorted Hubbard. "My wife has died and you are questioning her marital integrity?"

"Mr. Hubbard, your wife's infidelity presents a possible motive for her untimely death."

Len Hubbard looked at him with outright rage, his face red as the devil and his mouth wide and toothy. Only he could not hold on, and his emotional overload brought the tears coming back again.

Len studied his nibbled fingernails. "Mia did not have relations with other *men*," he emphasised the plural tersely, "in all our married life I am quite certain there was only one time that she fucked another *man*." Fournier raised his eyebrows, as Len continued. "And since our current discussion is voluntary, I have no intention of digging into that until such time that I have the legal obligation to do so. If my wife's death is no longer being treated as accidental, I shall be obliged to summon my legal counsel." He left it there for a moment, before adding, "Immediately!"

34

Sunday, 24 July, 1:47pm. Golfe-Juan, France.

Agent Fournier received a call from Agent De Brun of the Maritime Gendarmerie, whose patrol boat was chugging along the coast back towards Juan-les-Pins, a few kilometres away. De Brun had been visually sweeping the beach as they returned, looking for any suspicious activity – finding a dead body was not an everyday occurrence for him and adrenalin was ensuring he was mentally still on high alert.

Agent De Brun was aware that Fournier had lost one of the guests, and he believed he may have seen him on the town beach, near the Open Plage. Once again, bunking the Renault 19 up on the kerb, Fournier hurried to the spot that De Brun had reported, looking rather like he needed to relieve himself. He ran a few steps, thought better of it, walked quicker than fashionable, tried running again, came to the same conclusion as before and so he continued. When he arrived at Open Plage, there were only speedos and bikinis to be seen and not an overweight Englishman in sight.

The beach was now filling up, the ubiquitous African vendors trawling it for gullible tourists. Hats? Sunglasses? Coconuts? More hats? We got it. When Fournier retired, it would not be to a seaside town. No, he wanted somewhere more happening year round, with a good local pub. The thin beach came to an end towards Golfe-Juan, the coastline giving way to the huge concrete three-dimensional crosses of the harbour breakwaters. They looked like a scrap heap of unwanted crucifixes. He hoped there would be no more unfortunate deaths today, although anyone using the Roman's preferred execution method would at least leave no doubt as to the principal cause of death. In fact, he knew that death of the condemned in Roman times could take as long as four days and even then it was often caused by progressive asphyxia. Quite possibly Mia Hubbard died from the same lack of oxygen, although from a different cause. It would not have been an agreeable way to check out, neither for Mia nor the crucified. As he brought his mind back to the present, he saw Scott Dunster ambling along the harbour wall, hands in pockets. It was hardly the great escape.

"Monsieur Dunster, I must ask that you come with me immediately," insisted Agent Fournier, with what he hoped was a non-negotiable tone.

Dunster had an aura of surprise.

"Am I under arrest?"

"Not yet, no. But after you absconded from our amenable discussion, an arrest may very well be the next step, but I would prefer that you come volun-tarily."

Scott Dunster looked nonplussed. Fournier stood his ground.

"Okay, but if I don't like the way this is going, I will say nothing more without my solicitor."

"Just a friendly chat, Monsieur Dunster. Trying to be sure I have all the facts straight."

Back at the station, Agent Fournier thought carefully about how to deal with the older Dunster. He decided to go in with what he had, and see where it took him.

"Do you have a daughter Monsieur Dunster?" Scott Dunster got up as if to leave.

"Okay, okay." The small talk was not working. To the chase. "To start with, Mr. Dunster, I have to say your disappearance does not shed a positive light on you. Where did you go prior to the beach?"

"I needed some fresh air, Detective."

Hardly convinced, Fournier pressed on. "As you know, we are trying to piece together the final evening of Mia Hubbard. We already know you were having an extra-marital liaison. So tell me what happened." Fournier stared at Dunster expectantly, like a waiter might look asking what dessert he might like. Scott returned the favour with a practised 'what-the-fuck?' look. Scott said nothing while he gathered his thoughts.

Would he deny the accusation providing Fournier with a clear opportunity to expose his lies?

Dunster looked pensive, then began, "Okay. Well. This is sensitive. But since someone has already told you, yes, I have been involved in a holiday romance. But if that's anything to do with this, I can't think how," Dunster conceded.

"Did you not think it would be relevant that you have been having conjugal relations with the deceased..." Fournier was cut off.

"With the deceased?" Dunster interrupted, "With Mia? You have got to be kidding me? No, not with Mia, I've been seeing Stella Cooper."

Fournier scratched his comb-over balding scalp, and made some notes to cover his embarrassment. Of course, with Stella. That would explain the men's underpants. During his training, Fournier had been taught to have an interrogation plan, but his current questioning seemed more off-the-cuff than a cheap discarded beach watch. He pulled an eight by twelve inch print from his file and probed, "So are these your undergarments?" No sooner had the question left his mouth than he was struck by embarrassment. What the hell was he doing? Investigating a middle-aged man's moral indiscretions? Or was he trying, rather amateurishly, to make a case for this death to be considered suspicious?

Scott looked like the airline's ground staff had just told him that he had been bumped off a flight despite holding a confirmed reservation. His response to the question, made while walking to the door was "You have got to be joking. Is everyone here as incompetent as you, or are you specially trained?"

Agent Fournier looked at his hands and felt the sinking feeling in his stomach. The stinging came to his nose, and he knew a brief involuntary siesta was imminent.

Something about that man was still making him uneasy…

35

Me

Friday, 22 July. Off the coast of Nice, France.

Two days earlier

The previous night in Monte Carlo, Mia was the one who came rushing down the casino steps, asking if I was OK.

"What a bunch of wankers," I concluded in a classic English summation. "First they steal almost five grand, and when they've milked me dry, they eject me unceremoniously off the veranda."

"Only you could pull that off, Charlie. Although strictly speaking it was not actually casino staff that kicked you out," she said, smiling. Then she ran a warm finger from my chin, up behind my left ear, where she caressed me like a cat lover caressing a kitten. That erogenous zone stimulation, coupled with an emotional overload from the casino debacle left me fighting a hardening groin and welling eyes. Thankfully the others showed up and saved either getting worse. "Later," was what she whispered in that same damaged left ear.

Back at the boat, I just wanted to go to bed, but when Ana joined me and was gentle, I thought maybe she wanted to have sex. I engaged in earnest erotic legwork which was quite painful given the fresh bruises and scratches. I delivered much sensual caressing and stroking, and received rudimentary reciprocation from Ana. Seizing my chance, I repositioned myself, checked Len was not peering through the skylight, but was instantly told, "For fuck's sake, Charlie, can't we just enjoy a hug?" The painters were probably in.

My first conscious awareness the following morning was an ear-splitting pounding followed shortly by an intermittent urge to vomit. Len had started the twin diesel engines to power us out of the harbour, resulting in a less-than optimal customer experience in the port aft cabin. I found myself alone, Ana having already slipped out at some point. A glance at my Triathlon watch on the small night shelf betrayed my guess at the time: it was in fact 9:23am.

The relentless pounding of the motors – particularly the port aft engine, located seemingly under my pillow – thwarted all cognitive activity. Smothering my head with Ana's pillow did little to alleviate the constant drumming from below. As I was holding my ears, with two hands, the retching oily odour of diesel fumes hit me. I could literally taste it. In an instant my already misfiring brain experienced sensory overload and returned the problem to me as the feeling of excruciating nausea. Unable to cope any more with three of my senses rejecting their observations, I scampered across to the toilet in my boxer shorts. I would have made it, but someone was in there. I attempted to reroute my emergency to the bathroom, but that was also occupied. It would have to be the sea… but en route I gave in and heaved onto the white steps that had been mopped so thoroughly every day. Len was suitably unimpressed, but just pointed me to the bucket, rag and disinfectant. It made for an imperfect start to the day.

The leg from Monaco to Golfe-Juan was only 26 nautical miles in a south-westerly direction. However, the wind was westerly, so the going was slow. In French waters that day, within an hour we were tracking close to Saint-Jean-Cap-Ferrat, a built-up peninsular just a few kilometres east of Nice. From our view point, we could see some of the most expensive homes in the World, luxury properties of royal families and the extremely wealthy like Andrew Lloyd Webber and Microsoft's other founder, Paul Allen.

Scott was being his usual brown-nosing self, always there for Len's every request. If the skipper would shout, "Hoist the main sail," Scott would be there. "Tighten," and Scott would be pulling on the sheet, which apparently is the rope and not the sail. Len bored us the first day harping on about 'three sheets to the wind' meaning those flapping, unrestrained ropes are all over the place. By day two, the rest of us had all but given up and left Scott to it. He was like the teacher's pet, desperate to impress the skipper. "Ready to gybe," Len would yell.

"Gybe oh!" would reply the solitary forceful voice of Scott. The good thing about Len as skipper and Scott being the entire crew was that the rest of us could do what we wanted – drink beer and lounge about in the sun.

For lunch, the girls tended to throw some ingredients together. Stella was probably the best cook, so she generally led the food plan, although Mia also took charge on occasion. That lunchtime, on the last sailing day, it was Stella calling the shots.

As a sort of lunchbreak, Len gave the command to lower the sail, and we just coasted in the ocean, about four miles out from Nice. Stella laid on a spread of breads, smoked salmon, chicory salad, with egg, bacon and a delicious French dressing. She showed me how mixing mustard and vinegar, then extra virgin olive oil with a little seasoning made a better sauce then anything at a supermarket. Then, she said, we just needed some walnuts cracked.

Inside, Scott took on the search for a nutcracker, "In the drawer at the top," yelled Len.

Scott searched through all the drawers, comically pushing all the crap – the plug convertors, the pliers, the Sellotape – out of the way. But he found something else. He came back towards the galley, looking like a gangster waving a Glock self-defence pistol around, saying with a smile, "This should do the job!"

"Jesus, Scott, you don't know what you're doing, give that to me," ordered Len.

Scott stared at him, looked down at the pistol in his hand, then said, "Sure, I know what I'm doing." He returned the Glock to its hiding place in the drawer, and returned with the nutcracker.

After lunch, some of the magic had gone, Scott had crossed a line. Nevertheless he kept acting like Len's bitch; he hoisted the mainsail, and once again, I was unburdened by obligation. I messed around on Facebook and Snapchat, loading some of my stills from my Narrative Clip camera, generally just trying to inspire jealousy from my so-called friends back home.

Stella was addicted to a slushy novel on the rope nets between the twin hulls, and Ana muttered that she was going for a siesta. My phone died, so I stepped down into the living area to search for my 12-volt phone charger, quite like a dog digging for a bone at the beach. Raising the USB cable above my head victoriously, I became suddenly aware that two eyes were fixed on me through the open master bedroom door.

Mia was lying there on her belly, curved bum pointing upward. She was staring at me like I was a hare-brained animal. She did not make a sound, but she raised her eyebrows a little, and mouthed, "I'm horny".

I thought, 'Oh, shit'.

There was no question of me sneaking in to screw this women, who, while only four years older than me, was still technically my aunt. I nevertheless walked in and whispered, "Are you okay?"

Before I knew what was happening, she had whipped down my shorts and was greedily administering fellatio.

'Double shit', I thought. Using a free arm, she flicked the door closed. I looked through the exterior porthole window and thought how horribly wrong this could turnout.

Within a few minutes, it was to go predictably awry.

36

Scott

Sunday, 24 July, 2:20pm. Golfe-Juan, France.

Scott Dunster did not plan his disappearance from the station earlier that day at just after ten in the morning. Here is what happened. He had been holed up in that small-town police station interview room for over an hour. He acknowledged that he was no authority in the area of the judiciary, least of all the French legal system, but he was pretty sure he had no obligation to stick around. He felt as though some dozy backwater police detective was taking them for the unwitting chumps that they were proving to be. Having spent the week with Len acting the captain of the ship, Scott thought everyone was probably looking to his uncle for their next move, but, he decided, enough was enough.

The previous night – Mia's last evening alive – had turned in to a drunkard's paradise. There had been drinking games, seemingly endless bottles of spirits, and, on reflection, not a great deal to eat. A number of generous measures of sailors' dark rum were probably his last mistakes, and he paid for it that morning. If he had been in possession of a couple of ibuprofen and a venti drip coffee he could have brought the headache back under relative control. Only the hangover he had found himself experiencing was of a whole different magnitude. The musty aroma and beige walls sharply increased the likelihood that he would soon vomit, which was doubtful to help his case in Interview Room 4.

With his head in a fog and his stomach in a storm, Scott had gone to ask the police assistant for some tablets and coffee. It was not his fault that she was absent from her desk.

He had considered his options.

Scott had guessed that pharmacies in France were ever-present, much like pubs in Britain – every self-respecting street corner should have one. He stumbled towards the exit, expecting someone to stop him, but no one did.

Once outside, he had not been able to suppress the feeling of prison break. The headline might read, 'Dazed Prisoner Walks out of Jail in Broad Daylight.' His feeling of freedom was overwhelming. He had plodded unevenly down the street, sidestepping dog shit and polystyrene Quick hamburger packaging. Already he had been feeling better. Somehow, his pharmacy rule of proximity had failed to materialise and the only establishment he had passed was a petrol station, but not of the convenience store variety, more of the oil filter and lube persuasion.

Arriving at the waterfront, he had trudged under the Marseilles-Nice railway line and crossed the busy road managing to avoid being hit by one of the omnipresent mopeds. The thin strip of tractor-trawled sand had already been filling up with beach towels, stripy low folding chairs and straw mats, not to mention their balding and overweight owners, male and female alike.

To his right, had been a wrinkled woman massaging sun block into her sagging body. Farther away still, a man with an impressive beer gut had been attempting to secure his windbreak, sporting an unflattering speedo, the type that has remained perennially popular on the Continent. Having been comfortable in that world of low body ideals, Scott slipped off this T-shirt and flopped into the water.

The cure of cool sea – even if it was the stinky Med – was of the highest standards. Never mind paracetamol, he had thought, as he dipped his troubled head into the salty pond. Gratified by the watery intervention, he had slipped on his old scratched Ray-Ban sunglasses, had stretched out on the sandy beach and drifted off into a sublime morning nap.

After he had woken, some considerable time seemed to have passed, and he could feel he'd burnt in the midday sun. He'd been going in search of shade and water when that bumbling cop came into focus and persuaded him to come back to the station. Which was where he underwent the most amateur of interviews and ended up admitting to the police about his affair with

Stella. As he sat outside the station, deciding his next move, he recognized that there would be trouble ahead.

37

Mia

Saturday, 23 July. Off the coast of Antibes, France.

One day earlier

Mia remained quite sure that Len was trying to 'get into Ana's knickers', but she did not for one minute think he had been afforded the opportunity. She was, nevertheless, furious for the way Ana was leading him along. For someone to flirt with her husband is one thing, but to continue like this in front of her took the humiliation to another level.

Charlie, for his part, seemed oblivious to Len's advances on his girlfriend. The poor thing had really screwed up at the casino and the money genuinely seemed to mean a lot to him. Mia was in two minds whether to help him out with his loss, at least partially, but she could not figure out how to avoid it resembling unsought charity. So, she had not mentioned it, but would perhaps do so if the occasion materialised.

She had experienced a truly sappy side to Charlie when he lay on the cold stone steps the night before, after having been rather harshly treated by the hulks at the casino. She had found his demoralised demeanour curiously alluring and when she had touched his ear, she felt a certain chemistry between them, a feeling that had long since vanished with Len. She knew this was so-called 'limerence,' that natural feeling of infatuated lust. It had been well over a decade since she had enjoyed such fantasies about Len and that erotic desire to have her feelings reciprocated was beyond logical reason.

But Mia was an educated and patient woman and she had known better than to follow such animal instincts in front of the others, who by then were swiftly click-clicking down the steps from the casino in their designer shoes. She had decided to bide her time until a much less risky opportunity came along.

At around 2:30pm on the Saturday, that opportunity arose. She knew Len would not leave the vessel's wheel with so many inexperienced deckhands on board, and so after lunch, she stripped off her clothes and laid belly down stark naked on the bed. She had become accustomed to pleasuring herself regularly, especially when she suspected Len of affairs. Masturbating seemed like a valuable way to pass the time. She had only passed a few minutes with herself when Charlie started foraging through his bag for something. She lured him in and clicked the door closed. Charlie looked rather scared, like a first-time fare-dodger she thought, but that concern drifted from his face when she greedily took him in.

The blow job was only the starter, and Mia found the allure of Charlie increasing out of her control as he ran his fingernails sharply into her scalp behind her ears, massaging her hair in a masculine way as he did so. Charlie pulled her head away and Mia felt under his spell as he flipped her over confidently and pulled himself inside her. The moans she found herself making seemed to be coming from somewhere else. It felt amazing: fulfilling, sensual, consuming, with her route towards climax heightening with every thrust Charlie made. She regained her character and collapsed forward out of that subservient position, and roughly pulled Charlie's body, who leapt onto the bed, neither of them letting go of each other. She placed her hands on his chest as he laid on his back and she lowered herself onto him.

At that moment, she became aware that there was another voice in the cabin.

38

Sunday, 24 July, 2:34pm. Golfe-Juan, France.

Still at the mercy of the Rapid DNA results, Fournier called Michel Bichon at the Cannes pathology unit. Eventually, he was put through to the pathologist, a man he was somewhat acquainted with. The following conversation took place in French.

"Georges! Glad you called, we have completed our post mortem," Bichon began.

Fournier felt like he was about to receive his Baccalaureate results again. "Okay, tell me," he said flatly.

"I will email you over the full report, but the most interesting points are: One – the cause of death was respiratory impairment though submersion in salt water – she drowned. We found sea water in the victim's lungs, which suggest that she was alive when she entered the water," Bichon advised, Fournier listened intently. "There are two abrasions on the head and significant cranial bruising. One lesion is above the left ear, and the other in the centre rear of the skull. The latter is more

165

severe, has swelled significantly, suggesting it was sustained while she was alive, and could have caused her to black out, but it is unlikely to have killed her." At the mention of blacking out, Fournier's own heart started thumping irregularly.

"Cause of death, drowning, possibly after a blow to the head, then," verified Fournier.

"Yes, Agent. Two – based on the swelling of the corpse, the state of the vital organs, we estimate the time of death at between 12 midnight and 2am," Bichon continued.

"Hmmm. Low tide was not until 2:30am, so perhaps it was on the latter side of that window, or the body may have drifted out?"

"That could be, Agent."

"Three – there were various scratches and nicks across her body, but nothing of notable significance. The toxicology report confirmed that she had been drinking heavily and had a blood alcohol level of .32, which is extremely high. In addition, we detected that she had consumed a small amount of cocaine within the 24 hours preceding her death."

"How about the skin you found, any further potential DNA sources?"

"The skin under her fingernails was sent to the lab at 10:30 this morning."

Fournier rubbed his eyes and temples until he felt relief. Then he moved on to his hair, and massaged it brusquely trying to gather his thoughts.

"Anything else?" the detective asked.

"The cold salty water acted as a coagulant and we were able to retrieve traces of semen attached to her pubic hair. We sent that to the lab at midday. That's the main news, Georges, we don't expect anything more. For me, Detective, it has all the signs of accidental death by drowning, complicated by alcohol and drug toxins."

"Thanks, Michel."

All the head rubbing had not really helped. He had three hours to uncover enough concrete evidence to convince the DA that the death was not accidental. But if it wasn't accidental, what was it? Murder? Manslaughter? Suicide? If there had been foul play, as he suspected, at least he had a limited pool of suspects, didn't he?

Scott had admitted to an affair, but not with Mia, instead with Stella. If this was true, he did not have a lot on Scott.

If her indiscretions led to her death, then he needed to get to the bottom of that. The DNA results from the hairs found on the bed and the semen should be posted on the portal in about 45 minutes. He would then know officially if the hairs belonged to Charlie or Ana, who had volunteered respective swabs and unofficially if the hairs or semen was Hubbard's or Charlie's. If they matched none of those, nor that of Mia, they could have originated from Scott.

Fournier started to doubt himself. Was the DA's hypothesis correct? Was he so keen to prove it was murder that he had become blind to the obvious truth? Was this simply a case of hard-partying sexed up foreigners and an accidental death? If he was going to prove otherwise, he needed to advance on this line of enquiry without delay and did not have the luxury of time to wait for the results.

By now, his guests were hobnobbing around the chairs in reception, any futile separation had long ceased. Besides, most of them had lunched next door at the corner café, which only served to remind Fournier of his virgin baguette left by the printer.

"Charlie, could I have a word?" Fournier asked, in a chummy manner. Once in Interview Room 3, he went on the attack. "We know you were engaged in sexual relations with the victim, prior to her death." He watched Charlie for a reaction. Charlie simply stared at his shoelaces.

"Charlie, since you were with Madame Hubbard, then you weren't with your girlfriend Ana, which means you lied in a police investigation," Charlie continued to look at abstract points in the windowless room.

"It also means that you don't have an alibi, which makes me wonder where you were between midnight and 2am last night. You know, Charlie, this is not looking good, and the DA is pressing me very hard to look into this case." He figured it might encourage Charlie if he hammed it up a bit.

"I did not lie to you! I was with Ana at that time. I was with Mia before that," protested Charlie. "She went to bed, and I went to be with Ana."

"So, after you'd screwed the victim, you changed rooms and started over with your girlfriend?" Fournier was sounding venomous, or perhaps jealous.

"Is it part of your job description to make moral judgements, Detective? Mia wasn't a victim when I had sex with her on her bed. When I left her, she was alive. If you have any further questions, you can address them to my lawyer. I hereby request a state-appointed legal counsel. I am now going to have a beer. Au revoir."

Fournier considered the evidence he had against Charlie. He may have lied, but Jesus, they all had. A motive now pointed more towards a jealous partner than to Charlie. He was going round in circles.

As 3pm came and went, Fournier was losing his motivation to find a foul play case. Less than three hours remained before the deadline that the DA had given him would be reached. He had no resources and the next of kin had no interest in pursuing anything other than the conclusion of a swift accidental death. What did he have left? Only very circumstantial evidence against the Dunster brothers. Stella didn't appear to have any possible motive. Hubbard may have been overwhelmed with rage about his wife's sexual relations with Charlie Dunster. Ana may have been jealous on discovering her boyfriend's errant ways. These were clever people. Murder seemed too harsh and dangerous a punishment.

He needed those Rapid DNA results. He called the lab, feeling apprehension fill his body.

The results were ready.

Sunday, 24 July, 3:25pm. Golfe-Juan, France.

It had taken Agent Georges Fournier six attempts and twelve years to successfully transfer from the beat to the detective branch. His superiors' feedback had always been in the same vein 'Agent Fournier did not display sufficient intuition for detective work' and 'Agent Fournier failed to demonstrate adequate understanding of criminal law and judiciary processes.'

These structured formal criticisms had hurt Fournier deeply, especially as he saw younger and, in his view, less talented officers progress through the system. But Agent Fournier had nothing if not a dogged steadfastness, or perhaps an inherent stubbornness and eventually, seven years ago, he received his transfer. With it came a relocation from Annemasse, near Geneva, six hours away to Vallauris Golfe-Juan which was hitherto unbeknown to him.

Situated on the French Riviera between Cannes and Nice, it was the sort of outpost heavily requested and generally only ever granted to the proven favourites of the force. Fournier had neither requested it, nor did he hold any reverence within the administration. He reasoned like Tennyson describing the ill-fated Charge of the Light Brigade during the Crimean War, "Ours is not to reason why." What a wondrous and rare display of maritime cooperation that war had been between the French and British. He reckoned he could do with a bit more of that sort of collaboration on that Sunday.

Using his mobile phone, Fournier had finally got through to the DA and she had been her usual aloof, obstinate self. He walked back to his office and spoke into the phone in French, saying, "Good day District Attorney, Agent Fournier, Vallauris Golfe-Juan Police, Detective Squad."

"Yes, yes, I know who you are, get on with it," she responded.

"*Madame le Procureur*, I believe that we may have a situation with the body found in Golfe-Juan harbour this morning."

"Agent, your nose for criminal wrongdoing is like an Englishman's for wine. Off the scent. I have visited the scene myself – not that I saw you – and it looks like a cut-and-dried drunken maritime accident to me."

The DA sounded exhausted and exasperated. "Agent, we have a serial killer in Cannes, a gang problem in the suburbs of Nice, and the kidnapping of a high-profile French businessman's daughter. The pathologist has confirmed the victim had five times the legal blood-alcohol level to drive – she was corked!" admonished the DA.

"Right," responded Fournier, taking his turn to sound distinctly dejected.

"And, if that is not enough for you, she was high as a kite on cocaine!"

Fournier decided some disclosure was in order. "DA, I have been interviewing the victim's friends and family, seeing if their stories add up, seeing if I can flush anything out."

"Oh! Thank goodness!" Fournier stole a beat of lifting excitement that his hard work was finally being recognized, before the dispiriting realisation that the DA was employing her trademark sarcasm. "Agent Fournier, it is Sunday afternoon and I have already had a busy day. I am not interested in wasting any more valuable resources on your half-baked Inspector Clouseau treachery theories for this dead American lady on a boat full of foreigners. You have until 6pm to bring me a truly convincing case to charge someone, or I am closing it as accidental death. Good day."

Agent Fournier looked as his phone as though the outburst was its fault. The phone's clock revealed the time was 3:42pm. There were around 20,000 accidental deaths registered in France each year, excluding those relating to alcohol or drugs. This case was hardly unusual.

If this was indeed murder, he would have to make an arrest, and soon.

39

Ana

Sunday, 24 July, 3:47pm. Golfe-Juan, France.

Anastasia de Menzies was called into Interview Room 3, a small space that had recently been vacated by Charlie Dunster. Ana had been feeling a bit tired of the whole 'investigation' being conducted by this bungling imbecile Fournier – he just seemed so unprofessional. Besides, why was he working on his own? Surely the French Police could not be considering Mia's death as suspicious, or they would have a whole army of officers and proper CSI down here? Still, it was probably better for her if the investigation was kept small.

Ana decided in the morning that by flirting with the detective, he might be more likely to treat her with less mistrust. She was unsure whether to continue with the sultry temptress act, or to switch to something a whole lot more assertive. Len's plan to 'keep it simple' had hardly been a roaring success – she thought that it had just provoked the detective's suspicions further. She had lied to him this morning about who she'd been sleeping with last night, or at least, she had certainly been sparing with the truth.

With Ana's lascivious looks, she was used to getting any guy she desired. She knew Charlie rated beauty over intellectual capacity so had not been at all threatened by Mia. The dowdy, professional, well-healed lawyer couldn't have been an attractive proposition to him. But that afternoon, she remembered in perfect detail, she had wanted to borrow a book from Mia so had gone below deck to borrow it. Thinking Mia may have been sleeping, she silently opened the door, fully prepared to simply take the book from the table by her bed, but had instead been confronted with a very different scenario – Mia straddling her man, head raised to the Gods in ecstasy.

40

Fournier

Sunday, 24 July, 3:49pm. Golfe-Juan, France.

Agent Fournier began "When you found out about Charlie and Mia, what was your reaction?"

"What would yours be, Detective?" Ana shot back. Fournier was beginning to feel his case slipping out from beneath him. Just over two hours remained for him to present something persuasive to the DA.

"Why don't I do the asking, and you do the answering?" invited Fournier rhetorically.

"Well, I was pissed – how dare that bitch try to take him from me."

"Did you physically attack either Madame Hubbard or Scott Dunster?"

"When?" queried Ana.

"Well, any time after you found them having sexual intercourse?"

"No, I did not."

Fournier flicked through his notebook – a real physical A6-sized paper pad, not a laptop. "Okay, you said that you last saw Mia when she went to bed in her bedroom with her husband at around midnight or 1am, is that right?"

"Pretty much."

"And did you see either Mr. or Mrs. Hubbard after that time and before the morning?"

"No."

"Because you were in bed with Charlie that whole time?"

"Yes." confirmed Ana.

"You had made amends?" queried the detective.

"Charlie had explained how Mia jumped on him, aroused him – she took the lead totally, but that's not surprising with Charlie."

"Hmmm. I see," said Fournier. He was going to keep pressing in that direction when his mobile phone vibrated. He excused himself and returned to his office opposite the interview rooms. It was the technician at the Rapid DNA lab. As Fournier listened to what the caller was saying, his face turned from furrowed brow, to a quizzical grimace embodying disbelief.

He asked the caller to repeat the message, to be sure.

Frankly, Agent Fournier had reservations about each one of these foreigners. Still, he knew he could not chase all of them. The strongest hypotheses for a motive still pointed to Len, perhaps for rage, and Ana, for envy. He could find motives for the others too, but these two seemed the most credible.

The lab results were the clincher. The condoms had still not provided results, but the fingernail scratchings had been analysed. There was a clear match with the DNA that one of the suspects had provided. Fournier had long ago learnt not to presume that all criminals were men. While he had little experience of murder investigations per se, he had read many police bulletins and was fascinated by hardened female criminals – sex traffickers, cyber-criminals, serial killers etc.

The pathologist had suggested that the blow to the head was probably not severe enough to kill her, so again, could fit in with a potentially slightly weaker a female perpetrator.

He called the DA who advised, "You can arrest a suspect if you must, but only with relation to an accident. If you want to turn this into a murder investigation, you will need more than you have given me by the agreed time."

So, with the suspects growing increasingly impatient, he decided, in the interests of uncovering the truth, he must make an arrest.

Out by the coffee table, he called the group together. "Everyone, here, please, now. Thank you for your cooperation today. I realize it has been a long day and that you are grieving. But I have a duty to investigate deaths in this commune. I am now going to permit you to return to your boat," a look of relief fell over each of them, "Except two of you. One of you I will need to take into custody in order to follow our protocol in these situations, the other I have some further questions for in a voluntary capacity at this time."

The look of relief had deserted all of them as he looked from one to another. Stella made a show of inhaling a large intake of breath. Then he moved swiftly to the left and announced, "Anastasia de Menzies, I am arresting you on suspicion of accessory in the death of Mia Hubbard." He then read her the standard caution.

"Charlie Dunster, I ask you to stay behind, I have some further questions for you."

The three released guests stared at Ana in shock, and Len in particular adopted a look of, perhaps feigned, disgust. Fournier had kept his arresting statement deliberately loose, so as not to lose the case to the murder squad too soon and also because he was not overly confident.

He saw little need to handcuff Ana, but he led her directly back to Interview Room 3, where she had come from. Ana was looking crestfallen, shaking her head, unfocused eyes, like she was wrongly accused.

Agent Fournier began by explaining that everything they had said up to this point had no legal standing. It had been simply an informal chat, however, he did point out that he had the memory of an elephant and would flag up any inconsistencies in his report if she changed her story. Most importantly, he said, was her entitlement to legal counsel – she could bring in her own or be assigned one.

Ana asked for one to be assigned – one that spoke English. Fournier asked his intern assistant to track down a suitable legal counsel that Sunday evening, and announced that he would not take the questioning further without her lawyer present.

Fournier called the DA back, explained what his plan was, and requested a deadline extension, considering the time required to muster an English-speaking legal advisor. He could not fathom why the DA was being so awkward, but he knew better than to go up against her. She was as stubborn as a grass stain on white shorts. The DA agreed to an absolute final deadline of 8pm that evening for Fournier to provide indisputable evidence against Anastasia de Menzies, without which he had to release the suspect. This gave him a little less than three hours.

Sitting in his eight-square metre office, Fournier reflected that it had been one hell of a day, but he had a good feeling about how it would conclude. He was exhausted; this day was not like any other. His big break had been the lab's Rapid DNA results.

The lab technician confirmed that the fingernail scrapings had resulted in a DNA match. The presence of the skin under the nails provided concrete evidence of a violent fracas between Anastasia de Menzies and Mia Hubbard. He would ask her all about that when her lawyer arrived – perhaps he had not done everything that day in perfect order, according to protocol, but he was running this investigation alone, and he felt the weight of responsibility on his shoulders.

The Rapid DNA results had also put Charlie Dunster in Mia and Len's bed. The ginger pubic hair was confirmed as originating from the fair-haired Charlie, as was the semen extracted from the victim's body. This was not a great surprise – Dunster and de Menzies had both finally admitted as much. However, the woman had denied any fight between her and Mrs. Hubbard, which was key to his suspicions.

De Menzies appeared convincingly guilty of some level of homicide; he knew in France there were four degrees: *Premier degré* / murder; *deuxième degré* / voluntary manslaughter; *troisième degré* / involuntary manslaughter; and finally, *quatrième degré* / causing accidental death.

Agent Fournier hoped he could bring forward a case for third or fourth degree, which would mean he would most likely keep the case. If it was looking like first or second, the DA would transfer the case immediately to OPJ's murder squad.

Had de Menzies struck Mrs. Hubbard on the head in rage and pushed her overboard? Had she collaborated with anyone else? Could he penetrate the ring of half-truths the guests were spinning?

His usual approach, as a detective, was that he first searched for a hypothesis with motive, and then set about proving it. His premise was that at around midnight, when Len Hubbard was passed out elsewhere, Charlie Dunster got together with Mia Hubbard. On discovering her man's indiscretion, de Menzies retaliated against Mia Hubbard. Perhaps deliberately, perhaps accidentally, she contributed to Mia Hubbard's death. It did not appear to be premeditated, but that remained a possibility.

He was finally tucking into his probably germ-ridden room temperature jambon-fromage baguette when his mobile rang, now off silent, filling the station with the tune 'Criminal' by Britney Spears. He swiped the green button to answer. It was the lab, again. They had managed to get results from the condoms found in Ana's room – and it was another surprise. He touched the red handset button, and muttered for the umpteenth time that day, *"Putain!"* It was 5:54pm and about half an hour earlier he had released the very person he now most needed to speak to. He snatched the Renault's keys, dumped the half-eaten baguette and made for the door.

41

Mia

Saturday, 23 July. Off the coast of Antibes, France.

One day earlier

Mia quickly realised that Ana was not going to take this situation lightly. Yes Ana had caught her in bed with Charlie but the two of them were hardly serious. Her flirting with Len was surely proof of that.

"You fucking Bitch!" Ana yelled, not mincing her words and lunging towards her. Mia and Charlie had decoupled from their carnal embrace on Ana's outburst and Charlie was looking pathetic and limp.

She lashed out at Mia, clawing her off Charlie and leaving instantly red scratch marks all over her torso. Then she took her by the hair and dragged her off the bed, dropping her towards the floor. Mia instinctively tried break her fall, clutching at Ana's bare leg, drawing blood. Charlie stared from one to the other, shocked and horrified, then spoke, "Ana, stop it, for God's sake. Are you okay Mia?"

"Is SHE ok? Are you fucking kidding me?" spat Ana, rubbing her calf.

"I'm fine", Mia responded, getting to her feet. Charlie looked more uncomfortable by the moment, not sure to whom he should turn or what to say.

Ana lunged at Mia again but she was stopped with a clean, hard slap from Mia right across the face, which stopped her in her tracks.

"Fuck! You cow!" Mia screamed.

"I'm sorry but you've made your point Ana. Look at me. I'm naked and covered in scratches, and I think you've pulled half of my hair out. I understand you're cross, but enough. Can we just talk about this please?" said Mia, so calmly it seemed almost out of place under the circumstances.

"What is there to talk about? You're fucking my boyfriend! And you…" she turned her fury on Charlie now "How fucking dare you? What is your fucking problem? Look at her! Is this some sort of sick dare?"

By then, all the commotion had drawn the others below deck. Mia felt her world tumbling down around her. Charlie just wanted to hide. Ana wanted to scream some more. If only there had been a lock on the door.

Len was last on scene and when he entered the cabin, he just stared. First at his wife, then Charlie, and then Ana. Mia was frozen, her mind simply thinking how unjust this all was. All of these people were screwing around except her, and the first time she tries it, this is what happens.

"Mia? Your nephew? Jesus!" Len was speaking calmly, but with a touch of falsetto creeping in on some words. "Everyone get the fuck out of here…" he was not whispering anymore. Scott, Stella, Ana, and Charlie, with his shorts in a ball covering his genitals, filed out quickly.

Mia stayed right where she was.

42

Fournier

Sunday, 24 July, 5:57pm. Golfe-Juan, France.

Fournier called the mobile numbers he had for Len Hubbard, Stella Cooper and Scott Dunster. Each one went to voicemail, before the number even rang. Without leaving a message, he jumped into the unmarked trusty and rusty old Renault with an urgency that rarely accompanied him. He had a buzz inside which was both exciting and petrifying. Since he had been in the station, the weather had turned on its head and a heavy summer's rain shower could be smelt coming in with the warm evening breeze. He turned the key to a rapturous silence; the battery didn't even have the power to turn the starter motor over. Evaluating his options, and with no other police vehicles there, he rifled through his pockets and found the key to his own white Vespa scooter.

It was a practical choice considering the region's traffic, but he was not technically allowed to use it for police business, either from the administration's point of view nor his insurance company's. Given his current needs, he was willing to 'borrow the cat's paws', as they say in Japan.

He donned the open-face helmet that he kept in the scooter's top box and had greater success with the small Vespa engine than that of the Renault's. It took seven minutes to reach Golfe-Juan harbour, and a further three to push the scooter back on its haunches and walk over to the water. The harbourmaster saw him and trotted over in a semi-urgent kind of way.

"No one's out there," he said in French.

"You've not seen the English party?" questioned Fournier.

"Not since this morning – thought they were with you. Any news on the body? Rumours are spreading like wildfire that it was murder."

"We're looking into it," Fournier responded, with a grandiose that overstated the meagre effort the police were making. He could have said, 'the DA wants to do nothing about it at all, so I am single-handedly carrying the flag,' but he knew better than to 'air his dirty laundry in public' as the Anglo's say. He wondered who on earth airs dirty laundry, anyway.

"D'accord, merci."

Fournier needed to find the other bloody guests, or at least one of them, and time was preciously ticking away, like dry sand through his fingers. It was 6:25pm and those crazy Anglo-Saxons would most likely be thinking of drinks. He was struck how a Frenchman typically thought to drink wine with his meal and an Englishman might think to eat some food with his wine. Relying on this stereotype, Fournier completed a lap of the Golfe-Juan restaurants on the harbour edge, and then sped off down the beachfront road to the east.

The commune of Juan-les-Pins was immortalized by the 1960s Peter Starstedt classic, *Where do you go to my lovely?* Starstedt sang:

When you go on your summer vacation

You go to Juan-les-Pins

Well, Fournier was hoping he was right. He dodged tourists crossing the road in front of him, looked out for other two-wheelers passing him, despite his own impression of Godspeed. Watching teenagers drive their 600cc scooters resembled lambs controlling rockets as far as he was concerned.

Arriving in Juan-les-Pins, he cruised along the main drag, which, judging by the number of others motorists doing it, was appropriate Sunday evening behaviour. The beach there was only a stone's throw from the storefronts, and he scanned the beachfront restaurant terraces, the strip of sand and the pavements. After three tours of the one-way system, he had seen nothing resembling his Brits, when suddenly, there they were, all three together. They were queuing for ice cream – hardly the actions of international fugitives, he had to concede.

Fournier bunked his Vespa up on the pavement and rushed over to the foreigners. He was out of breath when he arrived, and almost tripped over a young girl with a purple fishing net. Fournier looked bedraggled as he surprised the three from behind.

"Monsieur Hubbard, I need to ask you to come with me, I have some questions." He was hyperventilating.

"Detective, I have spent my whole day at your disposal, a day when I have tragically lost my wife. Forgive me, but, going back to your grimy, stinky police station does not appeal."

"Some new information has come to light," Fournier stated.

"What new information?" asked Len.

"Some DNA evidence, I think we should talk about it down at the station," Fournier was still panting, out of breath.

Fournier weighed up his options. If he arrested Hubbard, he had already said he would take legal representation, and Fournier did not have enough time for this. He was going to have to try and get Hubbard to incriminate himself, right here, right now.

"We should at least go somewhere private to talk, perhaps over there," Fournier pointed towards a low wall that bordered the beach.

"Whatever you have to ask me, you can do so in front of Scott and Stella," asserted Hubbard.

"Okay," Fournier flicked through his notebook. It took longer than the action merited as he could not find the page. "Right..." he continued, stalling for time. "Here. You told me earlier today that you went to bed at about midnight after brushing your teeth and spitting over the side of the boat, right?"

"Yes," said Hubbard, somehow making 'yer-es' a two-syllable word, which was a new one for Fournier.

"And you stated that you saw no one else after you went to bed shortly thereafter," Fournier insisted, still breathless.

"Detective, we have been through this…"

"I found two condoms in Ms de Menzies' room, Monsieur, and forensics have confirmed that they were used in the early hours of yesterday. One condom contained sperm attributed to the DNA of Charlie," Fournier paused for affect, "And the other contained semen matching your DNA."

Hubbard blushed so red, it was like a traffic light at night. The rosy skin colour went right down his neck. Scott and Stella were both struggling to suppress smirks. Hubbard was preparing his response.

"I never agreed to give you my DNA, this is illegal," stammered Hubbard. "Now, if you have anything concrete, based on legally obtained evidence, then I would be happy to talk with you in the company of my own lawyer." Len scribbled a name and number on the back of his own business card. "Until that is the case, kindly go fuck yourself!"

Shit. Hubbard was right. In all his excitement, Fournier had taken short cuts that would now damage the case. Hubbard was hardly going to consent to providing a DNA sample now, and anyway, time was almost up. He would have to press on with Anastasia de Menzies and Charlie Dunster, but the confab with Hubbard had, as they said on board, taken the wind out of his sails. The chance of building a strong enough case in the hour and a quarter to follow was looking increasingly threatened.

43

Fournier

Sunday, 24 July, 7:05pm. Golfe-Juan, France.

Back at Vallauris Golfe-Juan police station, Agent
Fournier had one women in custody and one man
helping him with his enquiries. He was hoping
something fruitful would come from the discussion,
since he had effectively lost the opportunity to bring
Hubbard in, at least, for the time being.

Agent Fournier knew that he could be more direct
with Anastasia de Menzies, since she was actually under
arrest. By the time he returned from his little hiatus to
Juan-les-Pins on Starstedt's flawed advice, the state-
sponsored legal representative had arrived for de
Menzies. Fournier marvelled at some of the lawyers that
the state sent. They had two requirements when putting
them on the roster: a) cheap and b) available; neither of
which are attributes associated with getting the
defendant the best legal advice for them.

That day, the state had sent Louis-Charles Papon. He
wore a sort of wispy fuzzy moustache, which he might
mistakenly have thought made him look older. What he

lacked in facial follicles, he made up for with his attire. Papon was sporting a designer short-cut three-piece suit, probably tailored Italian. He wore a conservative tie and a smart, crisp shirt. As he clocked Fournier, he touched his glasses in a socially insecure way.

Fournier opened the interview, first in French, stating his own name, the location, time, interviewee and case number, before explaining on tape that the remainder of the interview would be conducted in English, at the request of the suspect, Ms de Menzies.

"Ms de Menzies," Fournier began. He had become accustomed to the uniquely Anglophone title of Ms during his marriage to his American ex-wife. The French language and society had no equal, the closest match that some people used was to refer to every woman as Madame, irrespective of their marital status or age. "Could you state for the record how you came to know the deceased?"

Fournier continued through perfunctory questioning, the legal advisor had no reason to object to any of the questions. Finally, after about 20 minutes, Fournier arrived at the previous day. "So, you went to the Hubbard's cabin, entered and what did you see?"

"My boyfriend having sex with Mia," replied Ana.

"For the record, that would be Charlie Dunster, right?"

"Yes."

Fournier went on, "How did discovering Charlie Dunster and Mia Hubbard together in bed together make you feel?"

"You don't need to answer that," interjected Papon.

Ana ignored him and continued, "Well I was pissed off. Annoyed."

"With who?" continued the detective, "Ms Hubbard, or Scott Dunster?"

"Mostly with Mia," Ana conceded.

"What time was this?" asked Fournier.

"Around 2:30, yesterday."

"Am or pm?" Fournier was used to the 24-hour clock.

"Pm" stated de Menzies.

Fournier furrowed his brow. Up until that point he had presumed it was 2:30 in the morning. Whichever way, he chose to press on.

"And did you strike Ms Hubbard physically?"

"I'd like to advise my client." Papon whispered something in de Menzies ear.

"No, I did not," affirmed Ana.

"Hmmm," started Fournier, going in for the kill. "Have you, in the past week, fought with Ms Hubbard?"

"No, I said," confirmed de Menzies.

"This document," asserted Agent Fournier, "shows the DNA results from some skin found under Mrs.

DEAD IN THE WATER

Hubbard's body's fingernails. It suggests that Mrs. Hubbard was engaged in a struggle with you, Ms de Menzies. A struggle that I suggest to you led to her death."

"What!" exclaimed Ana. She remained quiet while collecting her thoughts. Papon did not try to stop her.

"Okay, yes, I did fight with her in the heat of the moment, but it sure as shit did not lead to her death. Our fight was at was at 2:30pm and by the evening we were speaking again. You can ask the others."

Fournier was not entirely happy with this response, but he decided to persist with his other key piece of evidence. The DA viewed that it was entirely circumstantial, but Fournier believed it may lead somewhere. The clock was ticking like the countdown timer on a bomb. They were down to half an hour. He would give it a try.

"Ms de Menzies, as you know, I seized two condoms from your cabin this morning, shown here in this photograph." He passed her a photograph. "Could you confirm for the tape who those two condoms belonged to?"

"Charlie," she confirmed, as she had when Fournier asked her before.

"That would be your boyfriend, Charlie Dunster?"

"The one and only, although I am not sure I would call him that anymore."

"Ms de Menzies, one of these condoms had semen with DNA corresponding to Charlie Dunster's DNA." He again paused for effect, while Ana opened her eyes and mouth wide and placed her palms on her cheeks. It created quite a good impersonation of Edvard Munch's 'Scream' painting. "And the other contained the DNA of Len Hubbard. Tests have placed the age of the sperm as leaving the testicles some time in the early hours of this morning. Could you explain that?"

"I would like to advise my client." Papon again muttered something in her ear. Then he nodded.

"Yes, that is correct. One belongs to Len," stated Ana. "I think the term ménage-a-trois works just as well in French?"

Fournier could not help looking towards the ceiling, hoping for inspiration from above. He closed his eyes for a moment, shaking his head instinctively. He sighed audibly.

"I don't see how any of this leads to my client being involved in Mrs. Hubbard's death?"

"Well, Ms de Menzies has admitted fighting with Mrs. Hubbard on the day of her death. She has been having sexual relations with Mr. Hubbard." He turned to Ana, "I put it to you that you attacked Mrs. Hubbard again and, perhaps unintentionally, you killed her." There was little conviction in Hubbard's voice. Everything he heard now seemed to point to Len Hubbard, but with the time at 7:50pm, there was little point in following his hunch any further.

He needed a believable motive and concrete evidence and all he had was an implausible motive and, at best, circumstantial evidence.

Sunday, 24 July, 7:55pm. Golfe-Juan, France.

Given her credible responses concerning the fight and the condoms, Agent Fournier concluded that Ana was not, after all, his prime suspect. She had displayed wrath in the fight, but could she have taken it further?

Charlie had begun an affair with Mia, but the other five all knew about it, including Ana and Len, so killing her did not seem to serve any purpose. Lust?

For Scott, he struggled to line him up to any of the seven sins. Perhaps Mia had threatened to report his affair with Stella to his wife.

That left Len Hubbard. The husband. Could be avarice, wishing to keep his wealth to himself. Or it could be envy or wrath, so mad was he to find his wife in bed with his nephew.

Fournier could not think of a sloth motive for any of them. He could not 100 per cent rule out suicide, or another party, but both seemed unlikely.

At 7:57pm, Fournier made the call from his office phone to the District Attorney. He felt like he was sixteen years old again, calling his mother to say he'd be late home from the disco.

"Bonsoir, Madame le Procureur," their conversation was again in French.

"So, was it Colonel Mustard in the kitchen with the lead piping?" She seemed pleased with her cheap joke that Fournier had heard countless times.

"I think we have enough to hold the husband." He hoped maybe overstated confidence would help the DA see the light. He patiently and carefully explained what he had on Hubbard. The DA was less than impressed, or maybe she just wanted to get back to her Sunday dinner.

"Nothing you have said gives me any indication that this was anything other than an accident. We will not be investigating this death any further, Agent. You are to cease all investigative activities to do with this case. Good night, Agent Fournier."

Fournier was doleful, but not actually surprised. Perhaps he was well placed as a small-town police officer, looking after tourists losing their handbags and trying to find lost cats. He rubbed his eyes, hoping that a solution would come to him, but all he got was irritated eyes. He exhaled, wondered if the DA was right, and let Ana and Charlie go.

Louis-Charles Papon looked like he'd just scored his first hat-trick.

44

Mia

Saturday, 23 July. Off the coast of Antibes, France.

One day earlier

After her ill-conceived sexual indiscretions were uncovered by Len, Mia knew that she was deep in the mire. It was Saturday afternoon and she was sitting on the bed that they had shared so often, Len pacing up and down in an area barely long enough to do so. She wondered who else she could piss off. Charlie had looked almost irritated with her when she had seduced him; had she misread all the signs?

Her recently formed friendship with Ana appeared to have concluded before it had barely begun. It's not like the woman was married to Charlie. Ana had dementedly lunged at her, resulting in those cat-like scratches that may scar her abdomen.

Len turned to her and Mia could not think of a time when she had seen him so red-faced and angry. She had stood up and he pushed her roughly back onto the bed. "Get out of my way" he said as he did it. Her head whacked against the night shelf and she lay, now crying, on the bed, holding her bleeding head.

He sat down on the side of the bed and closed his eyes, lowering his face into his palms.

Mia took the opportunity to reach out and cover herself with a bathrobe, which was hanging within reach, next to a jacket that might have been Charlie's. She considered her next move and then spoke, "How many affairs have you had, Len? I bet you can't even remember. You know…"

"…Shut up! This is not about me, Mia. This is about you, and your truly poor judgment to fuck your nephew! I am mad, Mia, really, truly fucking mad."

Len got up and walked to the door. He turned and, pointing an accusatory finger at her, shook his head and walked out. Within a few minutes she could hear them all laughing raucously up on deck. What was wrong with these people? What on earth had they found to laugh about? Her?

Mia slipped out of the cabin to the store cupboard, where she found a screw-top bottle of Australian Shiraz, must be some cheap crap one of the brothers brought. She poured herself half a pint into the glass normally reserved for night-time water, and took a gulp. Almost immediately the alcohol began to numb her, both physically and mentally.

Looking again at the jacket hanging on the door, which she was sure belonged to Charlie, she got up and ruffled through the pockets, not knowing why but feeling trapped in the cabin and wanting to do something, anything. She pulled out a foil-wrapped package. Although not a big cocaine user, she knew what it was and how to use it. If ever there was a reason to powder her nose, this was it.

Feeling much lighter, she folded away her vanity mirror and slipped her bikini back on. For the next two hours, she lay on her bed nursing the Hardy's vintage Shiraz, like the solution was sure to be printed on the bottom of the bottle.

45

Me

Monday, 1 August. London, England.

I had been back safely on English soil for a week. By the end of our time in France, tempers were frayed. After the maladroit attempts by that inept copper to find a sinister explanation for Mia's death, that last day we were as quarrelsome and backstabbing as contestants on reality TV. Everyone seemed to be blaming each other for some part of the tragic chapter.

Except me.

I believed it was a twist of fate. A date with destiny.

The police had released us at just after 8pm on Sunday. Ana and I walked to a small one-star hotel in Golfe-Juan rather grandly called Hotel California – it seemed apt for Ana. It offered precious little more than two single beds for the night, which had suited us fine. Despite the drunken and adventurous threesome the previous night, the events of the previous 24 hours had been draining for all of us, and sleep and time to think were all either of us wanted.

I exchanged texts with Scott, who told me he and Stella would stay at a hotel in Juan-les-Pins. It seemed nobody had the urge to stay on the boat.

Ana and I had barely spoken since she had caught me and Mia together – how long ago that seemed! I suppose it would have been appropriate to apologise, but I had never willingly uttered the words 'I am sorry' in my life. And I was not planning to start now or any time soon for that matter. We exchanged practical details, how and when to reschedule our flights, how to get to the airport, when to pick up our bags, but our conversation steered well clear of Mia or Len.

I had expected to sleep immediately, but getting to sleep sober proved more difficult than passing out, our seemingly flawless approach for the six previous nights. I woke at 3:30am, an unintended consequence of a nightmare where I was drowning in a sea of wine. In my dream, the police had arrested me, because, they said, it was illegal to drown. My mind was awash with thoughts and I waited until 5am before getting up, Ana was restless too. Outside a calming cigarette and a long walk gave us a chance to reconcile somewhat. Ana had more to say than me.

The next morning, the harbourmaster had kindly ferried us to Len's boat, which remained silent and unoccupied. We collected our belongings and got the hell out of there. An airport taxi took us to Nice and an on-time 2pm flight into London Gatwick. When the airline seated us apart, we did not object. In fact we both looked relieved.

By the time we landed in England, I think we were both ready for the next chapter of our lives. Ana took the airport shuttle with me over to the Gatwick Airport train station. I bought my train ticket. We kissed goodbye. I hoped this wasn't goodbye.

Seated on the Gatwick Express, I spat out a Snapchat friend request to her. Maybe that would help with communication. I decided to send invites to Scott and Len too. Being alone and away from France, despite being desperate for my independence, made me suddenly really miss them. A tight bond had been formed, albeit due to terrible circumstances.

Stella was not due home until later that evening, so I arrived to our empty shared home on Bermondsey Terrace at 5:40pm and dumped my bag on the table. I almost shat myself when I looked up and saw an unshaven man sitting in my armchair reading a magazine, looking surprised to see me.

"Oh hi. I'm Hugh, your new housemate," he said.

"Um, we haven't started interviews for the spare room yet. How did you get in? Have you spoken to the landlady?"

"She's my aunt. We've sorted it out."

Hugh's haughty attitude pissed me off, so I went to my room and lay on the bed. I slept for the next twelve hours.

46

Ana

Monday, 1 August. Laguna Beach, California, USA.

Ten days earlier, Ana had been relaxing on a yacht, on the Mediterranean Sea. Her muscular English boyfriend, Charlie, had lounged beside her. By then, she could have described the other guests on board as friends, Len and Mia were a cool long-married couple, who she would have liked to have kept up with. Stella had become a close friend in the short time since they'd met, she probably spent more time talking to her than to Charlie. Stella had confided in her first about her relationship with Charlie's brother, Ana had told her to go for it! She had encouraged Stella, telling her that she could make Scott much happier than his wife could. The sun had been shining, and Charlie had whipped up some frozen strawberry daiquiris.

On shore, the mystical principality of Monaco had awaited them. Chic bars, well-heeled clientele, the company of wealthy friends to enjoy the dreamlike atmosphere. What could have burst this veritable bubble of euphoria?

Fast-forward ten days, and Ana was serving another condescending customer a giant skinny iced caramel macchiato. The sailing trip seemed a lifetime ago. She was back at work in a bohemian-style coffee shop by day and bistro by night on Laguna Beach – admittedly not the worst hangout on the West Coast. The catamaran only existed for her in memories, and one of her new so-called friends was dead. She was wondering whether it was over with Charlie – her compulsion told her to give him a wide berth, and that last wild drunken night on the boat with both him and Len – what animal instinct had come over her? That recollection at least no one could take away!

She had taken the same flight as Charlie to London – she would like to have sat next to him and talked, but Charlie had been head down and disinterested. At least she did not need not be worried that he was going to run away with Mia! At Gatwick airport, she had endured a five-hour wait until her connecting flight to LAX. She caught up on email and was pleased to at least see a Snapchat invite from Charlie. Perhaps she could convince him to see her again one day.

The eleven-hour flight to Los Angeles was marred mainly by the overweight woman impinging on Ana's window seat. But it was a daytime flight, and thus perpetually evening, so she indulged in the complementary Californian white wine. By the time she arrived in LAX, she'd been travelling for 24 hours. The final leg was the shuttle bus down to her condo, which was located at the back end of Laguna Beach, almost a mile from the ocean, which kept the rent affordable, while still remaining in the town. As she closed her front door, she could finally relax. She had flopped into her unmade bed and slept until late into the following morning.

Ana's first shift at the coffee shop was on Tuesday afternoon – her boss had been annoyed when she had delayed the date of her return to work. In her first day back, she earned $64 for her eight-hour shift, and over $100 in tips. She was glad she was not working in Europe – when they had eaten out, Ana had watched diners' gratuity behaviour – it seemed most thought they were generous to round their payment to the nearest €5. Ana thought that such generosity is hardly likely to incentivize good service! Money is the solution.

It was near the end of her shift – just after 11pm – when the Snapchat arrived from Stella. It showed an image of Mia, in bikini and sunglasses, pouting her lips. The message said: "more to follow." Ana wondered what on Earth Stella was playing at.

47

Chrissie

Monday, 1 August. Forest Hills, New York, USA.

It was a friend that had introduced Chrissie to OneSquare, a charity that provided at least one square meal per day to the neighbourhood's homeless. There seemed to be more and more people down on their luck, and falling into a vicious cycle of no-job-no-home-no-job. Chrissie pondered how quickly it could happen to her. Thank God Anabelle had only been in hospital overnight, but what if Chrissie or her daughter had longer-term problems? She was lucky to have her mom just a couple of hours away to step in.

Chrissie was already surprised when she heard that soup kitchens had been born in America during the Great Depression. She was astounded to hear that Al Capone, the infamous gangster, had opened one in his district in Chicago in the 1930s. Perhaps he saw himself as a bit of a Robin Hood. She didn't know if gangsters still ran homeless kitchens today.

Chrissie fitted one three-hour shift a week at OneSquare around her flying schedule. Her neighbour was happy to watch Anabelle as a favour. Chrissie found her friend benefited from the feeling of purpose she got looking after Anabelle as much as Chrissie herself enjoyed volunteering.

OneSquare did not espouse any religious undertones. At OneSquare, volunteers liked to call the homeless people they served 'clients' and they did not have to endure any hints of any particular faith in exchange for the nutritious sustenance.

She arrived at 4:50pm, a little ahead of her 'shift'. Although it was unpaid work, the hours were taken seriously and latecomers were marked in a book. Nothing ever came of having your name noted, but the very action of recording it was designed to dissuade unreliability – no-shows had a negative effect on the whole operation.

Chrissie's least favourite time was Thanksgiving. Sure, it was nice of the annual helpers make a special effort, but the contrast between the haves and have-nots seemed even more acute. Add to that the high number of once-per-year helpers, Chrissie wished they would show up at some point during the year too, rather than grandstanding in late November.

OneSquare tried to serve more than only soup and bread. Sometimes that was on the menu, but at other times it could be spaghetti Bolognese or vegetable stew, admittedly with the omnipresent bread. Some of the customers themselves helped out cooking and serving,

208

which pleased Chrissie. 'A hand up and not a hand out' fitted well with her philosophy on life.

That day, Chrissie was paired with Jelco. No one seemed to know if that was his real name. He did not look very homeless – sure, he sported a beard, but it wasn't ungainly. His clothes had been washed at some point. He didn't smell of roses, but he didn't smell of damp, either.

Jelco recounted the tale of Harold. He had been sleeping in the same place as him, a covered section just as the Brooklyn Queens Expressway went up to an elevated section. One day, two men in suits came asking for him. Naturally, everyone, including Harold himself, denied knowing Harold, and suggested another part of the city that he may be squatting. But as the suits were walking off, they left a business card, and said that we should give it to Harold if we saw him.

Well, it was over a month later, Jelco found it in his pocket and reminded Harold about it. The card said Frederick H. Steinberg, NY Probate Lawyer. Harold had no clue was a probate lawyer was, but another guy suggested it was someone who settled estates, like, after someone had died. Harold called them up, asked them what it was about. Well, his aunt had died in upstate New York and left him over two hundred Gs in her will!

Fascinating as the story was, Chrissie was not sure that she would want to be the recipient of such benevolence. She had worked hard for everything she had, and getting a handout for doing nothing didn't seem right.

"What would you do with two hundred Gs?" asked Jelco. For all he knew, Chrissie had such wealth.

"I don't know." Chrissie thought a little. "I think I would put half towards buying an organic flower shop, and the other half, I would split between my daughter's education and supporting causes I believed in."

Jelco smiled, and said with satisfaction, "I'd buy a Ferrari."

A few hours later, when Chrissie got home, she had a letter waiting for her. Not an email, not a message, a real handwritten note, on personal letter-headed paper. The letter was two pages long, and at the top had the name Len Hubbard Esq. followed by his home address in a place called Echenevex in France, and then a bold line horizontally across the page. The letter was dated 14 July.

A tear came to Chrissie's eye as she read how the results had come back from the DNA lab and he wanted to give the news a personal touch by sending a hand written letter. The results had proved that he was indeed her biological father. In his letter, he apologized for being an absent father as well as for his formality with the tests, but said now that it was confirmed he would 'look after her' and wanted to meet her 'as soon as practical'.

Despite the late hour, Chrissie called her mother with the news.

48

Scott

Monday, 1 August. Oxford, England.

It had been seven days since Scott's life had returned to 'normal'. Since being back at home, the daily grind always began with blitzing his dark roasted coffee beans in his electric mill. It made a satisfying screech throughout the house, which bothered him not one jot.

Alison seemed to have adjusted to life without him while he was away. It had been the first week of the girls' summer holidays, so his wife and children had been away for a long weekend. Apparently that was a lot more enjoyable without dad. His wife was yet to ask anything about the conference in Madrid. By contrast, Scott had asked detailed questions about their break, and received closed minimal responses. Yes, the weather was okay. Yes, they stayed in a mobile home in Devon. No, it was not too far to the beach. It was like getting blood out of the proverbial stone.

It came to a head when Alison revealed that she had seen Charlie's Facebook posts. 'Bloody Facebook!' Scott thought, he should have realised that Alison and Charlie were Facebook friends.

That's when she exploded. She would not listen to reason.

He had lied to her about going to a conference, he was, in fact, on a boat in the Med with a harem of bikini-clad babes. That, apparently, made it irreconcilable. On Friday, she was taking the girls to the Algarve. Scott was required to take them all to Luton Airport, but was evidently not invited to go any further.

In all fairness, he had spent the morning 'sexting' with Stella. He bought a pay-as-you-go phone SIM card to keep his fun private, from his employer and his wife. Being in the mobile telephony business and understanding the technology associated with that at least had some benefits. The messages had started off fairly low key, but had quickly escalated to images of naked body parts. It seemed like a harmless and exciting pastime. However, Stella hadn't responded for over four days.

The next day, he was glad to be going back to work. It gave him a goal to focus on, although his muted joy was unceremoniously short-lived.

Jeremy Smythe, the regional boss, had called him into his office. Smythe was normally a down-to-earth man, Scott would even have ventured 'friend' after a 'successful' barbecue last year. But he appeared to have been brainwashed during the six workdays that Scott had been away.

Smythe told him that management consultants had interviewed stakeholders to drill down into the key issues hindering deliverables. The company would be right-sizing their divisions and sun-setting some projects and positions. Going forward, they would be strategically targeting the best human capital with the right competencies to leverage their skills. At 'end of play', he was sure the organization would be more efficient and effective as a result.

"So…" Jeremy continued, "…As a result of this root-branch review, some of the chicken shops will be discontinued to purge the organization of the worst clock-suckers." He had a little sneer at this. "As a result of this contraction, I think you will agree, it is an optimal time for the company and you to execute a conscious uncoupling."

Scott looked at him in what can best be described as a 'you-arsehole' look, and said, "Is that a bullshit way of saying I'm fired?"

"No, not at all. Your position has been terminated, and as such we need to release you at the end of this week. You will receive six weeks' severance pay, one for each of for the six full years you have been here, and you are encouraged to look through the vacancies that will be posted starting tomorrow, to see if anything is a good match for your competencies and experience." Jeremy looked pleased with himself. "Oh, and we heard about the incident at Holborn Police Station."

Where the hell had it all gone so wrong… the thought of looking for work was beyond depressing. Alison worked as a part-time teaching assistant at the girls' school. Her salary was less than £9k a year. That would cover half the mortgage. Bollocks. This was a problem.

Leaving work early that day, Scott paid a visit to the Fox and Phone, an old pub with a new name that was close to the office. He knew the burly Yorkshire landlord well.

"Is it too early for *apero*, Mick?"

"Oh, dear, someone's been on holiday to the Continent," mocked the landlord.

"Right, sorry, yes."

"The usual pint of Muzzy Head, Scott?"

"Sounds good." Scott enjoyed the craze of micro-breweries for the hoppy beer created with such care, but less so for the we're-so-wacky ale names.

"Where were you? France?"

Scott told him about the boat, about Stella and of course about Mia. The landlord listened like he'd never listened to him before, even asking questions back. When it was time to go, Scott reasoned that he was probably just under the legal drink drive limit after three and a half pints so filled his mouth with extra strong mints and headed home.

Most evenings, Scott would covertly unscrew a bottle of Australian Shiraz, one of his favourites, to share with his wife. With Alison in the Algave, and nobody there to judge, he polished the bottle off in three healthy glassfuls. After the bottle of wine was drained, who wouldn't want a generous cognac to wash it all down?

He repeated this beer-wine-cognac routine each night that week, until Friday, when his otherwise brilliant and recurring plan was interrupted by an accident on the B480 and a subsequent fluoro-jacketed policeman instructing him to roll down his window. It only took one glance at Scott's watery dilated eyes, mixed with the tell-tale smell of strong mints, for the policeman to ask him to kindly step out of the car.

Another day, another police station, Scott thought. What else can you throw at me? His marriage was on the most slippery of wet rocks, he'd lost his job and to top it all, he would now lose his driving licence for probably two years, not to mention the fine.

The duty sergeant permitted him his one telephone call, which he duly wasted attempting to call Stella. He desperately needed some moral support, but instead he was greeted by her familiar voice, inviting him to leave a message after the beep.

The copper in charge had ensured that Scott removed his belt and tie before locking him in the temporary holding cell; suicide watch. Scott felt an overwhelming sense of disappointment with himself – what a screw-up. He closed his eyes and passed out, unsure if his life could deteriorate any further.

49

Len

Monday, 1 August. Echenevex, France.

Len had been subjected to a supremely crap week. After the guests had thankfully buggered off, he switched back to sleeping on the boat. There were hundreds of seasonal chores to complete on the boat, which nobody had helped with. He pulled it up to a mooring and spent much of Monday 'cleaning ship'. In-between phone calls he saw Snapchat invites – one from Stella and one from Charlie, the little runt. Len accepted the invite from Stella, but Charlie could go screw himself.

The death had finally been recorded as accidental and his wife's body had been released into his custody. Mia had never actually expressed any preference concerning a burial or cremation. With a forced tear in his eye, more a result of tiredness than anything else, he had expressed that Mia had always wanted to be cremated privately without a ceremony. To make it sound believable, he had added that she wished for a church 'celebration of life' service in the village they had made their home, Echenevex, six hours away, near Geneva.

Such an arrangement had raised no suspicious eyebrows and with only himself and the staff present at the Cannes crematorium, Mia's body was reduced to a handful of warm grey ashes on Wednesday. He had been given a white tub with her remains – a temporary urn – which rather resembled an ice cream container. Perhaps it was. Len had telephoned the parish priest at the village church in Echenevex. At first, he was shocked at Mia's passing, and then most willing to put together a small service to be held a week later.

It was that Wednesday when Stella had started sending the images – pictures of him attacking Mia. He had been shocked, then angry and finally nervous. He had misjudged Stella's capabilities. She came across as such a nice trustworthy girl, this was genuinely a shock… and something that needed to be dealt with.

On Thursday, Len closed up his boat and taxied to the Golfe-Juan station. First a local train, then a change in Nice to an InterCity Express eventually reaching La Spezia, the town where they had started their fateful journey just twelve days earlier. His Tesla was ready and waiting in the manned car park where he had left it.

Len had been driving for a little over three hours when he decided to take a pit stop, needing a break himself and to charge the car's long-range battery. Approaching the Mont Blanc tunnel on the Italian side, he used a supercharger station near Courmayeur, one of his favourite ski resorts. The twenty minute stop would half charge his battery, giving him plenty of range to get home. It had taken another three and a half hours to reach his rural farmhouse that the locals called 'Le Château.'

The house had a peculiar air without Mia. It was quiet. It was liberating, he thought guiltily. He could even start planning his move to Switzerland, and could bring women home whenever he pleased. Life was going to be easier! Condolence emails, messages and cards were jamming up his virtual and physical mailbox. He was surprised that he did not feel more regretful about what had happened. He tried to put on a sombre voice when fielding a death-watcher call, but that got boring very quickly and he stopped answering the phone. People would no doubt assume he was grieving. He was in the middle of daydreaming about his new life when a chime indicated another new email.

Instinctively, he glanced at the lock screen of his phone and saw an email from Stella with a subject of 'Read Me'. He did, and he regretted it instantly.

Her email demanded $100,000 to buy her silence. Bank details in the Cayman Islands were provided and a photo was attached showing Mia face-down in the water. The caption on the photo read, 'There are more.'

50

Me

Monday, 1 August. London, England.

I had heard Stella return home last Tuesday as I lay in my bed upstairs, bored of the thought of returning to work the following day. Stella had taken the later flight from Nice and I supposed she spent the day with Scott. I was still unsure what to make of our new housemate, and how he had arrived. I could hear them chatting downstairs, but did not want to talk myself. I resolved to catch up with Stella about it the next morning.

The extravagances of the previous week would take months if not years for me to repay. As I worked back over that evening at the casino in Monte Carlo, I kept hitting my head with my fist, calling myself a fucking idiot. I had got swept up with the expensive lifestyle on board, and forgot the reality that my IT job paid me barely enough to sustain life in London, never mind overdrafts and credit cards to repay.

At least I would not face public transport expenses. It was a perfect summer's morning and I responded to the clear blue sky by choosing to cycle to work. I enjoyed cycling, although I longed for open roads rather than exhaust riddled traffic jams.

London drivers were inexplicably hostile to cyclists, seemingly jealous of our swift passage. With the possible exception of the occasional red light jumped, I found it difficult to comprehend such a venomous hatred toward bikes, taxi drivers seemed some of the most aggrieved. The summer heat seemed to make them worse. I resolved to be extra wary of maniacs on the road and took to wearing my live-streaming helmet-cam as a matter of course.

I did not have a clear plan how a helmet-cam would save me, it relayed a real-time video feed and GPS location, but only I knew the URL. At work, nothing had changed, I just showed up, buzzed around for a few hours unchallenged, and trundled off home at 5pm.

During the evenings of that week, I went through the thousands of images I had from my Narrative Clip camera. I had worn the thing so often that people just forgot about the tiny badge-like device – smaller than a matchbox. Sometimes, one of the others would ask about it, and I would reassure them, "Oh, it's not on, a red light flashes when it's on." A lie, but hey, it worked.

It was admittedly a bit crafty to set up a Snapchat account in Stella's name. Some would say unethical, or morally unjust. Purporting to be someone else online can even carry a prison term. But surely my fellow guests would see my reasons. I had something I wanted to reveal and using Stella's credentials seemed like the best way. I had sent the first teaser images to Len, Scott and Ana. I reckoned if they had anything to say back to 'Stella' they would probably reply to the Snapchat message. Even if they used email, I was an IT geek, living in the same house as her and had helped her set things up so I could gain access as the administrator. On Tuesday, I had dealt with the email situation anyway, so any messages got forwarded to a new account. She would never know.

My ploy was directed at Len; the other guests were only really included in the invites to provide consistency.

On Friday 29 July, I upped the ante.

Searching though my photos that first night back in London, I had not expected to find the images that would change my life.

During the morning of that last Friday on the boat, I had left my jacket in Mia's bedroom, with the camera attached and facing outwards. Of course, I hadn't known that I would take a starring role at that point.

After the sex and rowing and all that bullshit, only Mia and Len had been left. Mia, Len and the camera. I had images of him pushing her onto the bed but then nothing happened for hours, apart from Mia crying, drinking wine and stealing my coke. At 11:52pm Len returned to the berth, visibly drunk. The camera caught Len pushing Mia again onto the bed. Thirty second later he was holding her by the throat. Another thirty seconds and it caught Mia looking up, like a hunted fox. Thirty seconds more and Len was blocking the view. The next shot was the money shot. It showed Len striking her with a metal torch – the kind the army use – on the right side of her head. Bingo.

51

Monday, 1 August. London, England.

On Stella's last night in Juan-les-Pins, she, Scott and Len all booked into the Hotel du Soleil just off the seafront in Juan-les-Pins. Scott and Stella had shared a room, but some of the spark had already drained from their holiday romance. Stella guessed it would be back to wifey for him, and back to celibate life for her.

The following day, they all collected their belongings from the boat and said goodbye to Len. Scott and Stella had separate flights from Nice in the late afternoon. She had felt a mixture of angst and freedom, being with Scott had been fun, but she had started to find him a bit pathetic – he wore pyjamas, brushed his teeth three times a day, and genuinely used expressions like 'oh my goodness' and 'golly'. That may have been part of her initial attraction to him, his Britishness, but it hadn't been long before cute turned to puke. Anyway, he definitely had an unhealthy love affair with booze, an instant turn-off in her view.

It was 10pm when she arrived home. A new guy had moved in, which was a bit disconcerting. He had dark features and big hands and was hairy like a gorilla. When he looked at her, it was with such intensity. When he spoke, it was like each thing he said had a weighty profoundness to it, however banal it actually was. "I have put the wheelie bin out," came across as "I have taken care of a most pressing chore, you should not worry yourself."

In the clinic, her fellow physical therapists were pleased to have her back, relieving them of some of the workload. On Tuesday, she had received a weird text from Scott. It read, "WTF???" They had been exchanging saucy texts and the odd picture, so she wasn't sure what he meant. Another reason to back off. She ignored it. More cryptic messages followed and by Wednesday, she blocked him. Time to move on. And anyway, after a few days of flirting, Hugh had rather presumptuously invited her to Cambridge for the weekend and, thinking about it, she hadn't been able to think of a good reason to refuse.

That Friday, Stella and Hugh caught the train to Cambridge. They had been sitting in a taxi when her phone rang. The caller ID showed it was an Oxford number – probably Scott. She silenced it and put it back in her pocket.

"Aren't you going to get that?" asked Hugh.

"No, it's not important, they can leave a message if it is." Stella responded.

52

Fournier

Monday, 1 August. Golfe-Juan, France.

Agent Fournier was sitting cross-legged on the single bed in the guest bedroom of his apartment. On the floor lay piles of papers, transcripts, photographs and recording tapes. He pondered the information in front of him, sipping a hot espresso. Recollecting the previous week, he had found it the most challenging of his career as a detective. He was by no means satisfied with the conclusion but had exhausted his professional options.

The coroner had formally signed off on Mia's death as accidental. There was no formal inquest. The coroner, District Attorney and pathologist all agreed with each other that the evidence did not warrant any further investigation. The death certificate recorded the official cause of death as drowning complicated by the effect of alcohol and drugs. Specifically, the cocaine seemed to have been the nail in the coffin, so to speak, motivating the judiciary to look no deeper.

The week had also been personally draining upon his health. He could count a total of five blackouts on that one Sunday. With the case formally closed, he had finally taken the long overdue trip to the doctor's office. His doctor, like almost all general practitioners in France, ran her own shop. Fournier had tried to explain to her that in many developed countries, doctors pooled together and shared premises and administrative staff. "We could not afford that," was her only defence, which was an odd argument as it would surely save money. So, as usual, Dr. Lamboley interrupted her appointment at least three times to answer the phone and discuss other patients' issues. The doctor decided his was probably a condition known as vasovagal syncope, a disruption in the balance of neurotransmitters that regulate the blood vessels and heart rate, causing a temporary decrease in blood flow to the brain.

While this sounded pretty drastic to Agent Fournier, the doctor assured him it was generally nothing to worry about and he should recover after some rest. She signed an *arrêt de travail* sick note to excuse him from work for two weeks and made an MRI scan appointment for him in two weeks' time. Until then, he was ordered to rest.

Fournier had managed to mope around his apartment for the total of one afternoon before boredom took hold. He could not let the body-in-the-water case go. The day the corpse had been discovered, his main suspect had been Len Hubbard, the spouse of the victim. But he still lacked a credible motive. Sure, he had Hubbard's avarice and wrath, after discovering his nephew shacked up with his wife. But Len seemed like a man more calculating than that.

Fournier massaged his scalp, then stopped when he became concerned that he was rubbing away his few remaining hairs. He thought back to the previous February, when he had been called out to an attempted burglary in the harbour. It had been Len Hubbard's boat.

The next morning, he decided to take a short walk to the police station, even though he was meant to be on sick leave. He signalled *bonjour* to the desk sergeant, as he did every morning, and scurried through the foyer, through the badge-controlled security door and up a few steps to his office. Normally, up to five officers and three support staff filled the space, but that morning, at just after 7am, it was empty.

Fournier collected up all of the Mia Hubbard case files, the ones which had been of such little interest to the justice system, and stacked them in a large box. He took the opportunity to toss the remainder of his doomed *jambon-fromage* sandwich and made his way to the archive room.

He unlocked the door, using a real metal key, no card-key on this door, and dug out the file about the boat breaking and entering case from five months earlier. 'File' was a bit overstated, there was a one-page handwritten document, and a photo of the boat called *Shooting Star*. Len Hubbard's boat.

Fournier delved into his memory, and recalled that the apparent thieves were not your usual scraggy unshaven pieces of human detritus. No, these crooks were more familiar with the gym. However he had no more details. The case had been closed with no further action on Inspector Ayad's orders, but it had remained on his mind. Who were the intruders, bailiffs maybe? If they were acting on a court order, they would have stuck around. Underground debt collectors perhaps, looking to take material possessions in lieu of unpaid loans. Buoyed by his new direction, but unwilling to risk a confrontation with other occupants of the floor, Fournier made his exit before anyone arrived for work.

Back home, Fournier took the business card that Len Hubbard had given him. It read *Stoilco* and included an address and phone number in Geneva. He looked up the accounting practices for private companies in Switzerland, and found they had been fantastically tightened in recent years thanks to scandals at banks UBS and HSBC amongst others. These scandals led to seemingly relentless investigations by the US and the EU into Swiss-registered businesses' tax practices.

Fournier read that Swiss bank UBS paid over €500 million in 2015 to US authorities to settle allegations that began in an investigation into the rigging of foreign exchange and Libor benchmarks. It had already stumped up over €500 million in 2009 to settle a separate tax evasion probe.

He also read that HSBC suffered from a crippling financial data dump by a whistle-blower, which resulted in the leakage of thousands of clients' bank account details and millions of euros of recuperated tax.

Together with a general move towards greater transparency, Fournier discovered that companies, even privately held ones like Stoilco, were now subject to a general duty to keep accounts and file financial reports if they had a turnover of more than half a million Swiss francs.

Perhaps to demonstrate that they were a large, dependable operation, and thanks in part to this new legislation, Stoilco had provided an annual report on their website with some bare-bones financial details for the group. Most notably, Hubbard owned a third of it. Fournier was no expert in balance sheets and P&L accounts, but the company seemed to have barely scraped a profit in the previous year. Could Len's apparent wealth be a house of cards, destabilized by the global financial turmoil? He certainly would not be the first to succumb to it.

Over the ensuing days, Fournier dug into whatever lead he could think of. However, without the use of the comprehensive police computer system, especially for the parts that were not even in the French jurisdiction, never mind his own municipality, progress was slow going, Fournier relied on a few favours and some borderline just-ethical private detective techniques. The most productive lead came on Thursday afternoon. He disguised his telephone number and called Len Hubbard, the man himself.

Although Fournier was used to fluffing and bluffing, he felt a flash of anxiety as the number rang. With the fear came adrenaline and confidence, and then Hubbard answered, "Yes?"

"Mr. Hubbard," Fournier had planned his lines carefully and practiced in front of his bathroom mirror, pushing the H from the back of his throat. When he really concentrated, he could sound nearly as American as his ex-wife. "I am calling about the life insurance policy that you recently amended."

"Yes." Hubbard snapped. Two words, two affirmatives. Better than 'no', Fournier thought.

"I am very sorry, but my colleague did not process the paperwork correctly, it is still valid, I just need you to confirm the details so that we can draw up the correct documents." Fournier was especially pleased with his line, which he felt should elicit important facts from Hubbard.

"Who did you say was calling?" Hubbard barked, alert now, like prey being hunted.

Fournier hung up, despite the limited information, Hubbard had confirmed that he recently updated his policies, no doubt significantly increasing the effective bounty on his wife's head. Fournier had a feeling he was finally making progress.

53

Moutier

Monday, 1 August. London, England.

Cédric Moutier had been doing Hubbard's dirty work for years. He was not troubled by moral dilemmas and reasoned that if he did not undertake his work, then someone else would. Hubbard paid well and kept him on a retainer even when there was no work that suited his expertise.

A couple of months ago, Hubbard had asked him to trail his wife. It was an easy job, and Cédric was pleased to have done it well. The wife had not even noticed him. Hubbard had become convinced that his wife had taken a lover. All Cédric had to do was trail her and see where she went. She only ever went to work, but he got paid regardless.

Cédric was French, born into a working-class family near Marseille in southern France. He grew up watching his father and uncles playing the ball game *pétanque* each afternoon, drinking glasses of Ricard to keep them seeing straight. The familiar clink of metal on metal, followed by anything between a murmur and a full-scale argument, peppered those summer days. He had moved up to the Pays de Gex in search of better-paid work, and when the more formal channels failed to provide for him and his young family, a friend introduced him to Hubbard. To begin with, the jobs were innocuous enough – roughing someone up, 'borrowing' files from offices, taking a look around someone else's property – but in recent times, they had turned somewhat sinister.

Cédric had heard last week that Mrs. Hubbard had died during a holiday on Hubbard's yacht. He had been away in Majorca with his family that week, taking advantage of Hubbard's absence to get some well-earned rest.

Three days ago, he had been given his latest job. He had done plenty of work in Switzerland for Hubbard, but this required him to cross the English Channel. Moutier was not particularly interested in England – after a school trip to London as a boy, he had never seen the need to return.

Moutier was hardly an intelligence operative, but he knew a thing or two. He knew that both France and England take hundreds of images of traffic, including number plate recognition, so he had a reliable contact make up some dummy plates before he set off. The plates were copies of a similar van's plates, so they would ring true if checked. He fixed them to his white Renault Kangoo correctly, as is done in France, using metal rivets.

He had planned to use one route there and take a different one home. Since he was not great with maps, he had programmed the address into his Satnav, raised an 'unlikely' eyebrow at the estimated arrival time shown, and had pulled out of the driveway.

As he disembarked the ferry onto British soil, he felt a moment of excitement that he was in a foreign land. Then he remembered the task at hand for a cash payment of €3000, plus expenses. He was looking at the signs, trying to work out where to go and to remember to drive on the left, when BAM! He smashed into the silver Volvo in front of him.

"Merde!" he shouted. Rolling his eyes, he got out, put on his most sincere smile, which in reality made him look constipated, and gave the driver a whole lot of baloney information. He got back in and drove on, this time more carefully.

It took Cédric over four hours to get to Bermondsey Terrace in North London. He found number 24 and parked up at the side of the road in the dark, nestled into the back of his Kangoo with his sleeping bag and tried to get some rest.

The next morning he woke to a parking ticket and the threat of the car being impounded. That would not help. After stretching, he moved to the front seat and waited. At 8.14am, the target finally appeared.

Cédric followed the cyclist, noting the clipped-in shoes. After 5 minutes, he pulled into a relatively quiet street, so Cédric sped up and rammed the bicycle. It made a scraping sound against the van and he wondered if his expenses would cover van repairs. He jumped out, syringe in hand, and exclaimed, "I am so sorry, I did not see you... here, let me help you up...". He reached out and in one swift move injected phenobarbital into the cyclist's right arm.

PART 3

Life is the sum of all your choices.

Albert Camus

54

Olga, (A&E Nurse)

Thursday, 4 August. OLVG Hospital.

When the patient regains consciousness, he is hyperventilating, to the point that he appears to be suffering cardiac arrest. With much squinting and winking, he partially opens the eye that is not heavily swollen.

"Mr. Dunster, can you hear me?" she enquires, for possibly the twentieth time today. He was brought in last night during the graveyard shift, and they amputated what remained of his right leg at the knee.

When she had come on shift, the duty doctor had mentioned that the police wanted to talk to him as soon as he regained consciousness. It was up to her to monitor and assess him and let the doctor know when she thought he was ready. The outgoing nurse had mentioned that he may have something to do with the patient in the next room, an off duty French policeman,, who also came in late last night, although she also mentioned with a grimace that his chance of pulling through seemed less likely.

"Mr. Dunster, can you hear my voice?" she persists.

The man on the bed shuts his eye for a moment, which she takes to mean yes.

She puts a hand on his shoulder and sets off briskly to find the duty doctor.

55

Me

Tuesday, 2 August, 9:43am. South-East England.

Two days earlier

My legs aren't numb, per se, they just feel entirely paralyzed below my waist. It's been much better since I managed to get the blindfold half off – I can't see properly, but then perhaps my eyes are swollen. After I came to, the van continued for another half an hour or so, and then slowed. We parked for a while and I tried to make some noise, but the duct tape hindered that enterprise.

Now, someone is opening the rear door. The man is wearing a baseball cap and pilot sunglasses, and probably has a darker complexion, but it is hard to be sure from my vantage point. He grunts "hmmpf" and slams the door shut.

Ten minutes or so later, after we paused for a while, rough metallic ribbing indicates to me that we could be boarding a train or a ferry. A few minutes more and it is clear that it's a train. I quickly realise I am being loaded onto the Eurotunnel at Ashford near the English Channel.

A further half an hour later and I am being hurtled around again as we re-join the motorway, presumably now on the French side. I read recently in *The Economist* that Eurotunnel will never technically turn a profit. I wonder if all Anglo-French collaborations are doomed. I settle down to consider my options about how to get out of this increasingly tight spot.

56

Scott

Tuesday, 2 August, 9:45am. Oxford, England.

Scott had time on his hands. Since being relieved from work, he had discovered daytime TV and the relaxation benefits of wine with lunch. Despite leaving a message on Stella's voicemail, she had not called back last Friday night. Alison was still with the girls and her mother in the Algarve in Portugal, so he found himself in charge of his own destiny. Scott had not heard from them since they left, so his wife was unaware of his lack of job, or his brush with the law. That would be another problem to add to his batch of tribulations.

He had spent most of yesterday and this morning on the Internet. His old employers had demanded the return of his laptop, tablet and phone, so when he saw Charlie at the weekend, he had borrowed his iPad later bought himself a phone. He found that many hours could easily be eaten up, trawling the web's job sites, and, of course, getting distracted along the way.

Right now, he is hovering over Charlie's list of bookmarked websites. The first one indicates a cycling store. The second is marked 'Work mail'. Not expecting much, he nosily clicks on the third site listed, marked 'Helmet-cam'. Charlie once told him how his helmet-cam relays through his Smartphone as a hotspot providing a live stream from the camera to the Internet.

What he sees on the screen disturbs him to his core. Scott struggles for a moment, shaking his head in a twitchy way, trying to compute the live feed.

Charlie's camera is evidently in the back of a van, the lens's angle is such that he can make out one of the spoked wheels of his road bike. The soundtrack is limited to the droning hum of the road. Scott's heart is now racing as the reality of what he is witnessing strikes him. He considers possible options. Scenario 1: Charlie is voluntarily in the back of a van, perhaps getting a lift somewhere to go cycling. Scenario 2: Charlie is involuntarily in the back of a van, with legitimate law enforcement commanding the wheel. Scenario 3: Charlie is involuntarily in the back of a van, with a bad guy at the wheel.

He saw Charlie on Sunday; surely he would have mentioned if such a plan was voluntary. Maybe not. The clock in the corner of the screen reads 10:03. He calls Charlie's mobile, it rings, and he hear a very faint muffled melody on the webcam audio feed. Charlie's such a jerk, he thinks. Who else would have an 'I'm too sexy' as a ringtone? After Right Said Fred opine for the second time how uber-attractive they are, Scott hears the ring tone go silent. A few seconds later, voicemail kicks in. He hears Charlie's recorded voice with an arrogant tone. "I'm busy. Leave a message if you want."

"Charlie. Call me ASAP," he speaks to the voicemail.

Shit.

On Charlie's iPad he opens an app named 'Find my iPhone' which should show him just where Charlie is. Some login information is helpfully stored on the device. He clicks on 'Charlie's iPhone'.

He waits.

And waits – how long does this thing take?

Then, the map zooms in towards South-East England and eventually a location marked as Ashford International Eurotunnel station. Scott stares at the screen like a demented lunatic, feeling utterly out of his sphere of control. He has a deep frown, trying to make sense of it, and wishing he had not had two glasses of Merlot for a morning pick-me-up. He glares at the spot, as it starts to move. Then it fails to move anymore. The app indicates that it is the last known location.

Scott's car is still impounded at the Oxford Police compound after his misadventure last Friday night. He had planned to collect it today; now that will have to wait. Looking outside, his wife's pastel pink Fiat 500 is sitting invitingly outside on the drive, looking like a dollop of blancmange.

Scott thinks. What should he take with him? That would be easier to answer if he knew his destination. He grabs Charlie's iPad, his phone, a twelve-volt USB charger cable, his passport, his imitation crocodile leather wallet and Alison's Fiat car keys on a woolly sheep key fob. He closes the front door, then thinks better of it. Back inside, he collects a pack of cigarettes (normally reserved for the evening), the other half of the bottle of Sainsbury's Merlot, and some barbecue flavour hula-hoops. Prepared for anything, he thinks.

Scott fires up his new phone's Google Maps App and enters the destination 'Ashford International' into the device. Dishearteningly, it proposes a travel time of two hours and eleven minutes, spelling out that whoever has Charlie has already got a head start of over two hours. Scott spins the little car's front wheels out of their suburban driveway making a satisfying screeching sound of rubber on asphalt, and is pleased to see that the tank is full, which the vehicle estimates will deliver him a range of 368 trouble-free miles.

By 12:05pm, Scott is at Ashford International, pleased to have made up a little time. Parked on the Eurotunnel train, the red LED panel indicates imminent departure. Given his preoccupation with driving at 85 miles an hour whenever possible, he had not tracked Charlie's phone's geolocation during his journey.

Scott connects to the train's Wi-Fi and clicks to find Charlie's phone and it is not good news – it appears Charlie is well into France. He checks the helmet-cam stream, no noticeable change. He notices the helmet-cam site also has a GPS location, but the news is no better. The train is now moving away from the station, and quickly down under the English Channel, or *la Manche* as the French prefer it. He turns on the Channel Tunnel radio to pass the time, then gets out of his car and paces up and down the vehicle transporter.

57

Me

Tuesday, 2 August, 2:02pm. Central France.

Now, I reason we are making hay while the sun shines, as the saying goes, and we must be motoring through northern France. We stopped once for about ten minutes which was logically a fuel stop, when the driver came around and offered me a second "hmmmpf". He then removed the duct tape on my mouth, but he failed to linger for conversation, perhaps over a cup of hot chai. I am sure we will not be exceeding the speed limit, given *les flics* propensity for the speed trap, so by my calculation, two hours after leaving the channel train, we are probably around 150 miles from Calais. This would give us a possible location in an arc from the border with Holland around to Normandy in France. Most likely, though, given what I know, we are heading south.

The cargo part of this little van has no windows, not at the side and neither at the rear. So my observations are based on sound and touch senses. I have noticed the brakes grind, which together with the general state back here, suggests the vehicle has already had some considerable years in service.

It is disconcerting to be so out of control – but there is also a freedom to be completely under the radar. No one knows I am here. In the other direction, they would have checked the van when boarding the train, but apparently stowaways in the direction of France are less of a concern. No plane or ferry tickets, no car under my name being watched by number plate recognition systems. No CCTV recording me. In the UK there are over six million closed circuit television cameras, capturing unwitting residents on average over 100 times per day. I am off the grid. The only exception is my helmet cam and phone. They are still on, and should be working. For whatever that is worth.

I am pleased that my abductor chose to throw my bike in with me. The saddle and handlebars are clearly askew and it now boasts some fairly severe paint scratches, but other than that it does not appear significantly damaged. It's my everyday bike, a Specialized Allez. It has an aluminium chassis, a carbon fibre fork and the Shimano 2300 crank set. Of course, I don't use this bike for triathlons. That would be embarrassing, and slow. For that, I break out my Cervelo R3; costs five times as much, rides five times better.

My mind is suddenly snapped back to the present crisis as we screech to an apparently unplanned standstill. I am thrown towards the front of the cargo area along with my bike, and a sleeping bag that my driver has left back here. I hear cries from the cab: *"Putain! Merde! Ça me fait chier! Connard!"* followed by a trumpeting of the *claxon*. My driver's adversary offers some horn in response, and presumably a similar amount of cursing. I conclude: my captor is French.

An hour or so later, we clear the in-road tollbooth without further ado, and I shift myself like a tired caterpillar back to a less uncomfortable position.

58

Tuesday, 2 August, 2:05pm. Northern France.

Scott's passage under the sea between England and France took just over half an hour. The Wi-Fi on the train was a godsend, since he was trying to make up time, he could not afford to waste 45 minutes without a connection. On the train, Scott tracked Charlie's phone's progress and designed a route to trail him.

Driving off the train's vehicle transporter at Calais, Scott was making no friends in the endless winding queues out of the terminal. He actively cut people off, used the Fiat's high-pitched horn without provocation and was generally an inconsiderate driver. He felt he would fit in just fine.

Now, Scott is navigating his way through the northern French port of Calais, and Charlie's dot is moving some three hours south, somewhere between Reims and Dijon. Scott cannot see how he can make up the lost time. He has his phone navigating him to the A26, the toll *autoroute* south. The land around here is flat and colourless. Villages and towns seem punished to be located there. It is a simple landscape, not a beautiful one. The uniform flatness does, however, afford rapid passage. After a while, Scott pushes the cinquecento up to 100 miles per hour. He does not know the speed that Charlie is travelling at, but he is giving the little motor everything it's got.

Two hours later, Scott passes the tollbooth at Reims. As he stops to fill up the pink Fiat, he chooses *sans plomb 98* hoping for a little extra boost. He clocks a white van parked a couple of bays over. Then he feels stupid to be hoping it would be that easy: he is nowhere near Charlie's GPS location, and the country seems awash with white vans.

Back on the A26, he is tracking well, and he returns to cruising velocity of 100 miles per hour. The road is empty, is seems that French drivers are all out to lunch.

59

Me

Tuesday, 2 August, 4:55pm. Central East France.

It has been a good couple of hours of monotony. I dropped off to sleep from the boredom. I have woken now, because we are coming to a halt. The door opens. My captor is still taciturn. I am subdued after hours in the car. "Could you take the rope off" I ask, gesture, as best I can to my wrists behind my back, "it's cutting my skin?" No reaction. Maybe he is deaf or does not do English. "Could I have some water?" I say, badly mimicked slurping from a cup, without the benefit of hands. Radio silence. Door slammed shut. He needs to go on a customer service course.

A further two hours pass and we are now in a very winding section of road. However, judging by the speed, it is still *autoroute*. Now we are coming off the motorway, and the driver seems to have paid the toll using cash at an automatic booth.

The road is bending a lot more and I'm being flung all over the place. My head hurts, but only my arm is in severe pain while my legs have miraculously come back to me. By now, we could be anywhere from Bordeaux to Dusseldorf or north to Denmark. But I know where we are, perhaps I've always known, but I did not expect it to happen like this.

We are winding and bumping all over the place now, clearly on country roads – we must be nearly there. I think I am grateful that the journey is close to over, but I have a feeling that Len will not be happy to see me. No bear hugs this time. No high fives. If I am lucky, I might get a sharp jab on the arm.

We crunch up a stone driveway with night falling. I would really appreciate a slap-up meal and a few pints of ale. The gravity of my actions strike me, and a sense of fearfulness overwhelms me before a warm numbness takes over my body. The rear doors open noisily and Uncle Len welcomes me by snarling, "Get up you little bastard!"

60

Scott

Tuesday, 2 August, 5:05pm. Central France.

An hour and a half after Reims, and it is 5pm local time. Scott is passing the city of Troyes at full speed, pedal to the metal. How do the French take all the letters of Troyes, and pronounce it "twa"? In his head, Scott made it rhyme with 'boys', sod their stupidity. Don't get him started on Reims.

The touristic road signs alerted Scott to the fact that Troyes, the city of a thousand colours, was home to one of his favourite tipples: Champagne. That is, the real stuff, made with Pinot Noir and Chardonnay grapes and aged in nearby damp caves. Wannebee wineries claiming to sell California Champagne, or Russian Champagne should be ashamed of themselves. It's a pathetic attempt to...

Shit. Sirens behind him interrupt his mental banter. Dark blue Renault Clio, emblazoned with *Gendarmerie*. In addition to the driver, he catches sight of two more cops in the small car. Scott pulls over to the hard shoulder. The policeman looks about 25 years old and is wearing a kepi – the hat worn by Steve Martin's Closeau, rather than Peter Sellers'. What he lacks in age, he makes up for in aggressive stance.

"Papiers" the short boy-like *gendarme* demands. Scott makes a show of looking through the glovebox. Clearly not a convincing show. He presents his driving licence, thoughtfully returned to him by the Oxfordshire Constabulary until the court date in two weeks. *"Assurance, Carte Grise."*

"Sorry, no have." He replies with an imbecilic grin. What primitive English has taken control of his mouth?

"La vitesse maximum autorisée est cent trente kilomètres par heure." It was fairly obvious what he must be saying, but Scott just isn't getting it. The cop loosens up a bit. "You do one hundred sixty kilometres. It is too many."

"Very sorry," Scott speaks with a demented intonation, "I slow down."

"It is €135 for no *assurance* paper, €135 for no *carte grise*. I give you only 20 kilometres over maximum, it is another €135. This makes €405 total. You pay cash now, or you must lose your car. What you want?"

"No money, look." Scott tries. However the credit card catches the policeman's eye and he smiles.

"We follow you to bank *distributeur*. Next *Aire de services. On y va.*"

Furious with the disruption, but grateful that all the misdemeanours can be fixed with cash, Scott sets off again. He takes the Fiat up to 140km/h even though the cops are following. Fuck them.

At the cash point, the machine spits out €500. The cop takes €420, "no change."

"Receipt?" says Scott.

"No receipt today," mutters the cop, turning his chin up to Scott. "Not so lucky next time."

Back on the A6, Scott racks up the kilometres. He passes signs for Dijon, Beaune and Chalon-sur-Saône. At Macon, he reaches again for the iPad, while on the move. Using the rumble strip to keep the car from leaving his planned trajectory in the slow lane for a moment, he clicks 'Find My iPhone'. Charlie's phone is not moving from the village of Echenevex, near Geneva in neighbouring Switzerland. Scott zooms in, pulls up the satellite imagery. Yes, there is no question.

Charlie is at Uncle Len's house. He doubts it is a family reunion.

61

Hubbard

Tuesday, 2 August, 7:18pm. Echenevex, France.

One hundred metres below Len Hubbard's property in Echenevex, physicists are inspecting the 12-foot wide concrete-lined tunnel. Particles in two adjacent beam pipes are circulating around the 27km loop 11,000 times in a single second, only marginally slower than the speed of light. Scientists working with CERN's Large Hadron Collider are hoping to prove whether the big bang actually occurred fourteen billion years ago. Len knew, through contacts, when the LHC was active, and Mia used to swear that it made them both a little crazy and anxious. That certainly described him now.

Len had liked his nephew Charlie, perhaps even seen him as his protégé. However, Charlie's affair with his wife ruptured that relationship forever; the ultimate betrayal. Images of Charlie unashamedly banging his now dead wife fill his consciousness. He shakes his head, in an attempt to shake the recurring picture of the two of them, in his cabin. Fucking. The bastard!

Whatever Charlie thinks he has on him is preposterous, but potentially also very damaging. However, the images that Charlie sent prove nothing. So what, he had knocked Mia about a bit after discovering her affair. What man wouldn't? Perhaps more disturbing than the bedroom sequence of pics that Charlie sent is the one shot, taken with a different camera, showing Mia's body in the water. How had Charlie got that? Certainly, it looks incriminating to him now, and he intends to find out what Charlie thinks he knows. If necessary, the hard way. No love lost.

Charlie is the one who is attempting extortion, not him. Len is just reacting. When those messages, first on Snapchat and then on email, came in from Stella, it just did not make sense. Len had called her and asked her what the hell was going on. Stella denied everything. What was the point of denying it, after sending him messages? So Len had a contact of Cédric's, who works at CERN, take a look at the email, after he had detached the implicating picture. Len knew the World Wide Web had been invented at CERN, so surely they would know a thing or two about email? Cédric's man tracked the IP address, and through some highly classified systems narrowed it down to a street in London. Bermondsey Terrace. Now that was where Stella lived - but it was also where Charlie lived.

Subsequent to the bedroom images being sent to the group, the personal email demand had come to Len with the body shot attached. The text read "I know what happened and can prove it. I have more photos. Lucky for you, my silence is for sale. $100,000 to be wired to the account below by Tuesday. Any suspicions that you have called the Police and the files will be released on social media. Don't be a fool, Len." Bank wiring details had followed.

Len remains livid. How fucking dare he? Those four words just keep singing around his head. How fucking dare he? Len looks up and sees a white Renault Kangoo crunching up the gravel driveway. Headlights off. At the wheel is a fatigued-looking Cédric, no doubt tired from his drive. Wake-up Cédric, he thinks, the fun is just beginning.

Cédric opens the rear van doors, and Len commands, "Get up you little bastard!" Charlie looks forlorn, beaten, scared. There is a pool of piss resting on the corrugated floor of the vehicle. Cédric grabs a leg and pulls him through the puddle of urine and straight out. Charlie's arms are tied behind him, and he manages to cushion the fall to the rough gravel drive. Charlie eyes Len carefully. Who is going to make the next play?

Len does. "Helmet," he says. Cédric reaches down to unbuckle the cycling helmet from Charlie. It is a misleadingly intimate gesture, like helping a child up onto a high chair. Cédric tosses it straight into the nearby wheelie bin.

With his eyes, Len signals to Cédric from Charlie to the barn. There are neighbours in the area, but they are a good distance away, properties like Len's in rural France are often acreages. Charlie is dragged by his legs to the barn – a stone building with a concrete floor and remnants of hay littering the edges. Leftovers from Mia's flirtation with horse ownership. Charlie's shirt is halfway up his back. What is his wearing? A man in Lycra has no shame.

"Get his phone" Len instructs Cédric. Cédric goes back to the van and retrieves the iPhone. "Chair". It's Len again. Cédric lifts up their prisoner and thrusts him roughly down onto a wooden chair. He secures Charlie to the chair with an orange electrical extension cable.

Time for some answers. This may get ugly.

62

Me

Tuesday, 2 August, 7:29pm. Echenevex, France.

'Holy shit,' I think to myself, 'this is going pear-shaped.' My abductor, the prized wanker, pulls me by my legs across the drive; I am quite willing to walk. My padded cycle shorts are proving a sage choice of trouser to cushion the clumsy landing. The brute sits me on the chair and then binds me to the seat with an orange extension cord. I am starting to doubt my ability to get out of this.

He's a well-built man – I guess you have to be in his line of work. He is wearing his hair longer than your average thug, and he's donned a grey sports jacket over a white T-shirt and blue jeans. He could be my dentist. A big difference is that I can see a pistol, quite probably a Beretta, tucked into his belt, something my dentist is not of a mind to do.

Len speaks. "Charlie, I have always treated you well, haven't I? I help you find work, I invite you to my boat, I showed you life..." I look up at him. He has a point. "And, Charlie, how do you repay me? You fuck my wife, you try to blackmail me. What's wrong with this picture?"

I venture, from my compromised position, "Len, you taught me to play my hand, use what I have. You use people and I won't be used anymore. I have some incriminating photos of you and I thought you might prefer to come to a financial arrangement, rather than taking the risk of what the police would do with them..."

Suddenly, I am struck from behind while seated on my chair, a sharp jab to the right kidney. I look around, Brute looks pleased with himself. "Wrong answer," informs Len. I tighten the muscles in my body, bracing myself for the next impact, but nothing comes.

"Charlie, this can be quick – and relatively painless – or slow and really quite terrible. Cédric here has a whole repertoire of ways make sure you are cooperative."

So that's his name: Cedric. "What do you want?" I ask, feebly.

"To start with, I want to see the photos you claim to have. All of them."

"I don't have them here," I try, it was partially true.

Bang. A blow to my head, just in front of my left ear. It was designed to make my head spin, but not take too much out of me. It worked.

"There are some on my phone," I admit.

The brute I now know as Cédric brings over my phone and asks me the code. I normally use the fingerprint login, so I have to think, which is not coming easily. I look up at him. His fist is coming towards my chin. "80-20," I spit out, quickly. Cédric takes the power out of the upper cut at the last moment, and it's not nearly as bad as it could have been. But it still stings like hell.

The two of them are fussing over entering the digits into the phone, Cédric repeating inanely slowly the numbers. I take the distraction to lift my arms over the back of the chair, extension cord and all. My mind is awash with potential outcomes, but I am hell bent on what I should do. If I don't take control of the situation, I will be sure to remain the victim, and that has never been my plan. If Len and Cédric keep me here, I am as good as dead.

In one zombie-like movement, I stand up, arms and legs still bound and in a split second crack my forehead into Cédric's chin. At first it seems to take little affect. Len looks on like I am a demented fool. But I carry on hammering my head at his man, who was not expecting this at all.

I feel no remorse – to start with this guy is no stranger to violence, and more importantly, he has held me hostage all day. As my head butt causes Cédric to arch backwards, he loses his balance and comes crashing unceremoniously to the floor.

I slip the big man's head between my legs in a deft movement – perhaps having them tied at the ankle actually helps maintain my leg-lock position. I snatch behind me, in an attempt to reach Cédric's body, but Len in standing above me, shaking his head.

In one lunging move, I clutch towards Cédric's writhing body, my hands still locked behind my back. Len seems almost amused, like he does not believe I am a threat. I realize I am doomed. I think about everything I have risked to arrive at this moment, and now it is all for nothing, disposed of by my own uncle.

Suddenly, I start to wonder if things will start to go my way. I still have Cédric between my thighs, but only a few seconds have passed, and I see Len stepping in if he thinks his man can't handle it. And I am coming to terms with the fact that there are two men against me, and my wrists are bound together...

As I feel Cédric taking control of the situation, I feel his gun settle against my hands. This is my chance. I unholster it, and feel my way around its form, by hands chafing against the rope. Although no gun master, training in the Territorial Army means I know technically enough to get the safety off. Without any line of sight, I flick the safety trigger that comes on the Beretta, relying more on luck than knowledge.

Len is now moving towards me, recognizing the threat. I try and point the gun at him, but I rate the chance of even a glancing hit very low. The trigger moves easily.

Suddenly, it all happens so quickly. In a flash of an instant, it is done. I have crossed a significant line.

There is a loud manly roar as Len rushes behind me, kicking the Beretta out of my hands as he passes. I spin myself around to see what is going on. Holy crap. I have shot Cédric in the stomach at zero range. The puddle of blood on the floor is spreading fast.

As Len takes off his jacket, I can see he is also carrying a gun, in a holster. It looks like the one we found on the boat. He seems genuinely concerned about Cédric, however, in my single-mindedness, I don't feel anything for him.

And in my current humour, Len's got a growing problem...

63

Hubbard

Tuesday, 2 August, 7:40pm. Echenevex, France.

Len had used Cédric Moutier a few times on jobs that had gone south, ending with unwelcome corpses, but this one was proving to be the most problematic of all. He slips off his jacket and tries to plug the hole in the man's belly, but it seems to do nothing to stem the flow and only serves to avoid a bigger mess on the floor.

When Charlie had pointed Cédric's gun at Len, he was ready to unholster his Glock and fire first with greater accuracy, but Charlie had wisely turned the gun to poor Cédric. Len looks at the man's face, but it is bloodless and the look of dread has been usurped by one of grim resignation.

Len turns his attention back to Charlie, adopting a heartfelt appearance of astonishment and incredulity. His words are not planned. "Fucking hell, Charlie."

Charlie looks like a small boy admonished for stealing coins that he did not take. "I'm not the one beating the shit out of me, it was self-defence."

"Ha!" Len's mouth forms a smile, betraying the deadliness of the situation. But it's a smirk of irony, not an expression of levity. "Sit back down on the chair." Len says, in a gravelly voice so monotone it could have been computer-generated. His composure has become quite robot-like in other ways too. He felt revulsion so acute for his nephew sitting before him but somehow could not act on it.

"He who betrays walks alone," Len lectured in a steady voice.

"I can live with my choices, Len," Charlie sniffed some blood back into his nose, "can you live with yours?"

"What the fuck happened that night?" Len barks.

Charlie looks up at him, defiant. Len launches into a flying, vicious kick which lands undeflected into Charlie's abdomen. They both hear a crack as a rib gives way. Charlie cries out in pain.

"What – the fuck – happened that night?" Len articulates precisely, like he is talking to a lost foreigner looking for the train station. Len takes two calculated steps back, appearing to be lining up a rugby try conversion, rather than another brutal crushing blow to his own nephew.

"Wait." Charlie pleads, eyes wide open, face dripping with blood, tears and sweat. "It was an accident."

64

Me

Tuesday, 2 August, 8:09pm. Echenevex, France.

Len's flying kick knocks me for six. I hear my rib crack. I feel my rib crack. I cry out. I am now fearing for my life. How much more pain will he inflict in search of answers? I have a few for him

"What – the fuck – happened that night?" Len says, I am struggling to find the words that won't make things worse.

"Wait." I exclaim, "It was an accident. Sometimes, in life, you have to make decisions best for you, not for everyone else," I am wincing as I explain.

"What the fuck are you talking about?" screeches Len.

"There are laws in each land, which represent the bare minimum legal expectations from the country's citizens. And above that legal baseline," I pause to groan and gasp air, "There are ethical and moral values that are the generally accepted group norms."

"You better take this somewhere soon, I am losing my patience."

There remains a substantial grey area between the two bands of a) legality and b) ethics. When one delves below the ethical line, dipping below the law seems enticingly within reach. I did not choose how the events that day were set in motion. There was no premeditation, no deliberate trap. Sure, I was a part of how they unfolded, but my involvement, I feel, was chiefly passive.

I will try to explain.

It has been established that my aunt instigated a sexual encounter with me. In many countries, like the US and the UK, it is legal to have sex with your cousin, but not your blood aunt. But Mia was only an aunt by marriage, so our sexual relationship was above the law – but admittedly below almost any moral values you choose to name. Mia was complicit in our sexual relationship, more than that, I would say responsible for it.

It's what happened the day she died that I have to live with.

"When Mia came to me, early in the hours of Sunday morning, she was bruised from a fight with you. She had blood in her hair and blue bruises on various limbs. I wanted to go and confront you about it, but she convinced me that she had given as good as she got. So I comforted her."

"Yeah, I know you "comforted her"?" jabs Hubbard, looking for more.

I look up at Len, a man I used to admire, and think back to that fateful night. By 12.30am, I had presumed Len was now in his cabin, and after our arguments, I knew Ana had called it a night. Everyone supposed I was sleeping on the padded bench seat in the galley. I am not sure where Scott and Stella were, but I'm fairly sure no one saw Mia and me embracing on the rope nets between the twin hulls. We had both drunk quite a lot, I had consumed the best part of two bottles of Médoc, whilst Mia was knocking back martinis like they were going out of fashion. Which perhaps they were. On top of that boozy base, we had shared the last of my coke for good measure. Mia got crazy horny and energetic on cocaine. For me, it made me feel paranoid, angry and tough.

"Mia and I talked on deck that night," I offer to Len.

Thinking back to that night, Mia and I had had sex right there, in the warm night air. Mia looked truly satisfied as she lay there afterwards, looking up at the stars. I had lit a spliff.

"You talked? Give me a break," sneers Len.

"We had sex – but she was wasted." I tried to explain myself.

"Obviously she was wasted to spend time with a runt like you," delivered Len through gritted teeth.

That night with Mia, as the drugs had mixed, I had felt a growing antipathy towards Len and Mia's lifestyle: them sipping martinis whilst I drudged away resetting passwords for numbskulls in Vauxhall. As we lay in silence, my delusional resentment and paranoia that I was inadequate in life grew. My drug-induced anger built on itself, while conversely, I felt completely spaced out and unable to move.

"Tell me why you killed her." He repoints his little gun towards my face. Further away, Cedric has ceased to convulse, he is clearly dead.

Mia was herself a successful career woman, earning five times what I did. Where did all this injustice end, I had thought? The following day, we were to head back to our respective lives, and it would be months if not years before I saw her again. It would be better if we ended whatever we had going.

After the sex, I had said in a low voice, "I'm going back to London tomorrow."

"Yes, you are," she had responded matter-of-factly.

"I guess that's the end, then," I had stated, not realizing how literally my words would hold true for her.

"Okay," she had said, and stood up barefoot on the netting. As she placed her foot on the edge of the hull, she looked up at me. That was all it took for her to slip and be sent falling towards the hull.

"I didn't kill her, Len. She fell and drowned." It was true.

That night Mia had smacked her head hard on the aluminium carabiner and entered the water heavily, sliding straight out of the safety of air. I had stared, paralysed by a mix of drugs, shock, disbelief and desire to let her go.

I had watched as she rose back to the surface after her fall, but she was unconscious, and her body became trapped by virtue of the boat's shape. I could see her convulsing as the air left her lungs and was replaced by water. But I didn't do anything useful, I just stared, like someone watching the embers of a flickering campfire.

"There wasn't anything I could do." I say as he levels the gun to my head.

"So you dived in to save her?" Len says rhetorically, knowing that I did not.

"I was wasted, Len, we both were. I was in shock. I passed out."

Any noise Mia had made was muffled by the water, and in less than a minute, she was hardly moving; I think she had vomited. Her body then submerged, almost out of view. After a few minutes, it had come up again, before it sank down below the sea's surface.

Now, I am aware that the responsible thing to do would be to enter the water, grab her and see if CPR could save her. In all likelihood, she could have been resuscitated in those early moments. But that is not what I did. I just watched, with dilated pupils, wide-eyed and terrified about what I found myself doing, or not doing as the case may be. Inexplicably, I took a photo on my phone.

At the time, I irrationally reasoned that I was bound by no lawful 'duty to rescue'. At least, I did not really know much about such legal semantics, but Harry at the White Hart pub had once recounted this very phenomenon. Harry had been the first on scene at a traffic accident involving two cars hitting each other head on. Harry had called the emergency services, and given their remote location had wondered what else he could do. He was able to help save one of the drivers, by dragging his bloodied body from the car and resuscitating him.

Another regular had piped up, "I couldn't do that, can't stand the sight of blood." Harry had said it was his moral obligation, but that, in fact, not his legal obligation to save such a soul in distress.

Grasping at that man-in-the-pub tale, I had been thinking: let her go, destiny has decided her number's up. I judged that there was a difference between active and passive response.

As her body drifted with the tide and current, I had been intrigued at how quickly life turns the page to death. My drugged up mind at the time told me that we were all going to die, so the only part up for debate was when, and how.

We had been anchored about 200 metres out from the inner harbour of Golfe-Juan, and the tide was receding for probably another couple of hours.

SIMON BOWER

I had picked myself up, passed across deck, and through the dark galley to the bench seat. Again I told myself it was not my legal obligation to save her. Searching the web on my phone the next morning, that belief turned out to be erroneous under French law. Failing to save a soul in distress carries a five-year prison term. Even more reason to keep it all quiet.

"I've had enough of this bull-shit," interjects Len in the barn.

Back on that night, I had hardly slept and at 6am I slipped into bed next to Ana. I had been lying in the bed against her soft warm body, realizing she was sleeping naked, when I became aware of someone sleeping on the other side of her.

"Funny how you weren't so principled when I found you with Ana that morning,,," I say.

Ana had stirred awake, and stroked my face. She had given me the cheekiest smile and, ever the opportunist, made the most of the situation – an Ana sandwich, so to speak.

Not that I want to think about that intimate moment now. I have managed to eke my right wrist a bit looser behind my back. But I don't think I can string Len along much longer. It is me or him.

"It was an accident." Len plays the words back to Charlie, slowly, pronouncing each syllable. Len again readjusts his pistol. It's a Glock 43, a small self-defence gun, intended to be concealed. He clicks back the trigger safety mechanism and is about to speak when a door creaking noise at the barn door interrupts him.

Len intuitively spins around, and fires off three rounds.

65

Chrissie

Tuesday, 2 August, 3:14pm. Forest Hills, New York, USA.

The buzzer sounds in Chrissie's condo and she checks the camera before pressing the door release button. A couple of minutes later, Chrissie is holding the apartment door open when her mom exits the elevator.

"Thanks so much for coming all the way over to pick her up." Chrissie gushes as she hugs Joyce.

"Not a problem at all sweetheart, I have the week off anyway and it will be fun to hang out just me and Anabelle, won't it Anabelle?"

"Hi, Grandma," Anabelle looks deflated as Joyce enters and dumps her purse on the couch. Chrissie zips back to the kitchen where cookies smell suspiciously like they are burning.

"What's up, honey? Did I tell you, you're my favourite granddaughter?"

"Yes, lots of times, Grandma. But I am your only granddaughter. I'm just sad because mommy's going away," Anabelle confides. The apartment is compact and Chrissie is in earshot.

"Oh, but we're gonna have fun the two of us. Just you wait and see."

It is summer recess and Joyce has agreed to take Anabelle so Chrissie can stay over in Europe. In the kitchen, Joyce speaks to her daughter, "So remind me which wild goose chase you are going on?"

"It's not a wild goose chase at all. After the DNA results, Len Hubbard has acknowledged he is my father."

"Well I told you, he is the only white man I ever slept with, so it was never a question for me."

"He said he remembered you, I'll show you the letter in a minute. So, I arrive in Amsterdam, and I go straight to my hotel for a nap. Then, at 9pm local time, which is 4pm Eastern Time, I meet him at another hotel. I have the next day free, in case it goes well and we want to hang out."

"Okay, well be careful, dear. I do worry about you when you're away."

"Mom, it is more dangerous in New York! Relax, it will be fine."

66

Fournier

Tuesday, 2 August, 8:36pm. A1 *Autoroute*, Geneva, Switzerland.

Fournier has spent the day driving up towards the *Pays de Gex* in his clapped-out Renault with over half a million kilometres on the clock. The trip from Golfe-Juan was long. Given the mid-summer traffic, he had avoided the weekend, and also taken the road less travelled. The Route Napoléon retraces the steps taken by Napoléon Bonaparte in his 1815 return from Elba. Also known as the N85, it took him up into the hills behind Grasse, the town of renowned perfume. The hills gave way to the Alps and the gorge of Verdon, popular with extreme sport fanatics and tourists alike, the road perilously hugged the side of the mountain, ducking through roughly-cut tunnels.

He had to admit, he had really enjoyed himself, free from the shackles of official police work, undertaking a little private detective work of his own. If it turned out that he was onto something, he would investigate it formally later. His hunch was that Hubbard would not know that his jurisdiction was strictly limited to the municipality of Vallauris Golfe-Juan.

Now, after passing the mountain town of Gap, the industrial city of Grenoble and the lakeside town of Annecy, Georges Fournier arrives at the border with Switzerland at Bardonnex. The road network is such that he must pass from France, through the canton of Geneva to reach the village where Hubbard lives, back in France. The Swiss pay no attention to his French official police car status and charge him the annual motorway toll all the same. He'll have to peal that sticker off the window to avoid awkward questions when he gets back.

Twenty minutes later, Fournier is entering the Pays de Gex at Ferney-Voltaire, named after the exiled philosopher Voltaire. Fournier knew that the Pays de Gex exists as a curious appendage to the rest of France, trapped between Geneva and its lake on one side, and the Jura Mountains on the other. Its residents work almost exclusively in Switzerland, where salaries are considerably higher than in France. It is a so-called tax-free zone, which, as a precursor to customs unions, exonerates many goods from the burden of taxes and dates back to 1815. To this day, it offers its residents an exemption on import duty, notably on cars, identifiable by their bright red number plates.

Fournier is battling the traffic, cars with all origins, Swiss, German, Italian and French. He has barely eaten all day and he stops at a decrepit pizza van offering half a pizza for €7. Swiss prices too, he muses. The margherita pizza is worth it, washed down with a much needed Coke to keep him perky.

Fournier's questions for Hubbard centre on the motive. It has become more difficult to investigate the actual circumstances of the death, since the body has somewhat unhelpfully been turned into ash. However, over the past days, Fournier continued to dig into what he could find out about Len Hubbard's finances and businesses. He called in a favour to an old colleague, Agent Saucy, in Annemasse. It was from Saucy (that rhymes with cow-sy and not horsey), that he learnt of Hubbard's reputation in the region.

Apparently, in addition to his legitimate businesses he also runs various less-legal endeavours behind the scenes, in both France and Switzerland. His contact talked specifically of loan sharking, but had suspicions about drug and prostitution rings. Squeaky clean, Len is not. It was this extra information that convinced Fournier that he was on to something. However, his man in Annemasse was not willing to tag along, explaining it was neither his jurisdiction, nor division. Neither arguments held much water with Fournier.

So, alone, Fournier is driving up the D1005 looking for the correct turnoff for Len's house in Echenevex.

67

Me

Tuesday, 2 August, 8:38pm. Echenevex, France.

I never truly expected Len Hubbard to dole out $100,000 to cover up a crime that admittedly he did not commit. Moreover, I do not believe that Len is truly distressed by Mia's death – knowing Len, he probably sees it as an opportunity. But I needed to execute part B of the plan without leaving any traces.

When I sent Len those messages purporting to be from Stella, I reasoned that he would come to London to interrogate Stella, or maybe me, if he figured that part out, which he evidently did. He would have needed to be very careful to arrive in London without leaving any traces, and hence would save me the trouble of getting to Geneva without being spotted. As it worked out, it went down rather well. The only evidence pointing to me is my mobile phone. There must be millions of potential phones, so provided I am not directly investigated, this will never be an issue. To be safe, I'll report that as stolen, but I need it for now. I will dump it soon.

The biblical message is that 'the love of money is the root of all evil'. I prefer the version that 'money can't buy you happiness, but poverty sucks'.

And after a run of bad luck, it is poverty I am facing.

Len and I are locked in an unequal glaring duel in the airy musty barn. He is holding a Glock gun to my head. I have the visible disadvantage of being bound at the wrists and ankles, however Len is unaware that I have wriggled my wrists free and the extension cord is now so loose that it serves no purpose.

Without warning, a loud creak emanates from the barn door, and Len turns towards it, firing three rounds as he does so. I take the opportunity of his distraction to separate my right wrist from the left and I launch myself towards Len, chair trailing me, I manage to deliver a crunching blow under his chin. In the commotion, he fires his Glock again. There can only be two rounds left. Holy shit.

I can see that a dog was responsible for pushing open the barn noise. It is still standing there, now barking. It might be Len's mutt, I don't know. He'd never mentioned a golden retriever.

The two of us are wrestling, grunting and shouting. Both of us have hold of his Glock. We are on the ground, and the gun is facing up, vaguely towards our faces, one head, then the other. Len tries to bite my nose, I try to knee him in the bollocks. Neither attempt is noticeably successful.

It is like a slow motion arm wrestle, the Glock never quite far enough in either direction to make it worth firing. Then the dog approaches Len, comes right up to his face and starts licking him (not a guard dog, clearly). It is just a split-second distraction but it may be enough. I pull the firearm up. The gun is now pointing towards Len's chin.

I consider the good times, the help he has given me in the past. But Len is not a good man, and I feel no sorrow. He has everything and does not deserve it. He doesn't give a shit about Mia. I did him a favour. And now it's me or him. If he goes, I win in more ways than one. If I go, well, fuck it. I'll be dead.

I force the trigger, against Len's resistance and, with an ear-splitting crack, it is over.

For Len.

Au revoir.

68

Scott

Tuesday, 2 August, 8:45pm. Pays de Gex, France.

It has been yet another two hours hacking through France. Scott really needs a break. The cinquecento really needs a break. Scott looks at the half bottle and it looks back at him. Absolutely, he muses, it must be wine o'clock. He pulls out the upturned cork and gulps at the contents, the Merlot sliding down his gullet without obstruction.

How it tastes all the sweeter for the way he has earnt it! The hula-hoops have long gone, so he stops at a McDonald's drive-thru in a small town called Thoiry and picks up a supersize meal. He checks the 4G-enabled iPad. Charlie's phone has not moved. The helmet-cam has gone dead. He tries calling, again, but most likely the chirpy ringtone is muted. Not so sexy anymore. He wonders what on earth has happened to Charlie. Scott has heard rumour that Uncle Len can be ruthless, and if Charlie has crossed him, Len will be swift to exert retribution.

Scott keeps pressing on, his phone satnav now

indicates only fifteen minutes to Len's gaff. What is he going to do when he arrives? Wrestle Len or one of his men to the ground? I doubt it. Still, he has come this far.

Scott is stuck behind a vehicle. It is a so-called car-ped, a four-wheeled 400-cc moped, which means a maximum speed of less than 30 miles an hour. He is desperate to overtake but a stream of cars is coming towards him. He looks – no mean feat with the steering wheel on the wrong side – and narrowly misses a large truck. He looks again and gives the little Fiat everything it's got, at which point the maniac driver swerves to make a left turn. The car-ped's side door is directly in Scott's path, and there is no alternative. He strikes the side of the Aixam-badged thing and sends it clean into the ditch. Scott's vehicle rapidly grinds to an unceremonious halt and ends up on the side road that the car-ped and its lunatic driver had been planning to take.

A man in his 60s gets out, swaying as he does. Clearly, he is expecting Scott to follow suit (getting out, not swaying, but either were possible). The vehicle in the ditch is a pastis-wagon, designed for career drunks who have lost their licence. Scott realizes he should be more sympathetic, given his own addiction, but he is a man on a mission, and an orange go-kart is not going to get in his way. Scott revs the engine and swerves around the astounded man, accelerating off to cries of "*Salop!*"

Scott is fairly sure he is not asking directions to Shropshire.

69

Me

Tuesday, 2 August, 8:46pm. Echenevex. France.

I look around this eighteenth century farm outbuilding and feel a great sense of relief. Despite the haphazard way things went down in the last half an hour, I reflect – this was the plan. Or something close to it, anyway.

Len is responsible for his own death, in a roundabout sort of way. He lies there pathetically in a pool of his own congealing blood, a circumstance caused by his very own self-defence pistol. For my part, I clearly have some tidying up to do.

First, I remove my cycling shoes. They are those annoying kind featuring a metal clip on the sole that create a sound not unlike high heels on a hard floor. I go outside to Len's slick Tesla Model S, it is open. He won't be needing to reach sixty miles an hour in three seconds any time soon. I look first in the glove box, but the rummaging is fruitless. Seconds later I find his driving gloves (a dying luxury, like cigarette holders) in the door pocket. They will do. I squeeze my hands into them, but really they are too small for me. I take the soft cloth that is also in the car door – perhaps intended for buffing the dash, or wiping windows. That's not what I'll be using it for.

Back inside, I start to assemble the scene. I move the chair and the extension cord to the corner and wipe them both well for prints. I collect up the duct tape and pocket it. I take Cédric's Beretta 92G and meticulously wipe it clean. Then I wrap it in a rag and leave it by the door.

On a roll with the gun stuff, I take Len's Glock and give it the same cleaning treatment. Then I put Len's hand and finger prints all over it, and his index finger on the trigger. Fuck! Jesus... the safety is on the trigger, and the last round just went off. It fired up into the ceiling. Never mind, that can add to the scene. I place Len's gun on the floor, in an it-just-fell-like-this sort of way. I figure that ballistics' analysis may show that it wasn't Len's gun that shot Cédric, so I search the scene and find Cédric's shell. I pocket that too, staying one step ahead, I hope. Len's head is a real mess, a gaping hole under his chin, the bullet helpfully exiting clean out of the top of his skull.

Over at Cédric again, best not to touch him, I try to think if any incriminating remnants of me could be on him. It is not the most convincing crime scene, but I think it should pass. Boss shoots henchman over disagreement. Boss realizes it would be a life in jail thus turns gun on himself. All probably done with the same gun, the Glock.

The dog buggered off somewhere after Len expired. Hopefully it hasn't done a Lassie, barking some fireman

into action. My mind is alert, focusing on the job at hand. I am not a cold-blooded killer, I am a practical man, finding solutions to problems. Both Cédric and Len had been involved in criminal activities – probably killings, maybe not, but they were bad eggs. I feel no sorrow for them and I don't imagine they will be missed much.

After our short-lived escapade with the wingsuits back in May, Len was so overcome with sentimentality that I had 'saved his life', catching him mid-fall. He told me he would update his will to leave equal parts of his estate to his surviving spouse, son, daughter and in addition any nephew or niece – at that time, it meant Mia, Scott and me. Len's will sounded like a huge potential windfall, that I could not get out of my mind. But what if he lived for another 40 years...? And could there be more beneficiaries? I had found out recently about his 'love-child' – shit, she will be wanting in. But are there more? Perhaps Len sowed his own demise when he expanded the beneficiaries of his will.

During the week on board, I had come to terms with what a total wanker Len truly was. I realised that anything he ever did for me, or for anyone, was actually with his own interests in mind. After he'd found me my job, he had never ending questions about the firm, to which I had always honestly replied – but it sank in that I was simply his mole. He invited us to his boat, but he was only interested in some company and some younger women in the vicinity, so he could try it on... However, I think the turning point for me was outside the casino in Monte Carlo. I was desperate, having lost pretty much everything I had. While Mia had been so consoling, Len simply said to me, "Once a loser, always a loser." And then the smarmy smile. I had definitely misread Len and on that night I vowed to make thinks even. Well, now they were.

And when Mia died – which I must insist really was an accident – I could not get out of my mind that I could have all the wealth I desired.

So this was a logical conclusion to events dealt by kismet.

I look around the barn scene. It seems good enough. I can't hang around for too long. Although this is hunting territory, gunshots echoing around a barn after dusk and Lassie bounding around God-knows-where could easily rouse interest.

I enter the Hubbard's farmhouse. I have been inside before, but it seems even nicer than I recall. Classy touches everywhere – hand-crafted furniture, Persian rugs on intermittent cherry hardwood and granite stone floors.

Adjoining the kitchen is a thoughtfully decorated drawing room, a suspended black fireplace is juxtaposed with exposed original beams and a diagonally tiled floor. There is a large blanket on one of the corner sofas. I am wearing cycling shorts and a long sleeved Lycra T-shirt, so the blanket looks useful. I take it. The mountains will be cold.

No more time for Escape to the Chateau. In the kitchen, I hope to find some cash, but I don't. I can do without. I'll have plenty soon! The love of money is the root of my future.

I see a calendar on the wall. Mia must have bought it. It has the *La Poste* logo on it, given, no doubt, in exchange for the postman's Christmas bonus. I study the calendar. On the line marked 'August 3 – Wednesday' there is a handwritten note. I had heard something on the boat about him meeting a long-lost illegitimate daughter. It read:

Chrissie. Hotel Steibel. 9pm.

Hoping for a little more, I flick though the mail rack. Bills, bills, a speeding ticket for 250 Swiss francs for doing 53 in a 40km/h zone... then I find a double-sided print of an email. On one side an email message signed from Chrissie, I'll read it later, and on the other a photo of an attractive woman somewhat resembling Halle Berry. I slip the papers into a white plastic bag for protection against the wet and then put the bag in one of the pockets stitched into the back of my cycling jersey, along with half a baguette from the bread bin.

The experience with Len and his lackey has made me realize it is so overpoweringly exhilarating to be in command of life and death. The mortal controller.

As I consider my next quarry I know that I really have to get the hell out of here.

70

Scott

Tuesday, 2 August, 9:04pm. Echenevex, France.

It is 9:04pm when Scott reaches Echenevex. He had programmed the satnav during his food stop to take him to the location shown on Find my iPhone. Now, he is ripping through the village much more rapidly than the suggested 30km/h. A pink streak of Fiat. The village is mostly dead, just a few people drinking and smoking outside a small *auberge*. He turns right after the church, and up the hill. All the roads are single vehicle width. Left turn at the end, and he is heading out of the village, towards the source of the Allondon River. It is here, just after the golf course at the start of a gravel track, that the phone satnav triumphantly announces, "You have reached your destination."

Scott turns into the driveway and follows it until he reaches some outbuildings about half way down the drive. He parks beside a conifer tree, in a spot somewhat hidden from the imposing main house, but few people would call the car concealed from view. All is quiet. There is a Tesla Model S with red number plates, he is not sure why they are red. Parked near it is a white

Renault Kangoo van, the sort bakers use to sell their baguettes from the back door. Scott approaches the van, sticks his head through the driver's window, which, of course, is open. It stinks like an abattoir inside. Scott crunches cautiously towards the Tesla and peers through the window, without touching it. What a fine bit of automotive machinery Len drives, he thought, then reflecting that in a few weeks, thanks to his drinking, he himself would not be driving anything at all.

Scott stops, and listens. Crickets are rubbing their knees incessantly. He tries to block out that pitch, and to a degree he succeeds. He can hear evening birdsong, perhaps a nightingale, but no sounds that could be described as human. Warily, and watching where he treads, he moves towards a barn, whose door is swinging in the light breeze just a few metres away.

He is sliding sideways through the door opening, not touching anything, when he spots Len's body. A voice from inside him breathes, "Oh my fucking God." And he starts trembling uncontrollably. His face has inexplicably turned a deep shade of crimson. His nose has started making a ridiculous squeaking sound that may have caused him to laugh at any other time. Now, Scott's legs have turned to jelly. He is embarrassed by his own reactions, but the only people here can't notice.

Scott is repulsed by the sight of the remains of Len's head. Next to his body, a gun not dissimilar to the one he found on the boat. He is aware there is another man in the barn, quite probably the assailant. He is much broader than Len and if a dead man can look angry, he does. There is a much bigger pool of blood around him, and Scott realizes he is tracking some of it though the barn. He is nauseated. He feels himself blowing out his cheeks like he's learning the trumpet, when he grasps what bodily reflex is arriving. He dashes for the barn door, but only manages to empty his Big Mac and supersize fries by the door frame. So much for eating.

Scott reflects that the good news is that he has not found Charlie's body. Nevertheless, after the gruesome discovery of two bodies, he is unsure what else he may uncover. He takes advantage of a nearby shovel – it looks like an antique – to move his unceremonious pile of vomit, and dumps it quickly in a nearby well-maintained water well; hopefully there is a farm dog to lick up the rest. However, at the geranium-bordered well, there is not the 1-2-3 splash he had anticipated, so he peers inside and glimpses a padlocked metal door, about three feet down. "Brilliant work, Scott," he mutters to himself, "Fricking genius!"

Scott pauses, trying to piece together what went down here. i.e. what part Charlie plays in this and where the hell he has gone. He walks over to the farmhouse, and slips off his shoes at the entrance. It seems a peculiar move, give the fate of the homeowners, but he has dredged enough blood around already.

Inside, he is struck by the modern interior of this old building, it has been really nicely finished. He feels a pang of sorrow as he acknowledges its residents won't be enjoying it anymore. He is looking around, not for anything in particular. He opens a drawer below the microwave, inside, he sees a wallet, inside it, €150 in notes. "Expenses" he mutters to himself, pocketing the cash. Above the microwave is a calendar, but after a quick look, there seems nothing of interest on it, he photographs with his phone anyway. He realizes that Charlie may have been reloaded into another van and was in the process of being transported elsewhere. Perhaps this was a pit stop. Or had he escaped? He literally ran back to the pink car and grabbed the iPad. "Shit, feet are feeling damp," he thinks, followed swiftly by "crap, no shoes".

Despite the awful situation, he is chuckling to himself about his folly when he clocks a dark blue Renault entering at the end of the drive. Bugger.

71

Me

Tuesday, 2 August, 9:10pm. Echenevex, France.

I retrieved my bike from the back of Cédric's Kangoo about ten minutes ago. Everything seemed to be in order after I had straightened out the handlebars and the saddle.

I spent a moment to consider: had I left any traces at the barn? I remembered my helmet and collected it from the black plastic bin, the helmet cam's battery is flat I notice. I cycled out of Len's place and have now just paused to reflect at a bus stop with a metal bench.

My socks look like shit. I take them off and add them to the small bag of duct tape to be dumped. I look down at myself. Quite covered in splatters of blood. It is getting dark and I need to get moving. I consider cycling to Geneva, that would be simplest, but I would need to cross the border to Switzerland, and anyway they may ask for photo ID on a plane or train out of the city. I could ride to Bellegarde – that is at least in France and on the main TGV line. But it is an obvious and hence traceable move and besides I did not find any cash in Len's house.

I resolve to go the direct but slow way, over the Jura Mountains. I could do with some exercise. I cycle through Echenevex village and to the main road to Gex. There are a few cars passing, and other cyclists too. We nod as we pass. The temperature is falling rapidly as I climb the mountain, and as dusk turns to night, I realize I have been careless not to have lifted some clothes from Len's house. I have used a small bungee cord to fasten the borrowed blanket behind the saddle – it looks a bit unprofessional, but it is effective.

The ascent up the mountainside is over 700 metres elevation gain. Half-way up, I see a small waterfall at the side of the road on a hairpin bend. Despite the cooling air, I must wash myself and my clothes. I whip of my top and lower myself into the waterfall plunge pool, shoes and all. It feels paradisiacal, my personal mountain Jacuzzi, watching the sun's red reflect on Mont Blanc.

But there is no time for relaxing, yet. I scrub my shirt, to the naked eye, the blood has washed out. I vigorously rub my skin, my face, my torso, my shins. I gulp the mountain fresh water like a camel at a much-needed oasis.

I feel a whole lot better as, dripping with water, I remount my bike, refreshed and rejuvenated, but it's getting very dark. Fortunately, my shirt has some reflective strips on, but it's a dangerous winding road with plenty of lorries, and I am going to need to bed down for the night at some point soon.

My wet body dries quickly in the summer air and pumping up the long steep mountain road, I warm up too. I wonder whether anyone has found the mess at Len's 'château'. When they do, it may make the news, but I can't see how anyone would link me to the scene. In fact, there is no definitive trace of me having left London.

After the *col* – the pass – the road levels out, and I rip along at a dangerous pace. I pass the villages of les Rousses and la Cure. It is almost completely dark now. My eyes have adjusted to the late twilight, but drivers' eyes perhaps have not. I am tracking around a bend, full tilt, perilously fast, taking the racing line when a low sports car comes out of nowhere. The driver's on full beams, coming unrepentantly towards me. This is the end. I close my eyes. I CLOSE MY EYES? The sound of a horn fills the night air, replacing the rush of the wind and then the noise stops. My time is up, karma has come.

When I open my eyes, just a few moments later, I am remarkably still alive. I realize with panic that I am now leaving the road towards the gravelly wet verge. The change in surface is too sudden, and there is an inevitability to the events as I accept that I am imminently to go down hard. I only hope I can engineer a safe landing. I brace myself for impact with the rough stony ground.

My past few hours have been filled with death and now I expect mine to come, but it doesn't. The fall hurts, but not like if I had hit that red car.

I scrape against the gravel, severely grazing my skin, and taking some bruises. I've injured my wrists, and cut my lip, but the wounds are superficial, I think. I start to doubt my own plan, is it going to work?

I realize it is time to find a quiet spot for the night. There is an information board proposing scenic walks a short distance away, it is complete with a tiled roof, which seems overkill, but will suit me nicely. The far side of the small structure is completely shielded from view of passing motorists, and I unfold my blanket for a well-earned rest.

I still have 23 hours to reach my destination.

72

Tuesday, 2 August, 9:15pm. Echenevex, France.

Fournier had seen a lot of death in his career, but most of it attributed to either traffic accidents or suicide. The scene he sees in front of him now is one of most grizzly memories that he won't easily be able to erase. Len Hubbard – the man he has come to speak to – lies in a pool of blood. He is missing an intrinsic part of his chin. There is a gun beside him, a Glock pistol. He hopes it will have some useful prints on it.

Another man is lying a few feet away. Also dead as charcoal. Fournier wonders if he is the driver of the pink Fiat with British plates, or the driver of the white Kangoo van, with local plates. This flash of realization that he could be compromising an active crime scene sends a buzz of adrenaline through him. Fournier does not carry a gun – he is not in the Armed Response Unit – and he wonders how secure cops in America must feel to carry firearms. Of course, for the most part, criminals in France don't need guns, and the country benefits from a less-armed society. He knows that in the USA, there is, on average, one gun for each of its 320 million inhabitants.

In France, residents share one gun between three people. In the UK, one gun serves seventeen. He backs slowly out of the barn, his sensory perception on high alert.

He digs into his pocket and calls it in, speaking French. He says, "Hello, this is Agent Fournier, ID 36229. Off duty. There is a multiple homicide at… " he pauses to look at the paper where he scrawled Hubbard's address, "2103, Route d'Allodon, Echenevex, 01170." Fournier knew that throughout France, house numbers denoted the number of metres from the start of the road, so he was just over 2km in. The police despatcher repeats his message to him, and has some follow-up questions: was he there on official business? No. Is the scene live? It may be. How many bodies? Two. Any chance they might live? No. The questions continued, and local police were already on their way.

Looking back down the drive, Fournier notices that the pink Barbie car has gone. He tells the despatcher what he knows about it, so that they can put an alert out. Fournier walks into the house – he is being cautious, and has donned some crime scene foot covers that he keeps in the car. Once the police arrive, he will be shut out. What was going on here? Using latex gloves, he peers in a wallet left beside the microwave. No money in it. Len would surely have some euros. He looks up to a calendar. He photographs it on his phone. His eyes scan a beautiful reception area, with a hanging fireplace, damn, this place is well put together.

In the drawer under the microwave, he sees some A4-sized papers. He pulls them out and looks at them. They are prints from a computer screen, with images. He carefully lays them on the kitchen counter and photographs them. The first shows Hubbard attacking his wife, the second shows her body face down in the harbour. Fournier concludes he was correct to have suspicions about this man. He is thinking through more of the case when he sees blue lights at the end of the driveway some 200 metres off. He places the papers as they were and moves outside, shoves the shoe covers in his jacket pockets. Doing so, he sees a pair of shoes – surely the owner would not leave his shoes outside? He photographs them.

Two *Gendarmerie* vehicles are the first officials on scene, the Armed Response Unit. They draw their weapons. Fournier stands still, hands in the air. He knows the drill.

73

Tuesday, 2 August, 9:42pm. Pays de Gex, France.

When the car entered Len's driveway, Scott shat himself. Not quite literally, but almost. He dived down behind the Fiat. Once the old Renault drove further up the drive, he snuck a peek. He could hardly believe it. It was the same bloody copper from the south of France. Benefitting from the gradient, he slipped off the handbrake and rolled down the drive, lights off and cursing the crunchy drive. He figured the cop was more interested by what he found inside; he probably didn't even notice little pinkie.

It's now half an hour later on Tuesday evening, and Scott is heading up towards a ski resort that the signs reveal as *Monts Jura – La Faucille*. If he was sightseeing, he may be more impressed with the beautiful vista of Mont Blanc, 100 miles away, rising out of a perfect sun stream. But he's not touring, so only has eyes for the road and the iPad. Scott remains eager to rescue Charlie from whatever fate has taken hold. Poor bro, he always seems to get himself mixed up in tricky situations.

Scott passes La Faucille on the winding mountain road, and by now, the dot is only about 30 minutes further on. It occurs to Scott that he might get implicated in Len's death. His shoes are there, his vomit is there, his car was there! Not a perfect situation. He is musing this over when he has a petrol fright – in his enthusiasm to chase Charlie, he has not filled up the tank since Reims. He checks his phone satnav – a petrol station is coming up in Les Rousses.

Another 20 minutes and he scrapes into Les Rousses, running on fumes. That was close, he thinks. After a splutter the car dies. It kangaroos a couple of times, before coming to a stubborn rest. He's in full view of any passing car. The road is on a slight incline and Scott opens the rose-coloured door and pushes the vehicle behind a parked van.

A short walk, and he is at the fuel stop. It is evidently shut for the night. His phone GPS shows the next nearest station around an hour away back in Gex. He checks Charlie's status. It's about 20 miles further on and appears stopped. He calls him, but it goes straight to voicemail.

Calling it a night, he wanders back towards the car, when he notices two people stumble out of a bar. It says PMU on it, and curious, he wanders inside. Customers seem to be watching sports and betting, but there are obviously drinks as well. Great, he was concerned about forced sobriety tonight. He orders a whisky. Doesn't matter what. It was a generous measure, and Scott takes another, and starts talking to a visibly drunk man next to him.

"Who's playing?" he ventures, pointing at the football match. His buddy does not appear to speak a word of English. But he understands the question.

"PSG - Lyon. Lyon est en train de battre le PSG." he says with a contented grin. Scott presumes this is good news, and buys the man another Ricard to show his support.

It is 1am when the barman lets Scott know that the drinking den is closing. He stumbles back to the Fiat, and takes a piss behind a battered Renault 4. In his car, he reclines the passenger seat, covers himself with his jacket and settles down for a poor night's rest.

74

Chrissie

Tuesday, 2 August, 8:15pm. Forest Hills, New York, USA.

It is 8:15pm on Tuesday evening and Chrissie is preparing to go to work. Her mom left with Anabelle shortly after 6pm and after accompanying them to the train station, she had walked back to her apartment on Booth Street. She showers after a day of chores, and puts her feet up for a while which should help her through the night shift.

Her company-issued uniform is carefully resting on the back of her lurid green sofa. Chrissie puts on her white shirt with oversized collar and red collar band. She chooses underwear a little saucier than the situation truly merits; Chrissie knows on the plane everyone notices her VPL and hates to disappoint. Her pants are conservative – but she prefers them over the slutty skirts that some airlines prescribe. She looks at herself in the mirror, and is content with what she sees. A 32-year-old professional woman, still in the prime of her life. No wrinkles whatsoever, Chrissie hopes she has inherited her mum's ageless skin. Her balanced diet when she is home is still counteracting the fast food she sometimes has to endure while on duty.

Chrissie had to bid for this trip. Every flight attendant gets familiar with the Preferential Bidding System and the more senior one is the easier it is to win the good flights. Chrissie had to submit her request to travel to Amsterdam, without specifying the dates and was smitten that her application was honoured. Some colleagues never seem to be granted the trips they request, but now that she has a few years of solid service under her belt, the system is working well for her.

The night is fresh as Chrissie makes her way to 67 Av Subway station for the 9:08pm train. She is by far one of the soberest travellers on the E Train tonight. She looks at a guy dressed like a rapper sitting near her, relying on the carriage windows to study him in the reflection. His flat peaked cap does nothing to hide his hollow bloodshot eyes, a look of utter desolation filling his face. She wonders if he is on his way home or perhaps he's just riding the train to keep off the streets.

It only takes her ten minutes to reach Jamaica Station to transfer for the AirTrain, for which she holds a free pass. It whisks her into JFK airport in just a few minutes. She reports for work an hour before the flight time of 10:40pm and makes her way to the crew lounge. Some of her colleagues commute to work – they live someplace like Rochester, NY, and are based at JFK. So in addition to their scheduled shifts, they must add another three hours each way – crazy to Chrissie's mind. They even have to wait around NYC on the six A-days per month, when they may get summoned to duty with two hours' notice. No thank you, not for Chrissie.

Chrissie meets the In-flight Service Manager, her boss for the shift. He's a short camp guy going by the name of Shawn, who aptly has a buzz cut. Chrissie has worked with Shawn before and knows him to be an obsessive maniac when it comes to guest care. On a flight to London some time back, she had joked to him that a Brit in 42C was finding the air con a little on the 'parky side'. After finding out what it meant Shawn had berated her for the lack of empathy and rushed to 42C with a blanket in plastic wrap. Another happy customer, Chrissie thought, tongue in cheek.

At 10pm, Chrissie gets ready for the march to the plane – which is exactly when Shawn informs the crew that the inbound flight is still two hours away. Adding the two hour turnaround for cleaning, maintenance, refuelling and refilling food, beverages, duty-free and other consumables, they were looking at a 2:30am departure. Fortunately JFK is not burdened by night curfews, unlike La Guardia airport.

She sits on an armchair in the crew lounge and ponders what she may say when she finally meets her father.

75

Me

Wednesday, 3 August, 5:45am. Jura Mountains, France.

I was sure I was dying when I woke at 4am. It was the most intense, overwhelming feeling of dread. I had been dreaming about Len chasing me with a gun, which turned into a Taser electroshock weapon. It fired something that looked like a sticky Spiderman web, covering me completely. As the volts started pulsing through me, my dream became reality. My whole body was convulsing, but I had just been shivering. Extreme shivering. Ironically, without Len's blanket I really might be dead!

I can hear an aggressive dog barking in the distance. It is getting light, so I pick myself up. Much to do today. Must stay focussed on my end game.

I use my mobile phone to check ways to get north. The emergency £50 note that I kept in my cycling shirt is not going to stretch far. Paying for train tickets is out of my reach, and fare-dodging would be very risky, especially in France where the job of ticket inspector seems unquestionably essential despite any other cuts.

I have a plan, but reaching where I need to be by 9pm is going to be a challenge. If the opportunity presents itself, I could steal a car – but I have no idea how to do that without a key, so it is not Plan A. I don't want to raise suspicions.

I pick up my bike in preparation to set off a little after 5am and my heart sinks. The front tyre is flat as a pancake and I am blatantly not prepared for this eventuality. I try to ride it, but almost fall off before reaching the road. I pick up my trusty cycle, walk across the road to where the barrier gives way to a steep incline and sigh as I throw it down the rock face. It clatters, bangs and comes to a halt against a tree.

With my wheels disposed, I start to walk. I feel stiff, sore, and I am limping a little. The cycling shoes don't help. But my mind is clear and I know what I have to do. In the first hour, three cars pass, none looking like they are going any further than the *boulangerie* or *tabac*, and none giving me more than a glancing look.

It's now 6:15am and I reach the mountain village of Morez. The sign at the entrance to the village states proudly that it boasts a population of 5,132 and is situated at an altitude of 750 metres. I am keeping my eyes peeled and half way through the village I see what I am looking for. It's not my first choice of garments – a pair of dark blue workman's trousers and a black cotton casual jacket are hanging on a clothes horse. They will have to do.

310

I decide to keep my new fashion accessories concealed from view for now. I figure my chances are better dressed as a cyclist than as a tramp. I put my thumb out as the road gets busier, no luck yet. I look quite respectable, I think, with the white supermarket plastic bag from Len's place, I look like a cyclist who's mislaid his bike. Which is fairly accurate. Apart from the Beretta in my bag.

My mood has darkened – will I ever get out of this mountain backwater? I am contemplating my options when I hear a vehicle approaching. It turns out to be a powerful motorbike, a red Ducati Streetfighter. I have put my thumb out more as a joke, but the bike pulls up just ahead of me.

I practically sprint up to the rider, and notice he has a spare skid lid on the back. I speak to the rider's helmet, and find that he is a she, blond, probably 30s, quite petite – perhaps a vixen? Her leather body suit is black with red and white on the arms and legs. It could be my tiredness, it could be my desperation, but she looks hot as fire.

"Where are you headed?" she has an American voice, not even trying French.

"Dijon," I reply, "or wherever". I am trying not to sound or behave like a mad murderer, not sure how that is going.

"Grab the helmet and get on."

We accelerate away from my standing point at an exhilarating pace, pulling out as a pink car rounds the bend.

The helmet is equipped with microphone and earpiece, so I can speak to my new friend, although judging by her enthusiasm to get to Dijon, 139km north, I should not distract her.

"In a hurry?" I say, a non-invasive question, I think.

"I just took my boyfriend's – sorry - *ex*-boyfriend's bike. He'll probably come looking!"

"Great." I say, meaning the opposite.

76

Scott

Wednesday, 3 August, 7:30am. Jura Mountains, France.

Despite the light, Scott lies comatose until 7:30am. He eventually exits the car to march back to the petrol station. It opens at 8am so he has a few minutes to wait.

At 8:00am, he buys a green plastic fuel can, a vacuum packaged sandwich and a 500ml bottle of Coke. The attendant has filled the can and he is handing over 20 euros when he sees *Le Dauphiné*, a local daily newspaper.

Enquête sur la Mort d'un Homme. La Police Recherche une Fiat Rose. Investigation into man's death, Police looking for a pink Fiat.

Shit. He desperately needs to dump Alison's car. But Charlie is only a few kilometres away. He elects to dump it soon. Scott makes a face, which he hopes looks like he forgot something. He added another green petrol container, a packet of Tuc biscuits and a bottle of water to somewhat disguise the late purchase, and *Le Dauphiné*. He also pays for another five litres of fuel.

Back at the car, he is all eyes. He is paranoid that everyone is looking at him. Perhaps it is just the car - it is not an inconspicuous automobile for a middle-aged man. Both cans filled the car's tank to about a third, not bad. It would have to be enough.

Taking a side street he avoids the petrol station. He knew that he had acted utterly and unnecessarily suspiciously around the attendant; no need to add fuel to the flames. Back on the main road, it is 8:35am and the iPad shows one minute to Charlie! Time to save the day

Scott rounds the corner, and sees a man in biking gear and a Carrefour bag – it has to be him. But he is putting on a motorcycle helmet and as he nears them, the powerful motorcycle accelerates off at a tremendous rate of knots. He is cursing and shouting. What just happened?

He now surmises that Charlie is not being detained contrary to his wishes. In fact his behaviour implied that he was more than willing. Find my iPhone is now moving away from him. Damn it! He gives the Fiat all it has. Again.

The sign says Dijon 10km. He really must dump this car. But the alternatives are too risky or too slow, and he doesn't know what Charlie's next move will be. Home to London presumably? He tries calling him again, but no change.

Scott ascertains from the newspaper article that the deaths were probably considered as murder-suicide. There would have been little doubt, except that a pink

Fiat had been spotted on the driveway, which the police were treating as suspicious. They are asking the driver of the Fiat to come forward. Idiot!

The iPad indicates Charlie's location as a bus station in Nancy. He is almost on him. Big brother sweeps in to rescue lost man. Scott parks in the station car park and takes the tablet with him. The location services are surprisingly accurate, bringing him to a small concourse, and a ticket office.

Noticeably a deficit of Charlie. He laps around again, but it's not a big bus station, and Charlie would be obvious in his cycle gear. Running out of ideas, he peers in a litter bin and sees some cycle shorts and wrapped in the shorts – Charlie's phone.

Scott runs to the departures screen, but the only long-distance bus in recent hours left half an hour ago. He is immensely annoyed with himself, and Charlie. He had expected the coach to be heading to London, but London-bound buses only depart at 5am and 5pm.

The bus Charlie must have taken is going to Amsterdam.

Shit. Shit. Shit.

77

Me

Wednesday, 3 August, 9am. Dijon, France.

I was blessed by good fortune that Lucy came along, especially that she would pass through Dijon. She is outstripping any expectations that I had.

It is 9am and she is expertly taking roundabouts, of which Dijon has many. I see a Police checkpoint, but they are busy terrorizing a young bearded Middle-Eastern chap. I am obliged to hold on tight to Lucy's waist, particularly when we take off. Although some men may scoff at my inferior position to the female rider, that is not me. On the contrary, I am positively turned on by her control on the power.

Lucy seems eminently aware of my awkward arousal, as she lifts my hands to cup her breasts. I have only seen Lucy's face for a few moments, but we have developed a rapid intimacy that betrays our fleeting companionship. I wonder whether Lucy is going to pull over. Maybe I have misread the situation.

Lucy is evidently decelerating, and in short order comes to a complete stop. I am still aroused and wait a moment too long as Lucy announces, "This is Nancy bus station. It was great to meet you."

"You, too," I manage, my face a flush and my cycling shorts hiding nothing. I nervously hold my bag in front of me like a randy adolescent schoolboy. Lucy pecks my cheek and is gone.

So long, Lucy.

I wander inside to the small terminal. It is his time to lose this phone, I certainly cannot risk being tracked to Amsterdam. The smelly toilets are equipped with what the French call Turkish toilets – horrible seatless pits. As if to rub salt into the wound, so-called Madame Pee-Pee wants 50 cents for the pleasure. I hurry passed her and slip into my pilfered workman's trousers.

A small booth with a Perspex window with a circle of holes drilled into it boasts 'Change', and I swap my UK pounds for euros. I know he is screwing me when he gives me €50 for my £50.

I buy my long-distance bus ticket to Amsterdam (€38) and it leaves in 25 minutes. There is a small market across from the bus station, and I acquire a white T-shirt with a band's name on the front that I have never had the opportunity to hear. If I know French bands, the songs probably have a story for lyrics and a questionable tune. I desperately require shoes, and I opt for a flimsy pair of espadrilles, chosen by price. My total spend here is €11. I have €1 left. I blow it on a bottle of water.

My new T-shirt, the natty beach shoes together with my purloined jacket and workmans' slacks makes for an unremarkable appearance, which is the idea.

It's 11:00am, time I board the bus. I settle down into a seat just in front of the coffee machine, which requires more euros to enjoy. I ponder my future fortunes. What is Len worth? Four million pounds he might once have boasted to me? I am aware that the French tax man will appallingly grab half – and society regards my actions as criminal? There are still three of us surviving to enjoy the spoils, so if there is two million after inheritance tax, it is currently sitting at 666 thousand each. Is that a devilish coincidence?

Six hundred grand and some change might just buy me a two-bedroom flat where I live in Swiss Cottage. I am not a man requiring opulence, and such a property would suit my needs very nicely. But I if there were only two heirs to Len's estate, we would both pocket a handsome million. That 333K could really make the difference; decent capital to start a business, or a few years off, or include a yacht like Shooting Star – perhaps even Len's very own Shooting Star, since that will soon be for sale.

Amid my dreams of soon-to-be riches, the humming and drumming of the bus beats me and I become hypnotized into a surprisingly deep sleep, to a world where Lucy and I loaf around a white painted loft apartment, the smell of coffee wafting up to our bedroom of love and petals and all that shit.

78

Wednesday, 3 August, 10:17am. Dijon, France.

Scott Dunster had seen the calendar entry on the kitchen wall in Len's house but had not registered its significance. Now, in the bus station at Nancy, he checked the photo he took. He googles the Hotel Steibel in Amsterdam, which reveals a mid-quality hotel near the centre. He had always known Charlie to be a driven individual and he had taken Len's death in his stride – after all, Len had had it coming, if not from Charlie, then from someone else. Although Scott has never met Chrissie, he knows who she is – the result of an affair Len had years ago. DNA had confirmed it just a few weeks earlier.

Now, Scott thinks through Charlie's next move: Maybe he is just going to meet her? Was she involved in Len's death? It is not really making sense to him. Scott's not aware of Len's will, but it suddenly strikes him that perhaps a windfall is coming his way. Could Charlie really be thinking of an inheritance? Perhaps the new daughter will claim everything, if there was no will? Could he really be planning to murder Chrissie, Len's daughter, in cold blood? Whatever the exact circumstances – and before last night he would not have thought like this – but it seems more than probable that Charlie is planning to do harm or even kill their cousin.

Scott must not allow Charlie to take his offensive to that level, he's caused enough harm. He needs to stop his brother, but he also needs a drink, needs new transport and does not know which to address first.

He realizes he's pushed his good fortune to the limit with the pink shrimp so parks it in the station multi-storey car park. He checks and learns that Charlie's bus is due to arrive at the Dutch capital at 8:30pm. The next bus he could board wouldn't get him there until 11pm. Way too late. The ticket seller tells him in broken English that the *gare* is a short walk away – trains are much quicker if time is a greater concern than cost. Then the seller sees that Scott is not wearing shoes, and wrinkles her nose.

Within ten minutes he is buying a train ticket to Amsterdam. It's an hour and ten minutes before the next train to Paris, so Scott gives himself a break. He starts to write a text to Charlie, before remembering that he returned Charlie's phone to the bus station litter bin. He feels an enormous responsibility, but can't call the cops as he and his brother are in this too deep. He wonders whether he can get a message to Chrissie – but he has no contact details and there is no suggestion she is even staying at the Hotel Steibel – in Europe, meeting at a hotel restaurant is frequently *de vigour*.

It is slightly before noon when Scott sees a shop called *La Halle aux Chaussures.* He walks in, tries on the first pair of shoes that he sees, switches to a larger pair – they'll do – yanks off the tag to present it to the cashier and pays in euros on the way out. Men's extreme shopping. Thank God for that money he swiped at Len's. He desperately needs some lunch to soak up last night's excesses. A self-service restaurant catches his eye. Minutes later he is sitting in front of an enormous plate of lasagne and salad and two half-litre carafes of locally produced Burgundy – not a bad drop of Pinot Noir.

An hour later, Scott Dunster is feeling refreshingly woozy and stumbles towards platform 4 for the TGV to Paris. On board, a thoughtful attendant with a shaved head and blue waistcoat proposes some Bordeaux, and Scott thinks that sounds like a mighty fine idea.

It is one hour and thirty five minutes later, 2pm local time, and Scott is in Paris. The train terminates at *Gare de Lyon,* so he is trying to figure out how to get to *Gare du Nord.* Is it really necessary to put travellers through this metro ordeal?

The helpful lady at Nancy station ticket office had used a pink highlight pen on his tickets to dissuade Scott from screwing up. He was grateful for that now and guided by the pink ink, follows signs to RER Line D. After only ten minutes, a white, red and blue *Réseau Express Régional* train headed towards Orry la Ville Coye pulls up to the platform.

321

At *Gare du Nord*, Scott obeys the signs for *Thalys*, which is a word that his ticket has on it. Quite frankly, the whole station is a bit of a blur, and Scott thinks it would be a good idea to switch to beer, to sober up a bit. The *Thalys* train is already waiting at the platform, so he finds carriage 4, seat 52 and settles in for the journey to Amsterdam. According to his schedule, he is on track to arrive before Charlie so can beat some sense into the idiot.

79

Chrissie

Wednesday, 3 August, 11:14pm. JFK Airport, New York, USA.

After a few false starts and numerous hours, Chrissie and the crew finally push past the grumbling queue of guests and board the aircraft at 2:30am EDT Wednesday morning. The passengers are not putting up much of a fight anymore, finding their seats, and getting as comfortable as they can.

A group of 20-somethings who are probably on their way to Amsterdam for a weekend of partying are being a pain in the ass in row 52. She provides them with some drinks, after all, they have been delayed over four hours, but she does not think they need much more.

Half an hour later, and the revellers' neighbours are pressing the call button and complaining about the noise from the drinkers. One woman suggests they have switched to bottles of duty free – which, of course, is strictly forbidden. To appease the complainant, Chrissie asks the loud group if they have any duty free, and they produce some full bottles, she takes it from them for the duration of the flight and warns them of the severe consequences if caught consuming duty-free on board. But it's a hollow threat, as she can't be sure what they are up to and everyone else is trying to sleep.

Back at the galley, Chrissie chats quietly with a couple of the other flight attendants in economy class.

"I am not going to get much sleep before my return flight," says one attendant.

"You've stacked?" asks Chrissie, referring to the normal practice of squeezing as many flights together, thus giving a break of four or so days before the next work day.

"Yeah, I always try to – I commute from Chicago," the slightly tarty looking Sadie tells her.

"I don't know how you do it. Me, I'm taking a rest day in Amsterdam."

"Wow, don't blame you. Big plans?" It's the other attendant now.

"I don't know if you'd call them big," Chrissie wonders about the seriousness of revealing intimate personal details – generally cabin conversations were limited to impersonal drivel. "I'm going to see my dad."

"Live in Holland, does he?"

"No, in France, near Geneva."

"I thought Geneva was in Switzerland."

"He lives near the border," Chrissie explains.

"Long time since you've seen him, I suppose?" offers the first attendant, looking like she was being left out.

"I've never seen him." Chrissie replied, suddenly overwhelmed with the significance of the trip. With a tear of happiness to be finally meeting her dad and also sadness that he had not played a part in her life so far, she confides, "I only found out who my dad was a few weeks ago."

"Wow, that's mental," utters the first, feeding herself more peanuts.

"Yeah, really." Says the second, before a customer interrupts asking for a glass of water.

Finally, even the partygoers are snoozing or watching movies and thus the cabin is quiet. Chrissie relaxes out of view of the passengers, except those visiting the washrooms. She isn't sleeping, but she is just staring at the coffee machine, in a sort of trance.

At 7:30am EDT, which is 12:30pm CEST, Shawn announces that breakfast is served. Normally they would serve it earlier, but with the delay, Shawn decided the customers would appreciate this arrangement. It takes almost two hours for the whole operation. While Chrissie is occupied clearing up the final uneaten croissants on board, 39,000 feet below a budget long-distance bus is fighting the traffic in Belgium, transporting someone towards Amsterdam who she probably would be better off not meeting. At the same time, a *Thalys* high speed train is hurtling away from

Paris towards the Dutch capital at a speed of 180 miles per hour. She should pray it is on time.

The Boeing 747-400 makes a heavy landing at Amsterdam Schiphol Airport, owing to blustery crosswinds.

It is now 3:30pm local time, and after all the passengers have departed, Chrissie makes a beeline for immigration and customs. Staff pass straight through and she avoids a nasty looking line-up to enter the Schengen passport-free zone in Europe. She takes the elevator downstairs to platform 6 for the next train to downtown Amsterdam. Chrissie is staying at the Royal Tulip Hotel, a five-star joint directly opposite Centraal Train Station. Her employer picks up the tab for the first night, and so she only has one night to pay, and airline employees receive a massively reduced corporate rate.

Chrissie checks in, and she refuses the porter's help to take her cabin bag upstairs – she has got this far alone. She is given a tastefully decorated room overlooking the busy station. It's compact compared to American hotels, which is fine with Chrissie. She sets her alarm for 7pm and settles down for a much needed siesta.

80

Scott

Wednesday, 3 August, 6:46pm. Near Amsterdam, Netherlands.

Scott wakes from his slumber when he inadvertently spills his latest glass of *Bourgogne* across his lap. A warm damp feeling – not a good one – permeates into his crotch. He corrects the guilty vessel, downs the rest of it, before there are any more accidents, and sets about mopping up the red stain with the quarter folded napkins thoughtfully supplied for such eventualities.

The train had slowed from its impressive 300km/h on entering Holland, and now, leaving Rotterdam station, the pace seemed veritably pedestrian. The time is 6:50pm and in 40 minutes, he will arrive in Centraal Station. He will need to be on the top of his game to locate and deal with Charlie. He orders a beer to steady his nerves.

A week ago, if he had realized that Charlie was going to Amsterdam to 'see' their long-lost cousin, he would have wished him all the best, thought nothing of it, hell, maybe he would have tagged along. But the events of the past few days had led him to view his brother in a much darker light. There was definitely a world of difference between shooting your uncle in self-defence, which he now thinks Charlie did, and actively hunting down an innocent woman. For money. Pre-meditated first-degree murder, versus manslaughter – the differences in sentences are huge, not to mention the state of his mental health.

Scott shakes his head back and forth violently at this thought, before realizing that fellow passengers are looking at him warily. He quits the jerky head movement show, but keeps his brain on track. He knows Chrissie should be at Hotel Steibel at 9pm tonight, but if he just shows up he may not have time to prevent Charlie's intentions. He won't stitch up his brother to the police, he can't imagine ever doing that, and anyway that would involve a lot of incriminating explaining. No, he would need to intercept Charlie at the bus station. Scott had very little with him, but he still had Charlie's 3G iPad, from his futile search for his brother in Nancy. He checks out where the Eurolines bus stops. Crap! It terminates nowhere near downtown Amsterdam, it stops at a suburb called Duivendrecht.

On arrival to Centraal Station, Scott wastes no time getting off the train. He takes a deep breath, and smells the unmistakably and calming whiff of cannabis.

He searches for a train for Duivendrecht and with the help of a guard, buys a return ticket and finds platform 14. The 'Sprinter' train, naturally for Holland, leaves 15 seconds before the scheduled time and whisks him efficiently to Duivendrecht Station in precisely 13 minutes.

The time is now 8:15pm and Scott is anxious to find the coach station. Presumably Charlie's bus may not come in exactly on time. Station staff point him in the right direction, "It's that way, take the Stationplein Arena exit".

Scott takes up his surveillance point – a stool at the station bar – at 8:25pm. The barman serves him a beer without asking, saying "Flutje" as he does so. It is already a small glass, he thinks, but figures he'll take what he gets. The barman cuts a bulky figure and wears a comedy Groucho Marx moustache. Scott's dismay continues, when he sees half of the beer is froth. When Groucho goes to scrape the top of the head off with a knife, he tells him to stop – enough already – and takes the opportunity to order a second one.

Scott is watching over the bus station, but his concentration is not his strong suit even when he's sober. And sober he is not. Buses seem to be coming in constantly and while he's looking for the Eurolines brand there are numerous such buses entering. And what if the bus is dressed in plain clothes?

Scott eyes the bus passengers like a hawk, or at least an owl, as streams of disembarking passengers pour off the vehicles.

81

Chrissie

Wednesday, 3 August, 8:08pm. Amsterdam, Netherlands.

Chrissie was nervous. What sort of man would Len Hubbard be? Would he be a complete ass who she would never want to see again? What if he never wanted to see *her* again? Maybe it would be completely awkward – he looked like some big-shot businessman. Perhaps he would not show up at all? She decided that if that was the case, she would wait a half hour, then he would have lost his chance. He had her cell number in case he was running late.

For 32 years, the only parent she has known is her mom. Growing up, Joyce was the most wonderful mother in the world, but still, she was a single parent. Mom had boyfriends on and off throughout her childhood, but they never lasted more than a year or two. Certainly no father figure. And now she will come face to face with the man that started all this, probably during a drunken night in Louisiana.

Chrissie showers and makes her hair up, just as she likes it: tied high at the back, swingy bangs over her forehead, with various curls falling at the sides. Her mobile phone rings.

The caller ID shows that it is the airline. She decides not to answer it. This is her day off and she needs to be focused on what lies ahead.

She applies the MAC eyeliner and blush and steps into her dress of choice – it is mainly black, but has a two inch red band around the front. It shows a respectful amount of cleavage – classy she thinks. She slips into her heeled black shoes and views the finished product.

She takes everything off again. Tries the canary yellow skirt and flowery blouse. Decides that it makes her look frumpy, so takes them off. She lets her hair down, fluffs it up a bit. Checks in the mirror. Hmm, okay, she decides. Puts the black dress back on, picks up her purse and shoal, and makes for the door, wisely without checking the mirror again.

Being fickle is a woman's prerogative, she reflects.

82

Me

Wednesday, 3 August, 8:31pm. Amsterdam, Netherlands.

My well-deserved nap must have lasted less than ten minutes. Some half-wit was trying to use the on-board coffee machine and when he couldn't get it to work, he thought that somehow I might be the authority on it. I almost punched the twat!

I have been on this bloody bus for over eight hours. A day's work, just sitting on the bus. I can see why it is cheap. We seem to be on the school run, going out of our way to stop at every place you've never heard of, and some that you have. We have made stops at Metz, Liège, Brussels, Antwerp, Eindhoven and Utrecht. Next stop is Amsterdam, although looking at the timetable on board, it seems we are stopping at some out-of-town suburb called Duivendrecht. I don't really have the time for sightseeing around countries that barely break sea level.

The guy in front of me looks Dutch – blond and tall – so I have asked him how to get to Centraal train Station from the bus station. I know that Hotel Steibel is a ten minute walk from there. He has told me he is also going to Centraal as well, so I should just follow him. Perfect. He looks like he'll have a good top speed.

I have been studying the photo of Chrissie Morris that I lifted from Len's kitchen. Very thoughtful of him to keep it for me. Couldn't be easier if she were wearing a rose between her teeth. I don't let myself imagine what life she might be living, what husband she might have. My relationship with her is practical. You need to keep it compartmentalized. She has come along and reduced my share of Len's pot, and I am simply readjusting the equation to take care of that.

People die every day in silly accidents. Two thousand people die every year in the US alone, falling down stairs, and for what? An unstable step? A wobbly cup of tea? I reason at least Morris will be dying for a good cause. She'll mean a good £330,000 to me.

I have rationalized them all. Mia fell and that was her own silly fault. Knocking off Len was instrumental to the plan and for all I knew, he was going to kill me. That's basically self-defence. His henchman was collateral damage. And Morris will be the last.

I think about Scott: I reckon he'd be disappointed with my actions over the past days – he shouldn't be. But he probably is, but then he's no success story himself. Right now, he's most likely propping some up bar, talking shit to some guy he doesn't know. I wonder what Ana would think. I hope she would be pleased, and would understand the choices I've had to make. It's not been easy, and there has certainly been sacrifice.

As to how Morris's accident will pan out, I like to keep my options open. I have the Beretta courtesy of Len's man, in case the accident needs to be dressed up as a bungled robbery. But I'd favour something less noisy and more spur of the moment. It helps inordinately that she won't be expecting me. I will certainly look for an instant expiry – I am not a monster, after all.

The bus is slowing, going over some speed bumps. I glance at my watch, 15 minutes late, it is 8:45pm I believe this must be Amsterdam Duivendrecht bus station – the end of the route. I don't even bother trying to pronounce it. I want to reconfirm my tour guide hasn't forgotten me. "Is this it, my friend?" I ask. As he stands, I notice he really is extremely lanky, unable to stand up straight in the interior of the bus. Blond and clean-shaven, he is all things Dutch in a can.

"*Ja*, follow me, I will show you where to get a ticket." Shit, I think, I spent my money on the water nine hours ago.

"They don't always check tickets, do they?" I ask hopefully.

"Probably not, but there is fine of €35 if you are caught without ticket, and you will need to jump the barrier."

"Bargain." I say.

As I sit back down to my seat, I peer out of my window and bugger me, there is Scott supping a tiny beer at the station bar. It is not surprising to see him at a bar, of course, but at Duivendrecht bus station it ups my nervousometer to nuclear levels. I cannot think of a helpful reason that Scott would be here.

Scott is one of those do-unto-others-as-you-would-have-them-do-unto-you sort of guys. He would never sanction the Morris operation. If he heard of it, he would psychologically, or physically, try to stop me.

The bus comes to a stop, at last, and its airbrakes signal it's time to go. I disembark the bus with my new friend, and he looks perturbed when I put my arm lightly behind him. I put it down, but remain unreasonably close to him, we look to any onlooker like old friends. Over at the station, he has his annual pass ready, and I am opting to jump the train. My new friend remarks factually, "The train leaves in two minutes."

I step up my pace when suddenly something that feels like a meteorite pummels me against the ticket office wall. The assailant has his meaty fists on my jacket collar. Scott says, "Charlie. It's not worth it. Chrissie has nothing to do with this. I won't let you -"

Suddenly, and without warning, a huge guy lifts my brother off me, although I reckon I could have done it myself if I had wanted to. My saviour wears a moustache like Groucho Marx and is heavily manhandling Scott back towards the bar he was at – normally Scott might like that. I can hear in that special Dutch brand of

English he is speaking clearly. "Polite customers pay their bill!" I can't hear him after that, and I make for the train, ducking the barrier on the platform. My Dutch friend exhales and frowns when he sees me approaching.

"Hi again!" I say as the doors close on the train known as 'M'.

I can see Scott running up the platform, but he is too late. We are on our way to Centraal Station, a 17 minute ride.

83

Scott

Wednesday, 3 August, 9:03pm. Amsterdam, Netherlands.

Scott is furious – that bloody idiot Groucho Marx barman had prevented him from stopping Charlie, that barman has blood on his hands! He was kicking himself for his own stupidity. But he had no time for putting the blame on himself or Groucho. Charlie was the one that had taken things off-piste. Charlie was the one who had the idea to take Len out one way or another. It's true that several hundred thousand quid would fix a lot of his problems. Not the drinking maybe, but the job, the house, the wife could all be assuaged with such a considerable injection of funds.

Scott has little sympathy for his uncle's dispatch. He knew enough about Len's activities to believe that he had this coming, if not from Charlie, from another adversary. Neither could he care much for Len's henchman being killed: the price you may pay at some time in that line of work.

He doesn't know for sure, but his brother might well have had a key part in Mia's death. He really hopes he did not kill her. He could not forgive him for that. Right now, he is fairly sure Charlie has his sights on ending the life of Chrissie Morris, and for that his has no tolerance whatsoever. He will not let it happen.

Scott runs to the departures screen, the Sprinter train is leaving in two minutes from platform 2. He runs down the steps and up the other side, no mean feat in his condition. The train doors beep, alerting passengers to stand clear. Scott lunges for the door, but he won't make it. Then a young man bravely puts his foot in the door, and it remains open a few inches. One hefty yank and Scott slips in, thanking the guy profusely.

Scott gets out the iPad, and checks the schedules. He finds that, by some good fortune, his direct train is due to arrive at Centraal Station one minute before Charlie's stopping train. The chase is closing in.

84

Me

Wednesday, 3 August, 9:04pm. Amsterdam, Netherlands.

I am celebrating my success at the mouse outwitting the cat. I know to look out for Scott and he's well behind me now. My new Dutch friend is no longer my friend, and he has turned his back on me. My adrenaline is pumping sky high, I feel like a man on a mission.

The train has quite a few stops. The on-board TV screen shows we will stop at Spaklerweg, Amstelstation, Wibautstraat, Weesperplein, Waterlooplein and Nieuwmarkt, before reaching Centraal Station. There are no seats left, so I am leaning against a vertical metal handrail, near an exit.

It is 9:04pm, so I am already late for my little rendezvous with Morris. Presumably she will give a bit of leeway. I hope so. I am thinking through the various ways I can finish her off. Most importantly, it must not be traceable to me. That would be disastrous; it would scupper the master plan. I wish I had access to some poison, or lethal dose syringes that would be easy to administer.

Ten minutes later, we are pulling in to Waterlooplein. Two stops to go. My eyes open wide as I see transport police. I decide I better get off, but that would serve nothing as they are standing right by my door. The short rotund one points and me and says, "*Hem*". I don't think he was stifling a cough.

Two of the police, both six inches taller than me, grab me by both arms, and pull me towards a seat on the station. "*Uw treinkaartje alstublieft meneer.*"

I look confused, ready to act the dumb tourist, but they are already on it, "Your ticket please, Sir."

"Yes, thank you, to Centraal Station, please," I venture, idiotically.

"It is written clearly in English that you must purchase a ticket prior to boarding the train. I saw you go under the barrier at Duivendrecht. It is a fine of €35, plus the cost of the ticket, €4.20 makes €39.20 total."

"I've lost my wallet…" I suggest, pathetically.

"So how were you going to pay for the ticket that you just asked for?" No time for an answer, "Where are you staying?"

I wing it: "Ibis Central". I don't even know if there is one. Did I stay there for a stag weekend, once?

"Okay, Ibis Styles Centraal Station," says chubby, making a note on a tablet.

After more discussion, they agree not to arrest me – for the first offense – but take my invented name, home address and hotel. But, they tell me, if they catch me again, it will be the police cell tonight.

The whole episode took far too long, and it is now 9:30pm. I don't know how long Morris will wait, but I need to get a move on. I would prefer not to switch to Plan B.

85

Chrissie

Wednesday, 3 August, 9:05pm. Amsterdam, Netherlands.

Chrissie arrived at the restaurant five minutes ago at exactly 9:00am, which should have meant that her father would already be there. He had sent a photo, so she knew what to look for – bald, tanned, fit man in his late fifties. There was no one fitting that description, although the restaurant of Hotel Steibel was busy.

Now, Chrissie is still trying to convince the Maitre D' that there must be a reservation, "Maybe under Morris?" Chrissie suggests.

The Maître D' looks on the computer screen, but says, "Sorry, no. We are full at the moment, but you can have a drink at the bar and wait? It might be an hour or so for a table, I am afraid."

Chrissie agrees to that, but was miffed that her relationship with her dad was starting badly. If he did not show by 9:30pm, she would go to a back street Lebanese restaurant she had been to before, that always has space for a solo diner.

Chrissie orders a gin and tonic, and when it eventually comes with plentiful limes and a straw, she nurses it, scanning anyone approaching the restaurant like she is presidential secret service. Although there are quite a few bald heads, none seem to belong to her father.

Dejected, Chrissie absentmindedly flicks through her iPhone to avoid unwanted attention.

86

Scott

Wednesday, 3 August, 9:18pm. Amsterdam, Netherlands.

On the train, Scott is buoyed by his smooth move of bypassing Charlie.

At Centraal Station a few minutes later, he looks at the arrivals screen and sprints – as best he can – over to platform 13. The passengers are already heading down the steps to the underground passage, but he has missed no one. He stands at the steps, checking carefully, but Charlie is not here. How can it be? He runs up the platform, looking in the train, but the train terminates here, and no one other than cleaners and a guard are on board.

Crap, he thinks. Charlie must have alighted before – why didn't he think of that? He knows the name of the restaurant, but has no clue what Chrissie looks like. It's almost 9:20pm and Charlie could already be there. Scott runs back along the platform, down into the tunnel and out into the warm night air. There is a tourist information booth, still manned at this hour.

Breathless, he demands, "Hotel Steibel?" The young bearded man looks at him, unimpressed. Then Beard takes a breath, looks bored, and says with a slight lisp, "Straight over the tram tracks, follow the large street there, called Damrak. Go past the Sex Museum, and it's another five minutes on your right, just before Dam Square."

"*Dank u vel*," replies Scott, exhausting his knowledge of Dutch.

A few minutes later, Scott sees Hotel Steibel around 100 yards away. However, by now it is 9:35pm. He sees no Charlie, and no one that looks like they might be Chrissie. Is he too late? He has no idea.

After a few moments, he clocks Charlie approaching from the south of the Damrak in his distinctive Charlie run. He ducks behind some bicycles with horribly bent wheels, chained to a fence.

87

Me

Wednesday, 3 August, 9:36pm. Amsterdam, Netherlands.

Once I got away from the transport police, my priority was not to get stopped again. I went into a four-star hotel, tried to look casual and unhurried and informed the concierge that I was meeting friends at Hotel Steibel, could he possibly point me in the right direction?

That was ten minutes ago, and I used the map that he gave me to run directly to the meeting point. Now, I can see the hotel's illuminated sign from some way down Damrak. I am close to reaching my quarry. I am excited, but not nervous, I know what I am here to do. I take a left across a small bridge and: SLAM!

It's my bloody overweight brother again. Déjà vu, bro. How did he know to come here? Am I that traceable? I thought I was invisible!

"She's not there," Scott says.

"Who's not there?" I am not giving him this on a platter.

"Our cousin, Chrissie."

I like to think of her as Morris, my prey, not Chrissie. I decide enough nicety – I don't want to hurt Scott badly, but I'll do what I need to in order to score my goal. I lay a firm punch into his stomach. It's just one big flabby bulk, and my thump seems to make no difference. I make a curling strike to his right kidney. Oooh, that one hit the spot. He is fighting back at me, not in a life-threatening way, just in a brotherly brawl style.

When we were boys in Berkshire, it was not a fair match, he was six years older than me. But as the years have passed, I have got fitter and smarter, and he has got fatter and stupider.

I push, he shoves, a group of lads is looking on, just laughing and jeering. I force Scott backwards, he almost catches himself on a bicycle with a bent wheel chained to a post, and then, with no grace at all, tumbles backward into the canal. The lads are lapping it up, whooping and chuckling.

A tram is coming, so I run towards it. Scott is out of the water, dripping wet, tailing me. I surreptitiously let him catch up, he's bright red in the face and looks pleased with himself. I enter the tram, ducking under the on-board turn-style connected to the electronic ticket reader. The guard shouts "oi!" and follows me down the tram. As the doors close, I see Scott diving under the barrier, unseen by the guard who is celebrating his own good work by kicking me off the front exit door.

The tram pulls away with a furious Scott on board. If it is true what he says that Chrissie is not there, then I must immediatey engage Plan B.

88

Chrissie

Wednesday, 3 August, 9:40pm. Amsterdam, Netherlands.

Chrissie is upset. Her dad, the eternal bastard, has not shown up. She remains hopeful that he will call, but deep inside, she thinks it's unlikely. He would already have called. Could there have been a misunderstanding? No, he had suggested the place and time, when she offered Amsterdam.

She decides he's had his chance. She orders the bill.

When she gets to the Lebanese restaurant, she will order lamb shawarma, falafel and some hummus and she'll console herself with a half bottle of Italian Chianti.

89

Me

Wednesday, 3 August, 9:49pm. Amsterdam, Netherlands.

I run back to Hotel Steibel, wasting no time now. I know I have about ten minutes before Scott gets himself off the tram, most likely at the next stop, and then wobbles back here.

Hotel Steibel has around 30 or 40 tables outside, all of them full. I scan them, but each one has two or more people at it. I look up to the bar, inside, and see the woman that I am looking for.

I run inside, dodging the waiter coming towards me at the entrance which is adorned with flower pots and a menu perched invitingly on a wooden stand. I recognize her hair from behind, I sidle up next to her and whisper, "Hi Ana," before planting a deep kiss on her mouth. Just as people are starting to look, I withdraw.

"Has it gone to plan?" she asks, huskily.

"Not exactly as we planned, but all on track for a million dollar windfall... but I'm a bit short of time to finish the job, thanks for coming all this way, it will be worth it. Did you track her?"

"Yes, she is at a Lebanese restaurant a couple of streets away. She ordered dinner a few minutes ago, so I came back here to wait for you."

"OK, let's go, Scott is trying to stop me, but I've shaken him off for now." Ana left €20 on the counter for the drink, and left.

90

Scott

Wednesday, 3 August, 9:50pm. Amsterdam, Netherlands.

Scott is seething with anger. After Charlie gave him the slip on the tram, the guard would not let him off until the next tram stop. It was too dangerous to stop, apparently. Scott had looked for an emergency stop button, but he only succeeded in dinging the bell to request, "Next stop, please".

Once off the tram, at Spui, time is short. He breathes deeply thinking how many years it had been since he had run.

Dripping with smelly canal water, he launches himself into a run, knowing it is up to him to save Chrissie from his own brother. He sprints as fast as he can towards Hotel Steibel, but he does not expect Charlie to be waiting for him.

The day of drinking is catching up with him, and Scott is not at his most alert. But he has a plan. At the end of the street, he can see Dam Square. There is not a great deal of traffic at this hour. Looking towards the square, he steps out into the road to short cut. The white Toyota Prius taxi strikes him with such power that his left leg is cracked in half instantly and he is projecting into the air, landing on the pavement a good ten feet away. It had been almost silent on its battery power, just the buzz of tyres giving its existence away.

The taxi driver is visibly shocked. A bystander calls an ambulance by hammering 112 into their mobile phone.

Within minutes, a bright yellow ambulance arrives. Two paramedics jump out in green uniform and assess the scene. The white male pedestrian, 40 to 50 years old, is, at least, breathing. He has been struck by a taxi, probably at some speed. They carefully strap him to a large wheeled gurney and load him into the ambulance before rushing him with sirens and lights to the nearby OLVG Hospital.

91

Me

Wednesday, 3 August, 10:50pm. Amsterdam, Netherlands.

I watch Morris from the street – she looks familiar but I can't quite place it, may be a common appearance. She seems to be enjoying her food. And she has a half bottle of wine in store. I feel like a bottle myself! But such pleasures must wait. I saw some sort of food stall one street back. I ask Ana for some money, and leave her watching Morris.

At the food trailer, I am literally salivating at that thought of eating. I order what they have, which is a sort of deep fried battered sausage and chips. With lots of mayonnaise. I am so ravenous, I feel sick as I eat, but I need it. I take my bottle of water with me and head back to the lookout.

Morris has almost finished. Ana and I chat about what the hell happened over the past 48 hours. I recount it slowly, not dwelling on Len's demise, focusing more on how badly he treated me and the adventure of it.

Another ten minutes pass and Morris has asked for the bill. I am on the lookout for Scott, don't need him ruining things after I have come this far. The bill takes forever to come – why, I don't know.

Finally she is on the move. Having Ana with me makes it much easier to follow her. Morris walks down Gravenstraat, and past the Best Western Hotel. I can't be sure where she is going, but don't want to shoot her here. I would prefer not to use the Beretta at all. We cross Nieuwendijk, and walk down Zoutsteeg. It is a dark street, and I could run ahead and finish her off now, but it's too risky without knowing the CCTV hotspots.

I am impressed with Ana – she is tough as nails, functional, like me. She sees the cost-benefit analysis, weighing up one unknown's life with hundreds of thousands of pounds. Some people are killed for the contents of a handbag.

At the end of the street, she turns left up Damrak. It's a wide shopping street, popular in the day, desolate by night. I track her barely ten metres back now, along the pavement on the left side. Ana and I are not talking. I see my opportunity.

Morris starts to cross the wide street, but slows as she notices a tram coming. There are no stops between Dam and Centraal, so it is travelling fast in the warm night. I feel for my gun, I stuff it in the front of my trousers for easy access.

She lingers mid-way across the boulevard as the white and blue tram approaches, showing the driver she has seen him. The tram driver dings the bell, making quite a noise about it. I spring forward, as though I am a friend of Morris, grabbing her torso. She is surprisingly light. I see Ana, giving me a look of approval, then Ana screams my name, but I don't know why. I think of my life and how it's going to be, Ana and me and luxury all the way. I feel a sense of pride and relief as I shove Morris forcefully into the path of the speeding tram.

92

Fournier

Wednesday, 3 August, 11:12pm. Amsterdam, Netherlands.

Georges Fournier runs from his position trailing Charlie Dunster and Anastasia de Menzies. He is not in good shape and the last 72 hours have been physically draining. As the Dunster boy pushes Chrissie towards the tram, he realizes too late this was the plan all along. The time was now.

He charges at them both, at a trajectory in the direction of the tram, which means he has disrupted Dunster's own path sufficiently so that they are in a gravity-defying position as the tram connects with his own backside, the tram driver hits the brakes. This extra push ensured that both Chrissie and Dunster are thrown clear of the tram's rails, and the glancing blow to his rear is at such an angle it is not all that painful.

However, Fournier feels a different pain as he goes to the ground. By now, the familiar thumping is in his chest and an overwhelming sense of nausea overtakes him. He thinks of his deductions he had made from seeing the pink car in Echenevex and studying the evidence he had, the calendar, the changes to Hubbard's will. It had brought him here, and he, Georges Fournier, has saved the girl. Admittedly, he thought that the perpetrator was the older, fatter Dunster, but the result was the same.

It was the sin of avarice, how predictable, that was right in front of him. The French writer Balzac had summed it up well, *"L'avarice commence où la pauvreté cesse."* – avarice begins where poverty ends. Fournier thinks, this young man, blinded by greed wanted wealth at any cost.

Georges Fournier has his eyes wide open as his heart attack takes hold. If paramedics arrive in the next few minutes, it might help him, on the other hand, it might already be too late.

93

Ana

**Wednesday, 3 August, 11:12pm.
Amsterdam, Netherlands.**

Ana is beside herself with excitement, annoyance, pride and fury. This is the moment they had been working towards, and it's largely gone to plan. If they can just tidy up these loose ends, the future will be rosy.

Admittedly, she is annoyed that that bloody cop has shown up. Had Charlie allowed himself to be followed? Was it Scott who led the cop here? She is proud of her part in the deception. It had been her that had teased the information about Chrissie from Len, while they were lying in her cabin, on night of Mia's death. It had been her that had tracked Morris to the Lebanese restaurant. She'd not had much success in her life, but her part worked.

However, she's furious that Morris was not taken out by the tram. It was so close. Charlie should have seen the cop. She had even shouted to him. Can they still get to her? Not right now, she thinks.

Charlie looks in unshakeable pain. She is going through the motions of comforting him, but he is much less attractive as a failure. She strokes his hair and whispers to him that they need to get going, urgently, before the police arrive.

"I'm sorry." Charlie whispers to her. Apologies don't buy lifestyles, she thinks.

94

Chrissie

Wednesday, 3 August, 11:16pm.
Amsterdam, Netherlands.

Chrissie had just experienced the scariest few minutes of her life. She had been pushed in front of a tram travelling at speed. Then pushed again out of its path... and was currently sitting on the side of the street, dazed, as two ladies fussed over her.

Chrissie did not know what had happened to her dad. Or why a man, presumably drunk, had pushed her like that, and who was the man who saved her life? Where was he? Was he ok?

All she wanted was to be home, with her mother and her beautiful, kind, lovely daughter who was very nearly just orphaned. She thinks of the flower shop she wants to own, that she keeps putting on hold, and promises herself she will start to plan. She will find a backer. Enough of all this.

95

Me

Wednesday, 3 August, 11:17pm.
Amsterdam, Netherlands.

That bastard idiot cop from the South of France? Are you fucking kidding me? What the fuck? How long has he been following me? What just happened? She's not dead. Is he, though? What the fuck?

It had struck me at the critical moment. Perhaps it caused the slightest pause in my deliberate actions. I had seen her on the early morning plane en route to the Philippines. Chrissie had been my lifesaver that morning six months ago. Had I returned the favour?

Ana says we have to go. Now. Urgently. I know she is right. I had almost taken the gold-digger down, either my conscience or that moron cop had intervened. The consolation is looking at him now, writhing on the floor.

I don't think he'll make it.

EPILOGUE

96

Scott

Sunday, 5 September. Holland, Michigan, USA.

Five years later

Scott moved delicately to sit on the side of the king-sized bed, so as not to wake his wife. He reached out to the chair, where he found and then fitted his below-knee prosthetic leg. Downstairs, he paused as he came to the wall calendar, he marked the number '1859' on the square for 5 September. There was a long sequence of such numbers through the months, as there had also been on the calendars that preceded it. Scott celebrated the number of days he had been sober, and although he still had days when he found it hard not to hit the bottle, he was proud of himself and this small routine helped to keep him on track.

His eldest daughter had recently spent the summer with them, and while there, she had taken some long weekends around the Great Lakes area. Niagara, of course, Chicago, and many of the beaches in between. Most of the time, though, she had taking the role of au pair for her half-brother, Sonny, now two years old.

Scott had been at his lowest ebb in Amsterdam's OLVG Hospital after being hit by the taxi. He had been in unimaginable pain, his left leg amputated, and desperate for a drink. He had felt totally isolated – at the end of an unhappy marriage and having to come to terms with the actions of his brother, Charlie. It had struck him that he didn't have a true friend in the world. And there were many dark days to get through as he tried to come to terms with losing a limb, a wife and a brother.

Both the Dutch and French police had come to visit him in hospital. They started off with aggressive questions, which softened somewhat as Scott cooperated with them. His wife's pink Fiat had been found in a car park in Nancy. Thames Valley Police had visited his Oxford home looking for the car's registered owner, Scott's wife, who was abroad with the girls for a short break, according to a neighbour. In the end, it had been Fournier who had alerted the police that Scott was in Amsterdam.

By then, they could place both his wife's car and his shoes at the scene around the time of his uncle's death. They had also collected a sample of vomit that they could match if needs be. Scott agreed that these facts did not look good for him. He decided that he was through with protecting his brother and hard as it was, he sold him out to the police, knowing it was the right thing to do. He told them that he had followed his brother to Hubbard's 'chateau'. The more senior French Police officer had warned him that he should be prepared to testify in court – not a duty he would await with any relish but one he would nevertheless uphold.

Two weeks into his four-week stay at the hospital, the nurse told him he had a visitor. It was Stella. He reflected later at how this was the turning point in his life, when his situation finally forked off from its dire trajectory. She didn't seem to pity him and instead spoke of her disastrous brief relationship with Hugh, the 'new' housemate, who had turned out to have an awful lot of relationships, often at the same time. Stella and Scott had shared an incredibly private and powerful experience; those days on the boat, and the consequences had bound them together in a way nobody else could understand.

Once Scott was released from hospital, he still had a long path ahead, with daily physiotherapist visits and regular psychologist appointments. Stella suggested he come to live in the same house as her while he recuperated. Initially he moved into Charlie's old room, at least that's where he left his minimal belongings – however in the months that followed, they realized there was something more between them.

Being called as a witness to his brother's trial was difficult. He had spent months trying to decide what to do. Eventually he felt there was little choice, he would be under oath in a British courtroom, and he was not willing to commit perjury. It the event, it was all over fairly quickly. Through an EU member state agreement, he was summoned to the local court, where a video link and an interpreter were used to relay his testimony to a court in Bourg-en-Bresse in France, where the trial was being heard. His testimony and the cross-examination all directly related to Len's house, how he had followed Charlie there, witnessed the scene, but not found Charlie and continued his chase into the Jura Mountains. The prosecution were not allowed to ask questions about Mia or Chrissie. He was not sure if his witness statement had influenced Charlie's conviction, but he had decided to sever all ties with his brother, anyway. It saddened him to lose Charlie, but his brother was the one who had chosen this path of destruction.

Moving to 'Holland' had started as a joke between Stella and Scott, especially given his recent spell at its European namesake. However, as they considered the idea more, and realized what was possible – aided in part by the inheritance from Len – they solidified the plans to actually make it happen. They married three years ago in November – just the two of them and witnesses grabbed from the bar – in a pub in Camden. A low-key affair.

Their married status helped provide Scott with a smooth path to relocating to Holland, Michigan, the following summer. Stella was happy to be back near her parents who were aging quickly. Two years ago, Sonny came along. Scott felt like a revitalized man, running his small business shipping batteries by Internet order, taking care of his family and enjoying every day of his new life.

97

Chrissie

Sunday, 5 September. Cape May, New Jersey, USA.

Anabelle, with her pierced ears, grown-up haircut and changing body shape was beginning to look older than her nine years. She crossed Park Boulevard in West Cape May towards a line of storefronts. The street was lined with veranda-boasting 100-year-old wooden houses, which is something Anabelle and her mother loved about their life in the Atlantic beach town.

After the familiar short walk from her house, she opened the yellow door of the florist shop, a familiar bell jangled high above her. Chrissie looked up from where she was working to greet her daughter. "Hi, Chrissie, did you have a nice lay in?"

"Until the cat came and woke me up," Anabelle grumbled in a good-humoured way.

"Oh, poor you! Do me a favour, honey, and take this bucket out the back and wash it out for me." Anabelle obliged.

Chrissie returned to her task of arranging a regular customer's favourite pink bouquet of carnations, peonies and roses. She loved her close and simple lifestyle. Supporting a greener environment, she sourced her flowers locally, wherever possible, and with enough time and money to finally do so, she would often walk home via a number of organic health food stores to pick up a healthy dinner for the two of them to enjoy in the small but perfectly kept garden.

There was not a day that she looked back with envy on her old life of airports, stress and miserable customers. Now, her clients almost always came in jovial; and if they ever did arrive without a spring in their step, they invariably left with one. Her persona and her craft simply seemed to breed happiness.

However, the years preceding the Amsterdam had been difficult. After the tram incident, she went through a period of distrusting anyone she did not know, and in particular, men. Although she was not hurt physically, the attack took a deep emotional toll on her.

A few months after Amsterdam, her mother had suffered a massive stroke and died a few days later at NYPQ; the same hospital that had treated Anabelle so well. Joyce had only been in her mid-60s, and Chrissie was not ready to lose her when, perhaps, she needed her most. Despite the trauma of losing her mum, her passing delivered the life opportunity of which her mother would have approved. Joyce had few material possessions, or spare cash, but, over time, she had managed to buy her condo in Fitler Square, which had since turned into a desirable neighbourhood. As a result, when her mother's estate was settled, and together with the money she had received from Len, she put the flower shop plan into motion and had never looked back.

Now that Anabelle was older, and her own work was more sociable, she didn't think twice when a friendship turned into a romance. She had always received a lot of attention from men, and had not expected for a relationship to blossom with another woman, but felt so comfortable in Cat's company it had happened so naturally. She understood Chrissie, knew when to back off and when to come close. Anabelle's maturity for her years allowed her to accept Cat, not as a parent, but as a friend.

Chrissie had never made any attempt to make contact with any of her late father's family. They seemed like bad eggs best left untouched. She wanted to her spend time with those she loved and trusted and in Cape May.

Life was good.

98

Fournier

Wednesday, 17 November. Lyons, France.

His neighbour from the 12th floor of his apartment block was there, as was his old colleague Agent Saucy and a couple of former colleagues. His only surviving sibling, his elder sister Edith, made the trip from Toulouse and then there were two acquaintances from the local PMU bar he frequented. There was, of course, the priest conducting the funeral ceremony. The turnout did not represent the life of a man who spent every hour of every day meeting people. However, it was little surprise to any of those present that Georges Fournier had finally succumb to the consequences of his chosen lifestyle.

It had been a rollercoaster for him since investigating the death of Mia Hubbard, now five years past. When he went on the chase to Amsterdam, he had been trailing Scott Dunster, and although it turned out that Charlie was, in fact, the perpetrator, his detective work had been an important and valued part of the case.

After the heart attack that night by the tram, when, in his mind, he had saved the young lady's life, he had been taken to the main hospital in Amsterdam, where they had performed percutaneous coronary intervention; a mechanical means of treating his heart attack. The following morning, still heavily drugged, he had made his final call of the case, to Agent Saucy, explaining the situation and where the Dunsters had last been seen.

When he was transferred from OLVG hospital to the *Centre Hospitalier de Cannes*, he was visited by his supervisor, Inspector Ayad. He was aware that the *Gendarmerie Nationale* may wish for him to retire from service, but he had not expected an immediate, though respectable, termination of his post. He was never to return to his post at Vallauris Golfe-Juan.

Later, when Charlie was summonsed to court in Bourg-en-Bresse in France, Fournier's testimony, together with the resulting police investigation, formed the foundation of the case. Charlie Dunster was to be charged with the double murder in Echenevex. The trial was by jury, around a year or so later, so the outcome was uncertain and his statement was important to the state prosecution. When not providing testimony himself, he sat in the courtroom listening intently to the witnesses and specialists.

Fournier had chosen the gastronomical metropolis of Lyon for his retirement, a city he had always enjoyed and in which he had spent his formative years. However, retirement had not suited Georges Fournier. He felt he lacked both purpose and stature in society. He fell into a strict daily ritual – he would get up, undertake some rudimentary chores until exactly 4pm, when he told himself it was acceptable to drink and smoke at the local PMU bar, normally until it closed.

In recent months, the 4pm rule had been brought forward to 2pm, while his diet had lost even the most basic of vegetal ingredients. The smoking had increased, and exercise was a pipe dream. It was suicide by lifestyle. He had died at home after a normal night out at the PMU bar. Retired Agent Georges Fournier simply went to bed and did not wake up.

99

Me

Saturday, 20 November. Bourg-en-Bresse, France.

The prison guard handed me the clothes that I had arrived in. They were kept in a clear plastic bag, together with my belt and wallet. They were musty, damp, cold and the first thing I needed to do was get some new ones. It may have been a routine process for the guard, but it was an emotional one for me. After more than five years holed up in three different prisons, I was returned to Bourg-en-Bresse to be granted my parole, earlier than the full prison term for my good behaviour.

My time inside gave me ample time to reflect. I had shared a cell for a while with a born again Buddhist, who told me about his daily practice of mindful thought and action in pursuit of happiness. I realized that my mind had been blinded by the addictive affect that Ana had over me, it was her who fueled my envy of Len and encouraged me to be greedy. I accepted that I had done bad things. I have nightmares, every night. But I have done my time, and I have learnt from my poor judgement. It was wrong to try to take an honest and good human being's life by pushing her in front of a tram. Again, looking back, they were all Ana's ideas, I was just the mug who fell for her plan.

Thank God the plan had failed!

Ana and I had fled the scene together. I wanted to get back home to London as soon as possible – only I was on mainland Europe, without my passport. I could have reported it lost or stolen at the Embassy, but that would draw great attention to my whereabouts. So, Ana flew back to the UK and made a visit to my home. Stella was in, so it was straightforward for her to enter the house, I had lost my own key during my journey. When she returned the following day, we met at Schiphol airport. She handed over my passport that she had gone to great effort to retrieve, however she appeared distracted and despondent. Then, without any further warning, she told me it was over, she said 'she had other plans'. She had already booked her flight home to California; it was decided. Over the years I had sometimes thought about her, the way her reckless plans seemed such a smart idea in the way she presented them.

Leaving Schiphol airport, I had placed my passport safely in my zipped pocket – and I had still wanted to return to the UK incognito – my plan had remained to deny having ever left the UK after the boat trip. I had hitchhiked down to Calais and bought a passenger ferry ticket under a name not quite my own – I knew that ferry staff were significantly less fussy about names than their airport counterparts. However, I had not reckoned on an exit passport check by the French – a deliberate plan of theirs, it turned out, to catch me leaving the Schengen area after a tip-off from that French cop.

At first, it was not clear why I was being held in the immigration containment compound that night. The facility was being paid for by the British, but under French jurisdiction. Then, without warning, two French *Police Judiciaire* bounded into the room and announced that I was under arrest on suspicion of the murder of Leonard Hubbard and Cédric Moutier. I have not stepped on British soil since. Perhaps I never will again.

Over the next year, I was held in the remand prison until the trial. My lawyers had requested bail, but the judge ruled that I was a significant flight risk. It was true, I suppose. I dreamed of nothing else. My anticipated inheritance had not yet come through from Len, and it was that money that I was planning to use to fund the lawyers. It had been explained to me that my part of the inheritance was at risk if I was found guilty of either murder or manslaughter, under the so-called 'slayer rule'. I had never heard of it up until then, but if I was found guilty, then my share would be divided amongst those who would inherit from me, as though I had died myself. This at least provided great incentive for my defence lawyers for us to win, in order that they could be paid promptly.

The trial seemed to take forever. By then, I had a bilingual legal team – it seemed that each lawyer saw the need for another expert, and with a life behind bars on the cards, I was not in a position to doubt their superior knowledge of the law, and money was still thought to be no object. It was around half way through the trial that my chief lawyer, a diminutive man named Dominic Chard, delivered the news. Len's estate had been preliminarily settled. It would be shared between Scott, Chrissie, and me – provided I was not found guilty of murder or manslaughter. So far, so good. The problem was that Len's estate was not all that it seemed. His house was heavily mortgaged, in negative equity owing to the strengthening Swiss franc in which he had borrowed. His company assets and shares were not worth much at all, the firm was barely turning a profit, and was no longer desirable for investors. Many of the other status symbols he paraded were either leased, like the Tesla, or imminently to be repossessed, like the catamaran.

The total of Len's estate was settled at less than €100,000, including his share of Mia's estate, her death having been recorded as accidental. My share of Len's estate, if I was even to get it, was to be a little over €30,000. I was struck by my own stupidity.

The legal team was swiftly reduced when it became clear that, at best, I had €30k in future capital. Dominic Chard often sent his deputy, citing another important trial that he had to attend. I found myself having increasingly suicidal thoughts. Up until then, I had believed that whatever I had done carried the good probability that I would never need to work again. Suddenly, the best case was looking pretty awful, and my legal team was one fresh-faced guy who seemed surprised by every assertion that the prosecution brought.

I had pleaded not guilty, and we had sought a trial by jury in the *cour d'assises*, since Dominic Chard had believed it improved my chances for acquittal. That route was only permitted since the sentence, if I was convicted, was over 15 years in jail, and quite possibly a lot more. Conviction required a two-thirds of the jury majority.

The prosecution's case stated that I had gone to Len's barn (they were indifferent how I had arrived there, despite Scott's testimony), tied up Len with ransom demands, then, when disturbed by his sometime employee Cédric Moutier, had shot them both, dead. Then, they said, I fled the scene. They presented a mapping of my route, using my cell phone's GPS signals until Nancy bus station. They had some CCTV footage from Echenevex village square showing a cyclist with a blanket tied to his bike riding away from the scene. They also showed exhibits that they said were ransom snapchat messages I had sent to Len. It was a strong case.

Our defense was basically the truth. I had been taken to Len's house against my will. I had sent the social media messages, but did not mean it. I had been tied up with an electrical cord. I had managed to escape and in the ensuing fights, two men ended up dead. I left. One of the key prosecution questions was why I had fled the scene and gone to Nancy.

On the day that the jury was to deliver its verdict, I was led back to the court, as I had done each day for the previous three weeks. My oral French had become quite passable and I needed no interpretation. As I stood there in the dock, heart beating uncontrollably, I listened to the charges laid against me. It sounded like it was someone else's life being decided. "...the murder of Leonard Hubbard. The murder of Cédric Moutier." But it was my life being decided by the nine jurors, and it was all my fault.

The jury had finally come to a decision. Their verdict was as follows: I was found not guilty to both counts of murder, not guilty for the manslaughter of Cédric Moutier (they determined reasonable doubt). However, I was found guilty of the manslaughter of Leonard Hubbard. When it came to sentencing, the judge was unsympathetic to my mitigating circumstances. He ordered eight years imprisonment, to be eligible for parole after five.

The next blow was to take another eighteen months. A French judge ruled that, given my conviction for voluntary manslaughter in the death of Len, I should not benefit from his estate. My share would go directly to my issue: my brother, Scott. Worse still, I was liable for tens of thousands of pounds worth of legal fees I had built up, expecting a financial windfall.

Around that time, the suicidal thoughts returned with force. I was an embarrassment, a criminal, I had no friends. To make matters worse, Scott had written a curt, typed letter to say he wanted nothing further to do with me. If I could have hung myself, I think I would have.

Now, leaving prison after five years, I am scared. The world won't be kind to me, I know that. I have serious debt, no job and, given my recent stretch, no prospects. At least, out here, I can choose when to end it.

100

Ana

Saturday, 20 November. Bourg-en-Bresse, France.

Ana's rental car was tiny. She had picked it up at Lyon airport after her flight from LAX, via London. She slowed the car as she came to the beaten sign proudly proclaiming the entrance to the *Centre pénitentiaire de Bourg-en-Bresse*. She parked up, and waited.

Ana had told her husband that she had been invited to a wedding in London. He had become so disinterested in her life, she knew he would not even ask to see photos. Ana had met José Maria Sanchez Gomez when he employed her to be his housekeeper. It had been no coincidence that she had applied for the job. She knew that he held the keys to a good easy life, one that Charlie had been unable to provide. His wife had died a few years earlier, and at 62 years old, he was sitting on considerable wealth. His wife's share of the family copper mining business had mostly passed to him after her death, while he was also a successful businessman. Before she met him, she had read in a San Diego newspaper that he was worth tens of millions.

One September afternoon, after months of flirting, he had finally drawn her into his substantial San Diego office and allowed her to give him the time of his life. José had proposed to her a few months later. Ana knew at that moment that she'd struck gold. However, once married, the romance was short lived. Before long, José increased his time away from their home. He travelled to Mexico weekly, and she began to suspect that she was not the only woman in his life. Still, that did not bother her too much, she was in the relationship for the lifestyle, not the man, and she was the woman with the ring on her finger; and more importantly, the bank account that accompanied it. In all honesty, having him away so often meant she could live her life in the way she wanted. One of her first moves had been to hire an experienced tennis coach, who conveniently resided in the garden house.

After three years of marriage, they shared a bed no more than once a fortnight – when he elected to visit their marital San Diego villa. He did not enquire about her daily life, and she no longer volunteered the information. Their conversations centred almost entirely around household staff issues, renovations, and for him, the San Diego Padres, and their performance in Major League Baseball.

Now, sitting outside the prison, she passed the time messing about on her phone. Ahead of her, the perimeter fence was around five metres high with the unmistakable concertina razor wire atop its length. A rudimentary online check had informed her of the Inmate Release Information Search, and thus she knew that today was Charlie's release day; he would not know what had hit him.

It was not until 3.30pm that a man came into sight, shown through the gate by an armed guide. Charlie had aged considerably, although, from a distance, he looked fitter than ever. He had nothing with him that she could see; no bag, no jacket even. He set off on foot in the direction on the train station. She watched as he walked into the distance, along the side of the street marked *Chemin de la Providence*, a road with no sidewalk.

She depressed the clutch, put the vehicle into gear, and turned the ignition key.

The badge on the steering wheel said it was a Kia, it had a stick shift and almost no trunk at all. It would serve its purpose. She exited the parking lot in no noticeable hurry, preferring not to do anything memorable for the gate guards to recall. She could see Charlie walking along the right-hand side of the road. Ana accelerated, holding the wheel firmly with two hands.

Charlie appeared unaware that a car was approaching – at least, he did not turn around even though he must have heard the engine turning and the tyres' friction on the road. As Ana reached Charlie, she almost clipped his arm as she came to a sudden stop, hemming him in, and opening the passenger door from the inside.

"Wanna lift?" she beckoned with a cheeky smile. Charlie looked shocked to say the least.

"How the fuck?" he managed, "Ana! Shit! Jesus!..."

"Are you gonna get in, or did I come all the way out here for nothing?"

Charlie just stood there shaking his head, and eventually climbed into the car. Ana apologized for not getting in touch, and they talked rapidly as she drove towards the *autoroute*. When they stopped at a red light, Charlie lunged towards her, grabbing her breast instinctively with one hand and pulling her head towards him with the other. As they kissed, she reached across with her left hand and felt his rapidly hardening penis.

A blast on the horn behind. An irritated van driver flashing his lights. They pulled off again.

She pulled over at the first quiet lay-by and they had hot, primal sex, reclining the front seats and making scarce effort to keep below the window line, though there were no pedestrians, only passing vehicles. Charlie was understandably satisfied as they sat there afterwards, in silence for a few moments.

Ana broke the silence.

"Charlie, you know, my husband is worth millions." She let the word hang there. "Tens of millions, actually". The cheeky smile again. "And he's a waste of space."

"Shit." Charlie said, rocking his head as he thought, "You're married?"

"Soon to be widowed," came the response as she reached into the door pocket and flung a maroon-coloured passport at him. "This is for you, 'Brian'…" She winked at him then started to do up her blouse.

"There's a place he goes to in Mexico all the time, a place called Hermosillo. He walks from the office to the hotel. It worries me terribly; the cars drive so fast around there and there's not much by way of protection from the road."

Charlie was eying her distrustfully again, like he had when she approached him on the road. Ana recognized his hesitation and moved towards him, tracing a gentle circle around his mouth, teasing his lips with her fingernails. Charlie exhaled in a nervous breath as she slid her hand down his abdomen.

"Mexico you say?" Charlie offered.

"Mexico I say…" They smiled at each other, not entirely genuinely. Then Ana turned her eyes back to the road and turned the key in the ignition.

Acknowledgements

I reserve the weightiest thanks to my editor, Kate Taylor, who challenged every loose end and spotted each opportunity to let the reader understand the thoughts that made Charlie tick. Her eye for detail taught me so much and her support ensured that my draft manuscript became a finished book. Middle Farm Press have also been wonderful in getting the book to market, always refusing to compromise quality, and believing in the charm of the physical book in our digital age. A special thanks to Sam Gray, who has played a key role in encouraging and connecting me.

I am most grateful to the readers of the draft manuscript, particularly my ever-patient wife, Laure Felix-Bower for the unbridled enthusiasm and candid advice that helped shape the final draft. I save a word for all those who supported me along the way, who told me it was possible, who urged me to publish my work and who promised to buy a copy. Finally a hearty thank you to my children, Manolo and Millie, who never doubted their dad's writing talent for a moment, and who may choose to read *Dead in the Water* one day.

To you all, thank you.

Simon Bower

May 2018